"Mr. Bishop?"

Turning, Grant recognized the woman approaching him at once. Her long hair was pulled back from her face, but the warm glow in her eyes was just as he'd remembered.

He'd told himself he'd imagined the woman's effect on him the last time they'd met—four years before. She'd had a wedding ring on back then. She didn't now.

"Lynn," he said. She held out her hand. He took it. And didn't want to let go.

"You don't remember me," he said, quickly shoving his hands into the pockets of his jeans as he faced her in the empty, fluorescent-lit hallway. He'd heard that The Lemonade Stand was beautiful, a haven, resortlike. The commercial beige tile and white walls didn't give him that impression.

"I do, actually," she said. "Now that I see you. I recognized your name when you called, but I wasn't sure why. You're the one with the brother. Darin, right?"

"I'm impressed." Grant smiled. "You were his nurse for one day. You've got a good memory."

"Darin was memorable. So what can I do for you?" Lynn asked, that not-quite-smile he'd remembered curving her lips, and hitting him where a guy only liked to be hit when he could do something about it.

He'd hoped she'd remember him, too, and she had. More important, she'd remembered his brother. With enough affection to pull strings and get Darin into their physiotherapy program?

The Lemonade Stand was the only option he had. This had to work.

Dear Reader,

Welcome to The Lemonade Stand. Life hands all of us challenges; happiness comes through the choices we make in the face of those challenges. And sometimes the choice that brings happiness is the decision to reach out for help.

I know that sometimes life feels as though there are no options left. No hope for true joy.

And then there's a place like The Lemonade Stand, a very special shelter for women. *More* than a shelter. It's a place that shows women that they have the right to be happy. *Wife by Design* is the first of a series called Where Secrets Are Safe—and that refers to both the secrets that some women hide *before* they come to the Stand and the secrets, the hidden selves, they're able to reveal and explore once they're there. I am deeply committed to these books. And to the hope that the decent men and women at The Lemonade Stand have to offer. There is true joy and deeply peaceful happiness available to every one of us.

Because, after all, when life hands you lemons, you can choose to make lemonade!

Please let me know what you think of this book. And join me in the fight against domestic violence, which afflicts a shocking number of women in this country and worldwide. You can reach me at www.tarataylorquinn.com.

Tara Taylor Quinn

TARA TAYLOR QUINN

Wife by Design

Gloria –
So great to see
you !!!
Tara Taylor

◆ HARLEQUIN® SUPER ROMANCE®

Recycling programs
for this product may
not exist in your area.

ISBN-13: 978-0-373-60830-0

WIFE BY DESIGN

Copyright © 2014 by Tara Taylor Quinn

Printed in U.S.A.

ABOUT THE AUTHOR

With sixty-five original novels, published in more than twenty languages, Tara Taylor Quinn is a *USA TODAY* bestselling author. She is a winner of the 2008 National Readers' Choice Award, four-time finalist for the RWA RITA® Award, a finalist for the Reviewers' Choice Award, the Booksellers' Best Award and the Holt Medallion, and she appears regularly on Amazon bestseller lists. Tara Taylor Quinn is a past president of the Romance Writers of America and served for eight years on its board of directors. She is in demand as a public speaker and has appeared on television and radio shows across the country, including CBS *Sunday Morning*. Tara is a spokesperson for the National Domestic Violence Hotline, and she and her husband, Tim, sponsor an annual in-line skating race in Phoenix to benefit the fight against domestic violence.

When she's not at home in Arizona with Tim and their canine owners, Jerry Lee and Taylor Marie, or fulfilling speaking engagements, Tara spends her time traveling and in-line skating.

Books by Tara Taylor Quinn

HARLEQUIN SUPERROMANCE

HARLEQUIN MIRA

*Shelter Valley Stories
**Chapman Files
***It Happened in Comfort Cove

Other titles by this author available in ebook format.

HARLEQUIN SINGLE TITLE

HARLEQUIN EVERLASTING LOVE

To the women whose pictures line the wall of
my private office at The Lemonade Stand:
Penny Gumser, Phyllis Pawloski, Leeanne Williams,
Patricia Potter, Lynn Kerstan,
Kim Barney and Paula Eykelhof.
Each of you plays a vital role in my Lemonade recipe.

CHAPTER ONE

Three years earlier

"WE HAVE TO talk."

Glancing from the baby in her arms to the man standing in the doorway of their bedroom, Lynn nodded. Brandon had been acting odd since before Kara was born, moving into the spare bedroom ostensibly so his tossing and turning didn't make Lynn more uncomfortable than she already was.

And now five weeks after their daughter's birth, he was still using the spare room.

"Come on in." She patted the bed beside her. The baby had just finished her 9:00 p.m. feeding and should sleep until midnight. Lynn had napped that afternoon. She could manage without more rest. And even if she couldn't, she would. Brandon was her life—and was obviously having a hard time adjusting to sharing their world.

At least, she prayed that was the problem.

He joined her on the bed, and she placed his pillow against the headboard so he could sit propped up beside her. Ignoring the pillow, he turned his gaze to Kara and remained seated on the edge of the bed. The sadness in his smile scared her.

"Brandon? What's going on?" They'd been best friends since the ninth grade. Knew everything about each other.

He looked from her to Kara. "She's perfect, Lynn. Everything we hoped and more…"

But? She heard it there. His chin taut, he stared silently at the baby.

"You want to hold her?"

Nodding, he reached for the soft, blanketed bundle sleeping against her. Cradling Kara's body easily on one arm, the baby's head safely nestled between his biceps and chest, Brandon looked comfortable, natural, as though this was his fifth child, not his first.

His gentleness, as always, touched her deeply.

"She's great, isn't she?" he said, his voice thick with emotion. Reminding her of their wedding day, of standing at the front of the church that was filled to capacity with their friends and loved ones and hearing the catch in his voice as he vowed to love her forever. There'd been no mistaking his sincerity. Listening to him, she'd known very clearly that he spoke a truth beyond words. Brandon's love was real. The kind that came from someplace more powerful than the human mind or heart. From that point on she'd never worried that they'd make it. She'd known their marriage was safe.

Taking comfort in the memory, Lynn smiled. Nodded. "Yeah," she said, loving the sight of her engineer husband holding their infant daughter. "We made a beautiful baby, Bran, just like we always said we would."

Looking at Brandon, she waited for him to raise his eyes to her—for their eyes to meet in the silent communication that had been their gift even in high school. The private smile that soothed her deepest fears. Or made her heart race, depending on the moment.

Brandon didn't look up. And her heart raced. With fear. "Hon, what's the matter?"

Had Kara's advent into their lives created a gap between them? She'd read about the possibility. About husbands feeling rejected, neglected, a little jealous even.

"She hardly ever cries," he said. "I expected a lot more crying."

"We're lucky she's not colicky." Any other time Lynn would have been happiest sitting with Brandon, talking about their baby.

"Diaper changing is a breeze, too," he said. From day one Brandon had insisted on being a full contributing partner in their daughter's life. Apart from the feedings that, biologically, he couldn't manage. "A lot easier than those plastic dolls they made us practice on."

He'd knocked the baby stand-in onto the floor the

first time he'd tried to get the slippery disposable diaper fastened around it. She grinned, remembering. He didn't.

Kissing the top of the sleeping baby's head, Brandon transferred their daughter gently back to Lynn, still not meeting her gaze.

If she didn't know better, she'd think he'd just said goodbye.

Feeling desperate, she said, "I was thinking maybe we should plan a night out, just the two of us, next weekend. It's my six-week mark."

The doctor had said they could start having sex again at six weeks postbirth.

"Lynn, we need to talk."

Suddenly she didn't want to continue with her attempt to draw him out. She was tired. Postpartum.

And...Brandon was struggling. Of course she had to listen. Just like he always listened to her. Every time.

She was waiting. He still wasn't talking. She drew strength from the baby in her arms. Those sweet little lips. The eyelids that were closed to a world that could be so confusing at times. Flushed cheeks and little hands clenched into fists, even in rest. "Do you still love me, Bran?"

His gaze shot to hers. Finally. "You know I do."

He looked away immediately, but that depth of emotion was there in his voice again. His words trembled with it.

He wasn't a macho man's man, like her little sister Katie's ex-husband had been. But Brandon had never lifted a hand to her, either, or attempted to control her, as Katie's ex had done to Katie.

Taking Brandon's hand in hers, she held it between them on the bed, focusing wholly on him while the baby lay sleeping against her breast. "And you know I love you," she told her husband of eight years. "We'll be fine, Bran, just please tell me what's bothering you."

As she said the words, fear struck anew. The one thing that had always made her and Brandon so good together was their ability to talk things out. They'd always been able to tell each other anything. And everything. Until then.

"We aren't going to be fine, Lynn." It was the tears in his eyes, when he finally held her gaze, that cut through her, far more than the death knell in his words. Words could change.

His sandy-blond hair, short and pristine, just as he'd always liked it, made him seem vulnerable to her in that moment. Exposed. The rest of him—his tight, in-shape, average-height body—just seemed dear.

Laying the baby in the basinet beside the bed, she moved over on the mattress to sit directly facing her husband. "Are you sick, Brandon?" Had someone given him a frightening prognosis? Just now, when they were embarking on the challenge of a lifetime with their new offspring to raise? "You know doctors aren't always right, hon. Whatever it is, we'll deal with it. Get second opinions and treatment…" If she just kept talking everything would be all right. She was a nurse. She'd nurse him.

With a finger against her lips, Brandon shook his head. "You can't fix this one, babe."

Babe. He hadn't called her that in a while. She hadn't realized how much she'd missed it.

"You're scaring me."

"I'm scaring me, too."

"Is it cancer?"

Whatever was wrong, it was so awful that her husband didn't know how to tell her about. So she'd help him. Guess all night if she had to. She'd said they'd get through it together and they would. She'd show him. She had enough faith for both of them. They just had to—

"No, it's not cancer," Brandon said, shifting so that no part of him was touching any part of her. The movement was subtle. Moving a knee. But she noticed. "I'm not sick," he added.

"Then what?" His expression, no matter how hard she studied it, told her nothing. Except that he was hurting.

She racked her brain, trying to think of anything that had happened, anything she might have missed. Tried to figure out when the problem had started. And still drew blanks.

It had to have something to do with Kara. Everything had been fine...normal...until shortly before the baby was born.

The baby was fine. Not only had all the doctors said so, but as a nurse, Lynn would know if something was wrong with her infant daughter. Kara had a healthy appetite. Slept well. And, as her father had just pointed out, didn't cry much at all.

She was fine. Kara was fine. Which, in her mind, only left one other possibility. "There's another woman." While she'd been fat and pregnant, and uncomfortable and unable to have sex, he'd met someone else....

"No! Whatever else happens, Lynnie, you always have been and always will be the only woman I ever wanted or had sex with."

There was no mistaking the truth in those words. They spoke straight to her heart. Breathing a little easier, Lynn reached for his hand again. "Just tell me, hon." They were a team. Partners. For better or worse. "Things always seem worse until you get them out."

His family was close by. And hers had visited twice since the baby's birth. They'd help with whatever the problem was.

Maybe that was it. Maybe he was tired of both sets of parents camping out on their doorstep now that Kara was there.

"Please, Brandon. You're making me crazy with worry. What's wrong?"

She braced herself. Knew, when he met and held her gaze, that her life was about to change forever. And still wasn't prepared for his reply.

"I'm gay."

Present

THIRTY-EIGHT-YEAR-OLD Grant Bishop wasn't an emotional guy. He was a busy guy—too busy to get tangled up in things he couldn't control. Except for the things he couldn't let go.

He couldn't let go of Darin's condition.

Sitting in the silence of his older brother's hospital room that balmy February morning, he rested one ankle on his knee and beat out the rhythm playing over and over in his brain. *Da da dah. Da da dah. Da da dah. Da da dah.*

Dr. Zimmer's Tuesday-morning rounds were at seven-thirty. Grant wanted to be at a job site across town by nine so he could be back to make sure Darin got up in his chair for lunch. As long as his brother cooperated, he should be able to have Darin back home the next day.

Assuming the doctor told him the previous day's surgery had gone as well as he'd thought. That Darin was responding as expected. His forty-four-year-old brother had still been groggy from the anesthetic the night before when Grant, after spending fourteen hours at the hospital, had finally gone home to shower and get some sleep.

Darin, with a big patch of gauze taped over one side of his head, didn't look much different nine hours later.

More than two nights in the hospital was going to be a financial hardship. But if Darin wasn't ready to go home Wednesday morning, they'd manage. He'd paid off the loan against his landscaping business and could borrow again if he had to.

And if there was a long-term problem? If the surgery hadn't been successful? If the infection that had formed around the bit of irremovable stingray barb lodged in his brother's brain was still active?

If Darin experienced any of the numerous side effects that could have resulted from the craniotomy itself?

Hands clasped, he pounded his thumbs together, keeping the beat with the rhythm rocking his foot.

Darin was going to be just fine. The brothers had been dealing with this—Darin's accident—for seventeen years, and things always worked out.

Maura, the sixty-year-old widow next door, checked in on Darin for Grant on the rare days his brother couldn't accompany him to the job site, in exchange for handyman work whenever anything needed fixing at her place. She was all set to nurse Darin through the two weeks postsurgery the doc had said it would take before his brother was able to return to work.

Arrangements had been made. Details tended to.

It was 7:40 and the doctor was late. Standing, hands tucked into the pockets of his jeans, Grant walked to the door of his brother's room, pulled it open and stood in the entryway, watching the hallway. Nurses went to and from rooms; an orderly pushed a cart with breakfast trays up the hall, stopping at doors, delivering trays and moving on.

Darin was still on IV. He should have progressed to a liquid diet the night before but hadn't cooperated enough to sit up and drink. He'd barely regained consciousness and hadn't known Grant was even in the room, prodding him.

Running his fingers through thick black hair that hadn't yet begun to show the gray that had started to appear on his older brother's head, Grant rolled his shoulders and sat back down. He'd built extra time into his schedule in case the doctor was late. This wasn't his first hospital run. He knew how things worked.

And Santa Raquel, the coastal California town where he and Darin had settled after Darin's accident, wasn't all that big. He could make it across town and to his job site in less than twenty.

"Grant?" The deep voice had Grant out of his chair and at the bedside in one second flat.

"Right here, bro," he said, pushing the hair off

from his brother's forehead as he took Darin's right hand in his and held on. "Just like always."

Darin studied him with eyes that appeared to hold recognition—and more.

"How you feeling?" He started out small, not sure what kind of cognition Darin would have left. Or what further damage might have been done.

"Head hurts."

"You just had surgery."

"Not *just.* I had a night since then."

With a grin, Grant nudged his brother's shoulder. "You're right, bro, you did. And if you'll cooperate with the nurses today, tonight will be your last one here. You ready to come home?"

Darin made a face, scrunching his lips up toward his nose. And did it again.

What the hell was that?

The covers moved above Darin's left hand. And then moved again. Darin made that face again.

"Nose itches." Pulling his right hand free from Grant's clasp, he scratched.

And Grant grinned a second time, letting go of a deep breath. The day before had been slightly alarming, he admitted to himself now that Darin was back. His brother hadn't come out of the anesthetic as the doctors would have liked—the way he had for all previous surgeries.

He hadn't really been coherent, either, even when he'd opened his eyes.

But Grant had known Darin would make it through just fine.

Still, it was great to—

"Good morning." The tall, gray-haired doctor entered the room. Dr. Zimmer was Grant's kind of doctor. No-nonsense, tell it like it is. With a nod toward Grant, he focused on Darin. Asked a couple of questions. Slowly. Kindly. Lifting the sheet to look at his brother's feet, he asked Darin to move his toes. Asked about pain and other sensations. He studied Darin's eyes, had his brother follow a penlight with his gaze.

Everything was going as expected. Fine. Grant would be out of there soon. He'd get to work on time, come back to spend the evening with Darin and then go home to prepare the house for Darin's return the next day. All in all, they'd come through the potentially life-threatening episode with only one day of missed work. "Your left hand, Darin. Can you lift your left hand?"

Grant watched, nodding, waiting. The covers moved. And…nothing. The left toes had moved. Hadn't they? Grant hadn't paid that much attention.

He wanted Dr. Zimmer out of the way so he could check again. Just to make certain.

Moving to the left side of the bed, the surgeon lifted the cover, setting Darin's hand on top of them. "Now," he repeated gently. "Move your fingers for me."

And Darin did.

Thank God.

"Lift your hand."

Grant stared. Willed the hand to move. And it did. Okay, not a lot. But the movement meant that Darin was capable, didn't it? That there was no permanent damage to his brother's motor skills resulting from the latest surgery?

They'd been through this before. Through worse surgeries. Like the one right after the accident when they'd had to go in to remove the barb the stingray had left in his brother's brain. Grant had been a senior in college at the time. A mere boy.

Darin, once a force to be reckoned with in the business world, had been forever changed. He had his normal moments. And childlike ones. Stress made things worse. He couldn't figure out basics, like monetary value.

But they'd survived. Made a fine life for themselves. Just the two of them. A satisfactory life. Other guys had wives. Kids. Grant had Darin.

"Can I speak with you in the hallway?" Dr. Zimmer's request interrupted Grant's silent pep talk. The look on the surgeon's face put a blight on the positive outlook he'd been trying to create.

"I'll be right back." Grant squeezed Darin's hand. "You get ready to spend an hour or two in that chair over there." He nodded at the high-backed leather seat in the corner by the window. He knew the drill.

Darin had to be up, able to walk and get to the bathroom before they'd release him. And it all started with the chair.

"I can't lift my hand, Grant." Darin's voice was low. "Why can't I lift my hand?"

"Because it's asleep," he said, keeping his tone light. Lightness was the last thing Grant felt as he uttered his asinine response and followed the doctor out the door.

CHAPTER TWO

"I'M PUTTING BUTTERFLIES on this, but it needs stitches," Lynn Duncan said, her tone as matter-of-fact as she could make it while tending to the brutalized skin of the twenty-four-year-old brunette sitting on the table in one of the two small examination rooms at The Lemonade Stand Tuesday evening.

"I hate hospitals." Regina Cooper wasn't crying as she gave yet another reason she was refusing to allow herself to be stitched. Lynn almost wished Regina *was* sobbing, even though that would make her task more difficult. The younger woman's voice was deadpan, her words slurred as she formed them through cut and swollen lips. Like the life had been beaten out of her.

"I can do it right here," Lynn said. Technically she was off shift, but when you lived on the premises of one's job, you tended to be on call 24/7. Not that Lynn minded.

At-risk women came to The Lemonade Stand in coastal Santa Raquel, California, to find shelter. Lynn had found her life's purpose here, nursing them.

Tending to the third of three ugly cuts on the woman's chin and neck—one the result of a knockout punch to her mouth and the other two gashes from the glass that broke when it had been thrown at her—she said, "These are going to scar, Ms. Cooper, if we don't get them stitched properly."

"I don't care." Regina hadn't said much in the half hour since she'd arrived at The Lemonade Stand, partially, Lynn suspected, because it hurt too much to talk.

"You're a beautiful young woman," she said. "You've got your whole life ahead of you. And we need to get these taken care of properly."

Sara Havens, one of the Stand's counselors, was outside, waiting to take Regina under her wing. She'd know better what to say. But they didn't have weeks, or even days, for counseling to change Regina's mind about these cuts.

A member of the Stand's small full-time security team was there, too, standing guard.

Lynn's face was inches from the other woman's as she gently worked the torn skin together as well as she could. Regina's pretty blue eyes met hers. "You see where my beauty got me?" she asked in a near-whisper, her eyes growing moist but not enough for a tear to fall. "I can do without it."

"You'll remember him, and the beating you just

took, every single time you look in the mirror if we don't get these properly stitched," she said.

"I'm going to remember anyway."

"You want to wear his anger? To keep him with you every minute of every day for the rest of your life?" Nursing school had taught her how to tend to bodies. The year she'd spent in grad school after Kara's birth had provided her with her advanced nursing midwifery certification. The two years she'd been living full-time at The Lemonade Stand had been a completely different education. "You want to let him mark you that way?"

Tears blurred the hurt-filled blue eyes. "I can't afford stitches," the woman said. "I don't even know how I'm going to pay for the butterfly bandages. I can't use my health insurance. It's through his work and he'll know where to find me...."

Stopping her work, Lynn studied the younger woman. "That's why you won't agree to stitches? Because of the cost?"

Regina nodded. "I went to the ATM as soon as I left, but he'd already drained our account. I've got a hundred bucks on me, this week's grocery allowance, and that's it."

Regina spoke slowly, sounding as if she had marbles in her mouth, but she made herself understood.

Going for stitching supplies, Lynn pulled on a fresh pair of sterilized procedure gloves. "Your care here is free, Regina," she said. "I thought you knew that."

"Medical care, too?"

"Everything. For the first four weeks you're here, you have access to all services, and pay only what you can afford to pay. If that's nothing, then nothing is what you owe." She smiled at the young woman. "Now, are you going to let me take proper care of you and get this stitched?"

"Yes, ma'am." Regina's mouth wouldn't allow a smile, but the relieved look in her eyes spoke volumes.

And twenty minutes later, when Lynn turned over her newest patient to Sara Havens, who would see Regina through the admissions process and get her set up with clean clothes, toiletries and a safe place to sleep, she was fairly certain she'd managed to minimize the damage Regina's husband's brutality had inflicted.

At least on the surface.

"LYNN?" THIRTY-FIVE-YEAR-OLD Maddie Estes, one of only a few permanent residents at The Lemonade Stand, looked upset as she hurried toward Lynn just after Sara escorted Regina out of the three-room health clinic located in the main house.

"What's up, Maddie?" Lynn smiled at the pretty woman who was three years older than her by birth, but fifteen years younger in mental acuity. Maddie's developmental challenges, present since a premature birth, caused the sweet, gentle woman to worry over small things.

But with regular weekly physical therapy sessions, Maddie's motor skills, while slow, were finally within the normal range.

The woman's hands were flailing as she moved.

"There's a man here. He's been waiting to see you for a long time. He looks like he might be getting mad. You know, walking back and forth and back and forth in the hallway and slapping his baseball cap against his hand."

Maddie emulated the motion with jerky movements, her gaze meeting Lynn's only for a brief stop as it traveled around the space they occupied—the empty waiting room at the clinic. Lynn held regular, well-check office hours. They'd long since passed on that particular Tuesday in February.

"A man?" Lynn frowned, more concerned by Maddie's agitation than any visitor she might have. "Did he say who he was?"

After suffering for fourteen years at the hands of a man who'd once adored her but had grown to hate the sight of her, Maddie was extrasensitive to any sign of male aggression. And Lynn was particularly protective of Maddie.

"Grant...I can't remember what. I'm sorry, Lynn. I know I should remember, but he's just so upset, and your treatment light was on and I didn't know what to do so I took him to the bench in the main hall and waited back here for you."

"Grant Bishop!" Lynn said, remembering. She'd had an appointment with the man almost an hour ago. And had completely forgotten.

He'd called that morning, said he couldn't get there until four-thirty. And if he had a woman in jeopardy, she'd just made them wait even longer.

"You know him, then? I'm sorry, Lynn, I probably made him mad, but—"

With one hand stilling Maddie's twisting hands, Lynn looked the woman straight in the eye and said, "It's okay, Maddie. You did the right thing." Maddie's fidgeting stilled instantly.

"And now, can you do a favor for me?"

"Of course!" Maddie smiled. She agitated easily, but she settled easily, too.

"Kara's in the playroom," Lynn said, picturing her curly-haired three-year-old with a crayon in her hand and her tongue sticking out of her mouth. "I was supposed to pick her up at six and it's almost that now. Can you collect her and take her home for me? There's some leftover macaroni and cheese in the fridge. I'll be there as soon as I can be."

"Of course!" Maddie said again, hurrying away down the hall, but turning back before she got far. "Can I give her her bath, too?" Maddie asked.

Lynn liked to reserve bath time—and bedtime story reading—for herself. To keep some semblance of normal family and routine for the preschooler who was growing up so untraditionally in the arms of so many people who loved her.

"How about if we give her her bath together?" Lynn suggested, now conscious of the man waiting for her. Bath time was at eight, as delineated by the detailed schedule Lynn kept on her refrigerator. A schedule that Maddie followed religiously. "I'll be home in plenty of time," she assured the short but slender blonde woman.

"Okay, Lynn." Maddie's expression was serious. "And we'll save some macaroni for you, too. You'll get hungry if you don't have dinner."

Bless Maddie. She might struggle to understand the monetary value of coins and dollars, to connect the heating and lighting in her room with a bill that had to be paid, or to ascertain the nuances of human interaction, but she knew how to pay attention. To nurture.

And she was adamant about nurturing Lynn and Kara most of all.

They were lucky to be so loved.

FOR THE UMPTEENTH time Grant looked at his watch—and pulled his cell phone out of the holster on his belt, just to verify that the time he'd read on his wrist piece was accurate. He'd hoped to get to Darin by suppertime. To make certain that his brother ate. And did it sitting in his chair, not lying in bed.

The doctor had said Darin could get up as soon as he was ready. And he didn't need his left hand to feed himself. Or to chew and swallow, either.

Almost as soon as he'd returned his phone to its holster, he felt it vibrate. Darin, wondering where he was?

Pulling the cell phone out, he was already answering when he saw the caller ID. Luke Stellar, his right-hand man.

"This is Grant," he answered as he always did.

"Fountain's in and running."

A rock edifice he'd designed to the homeowner's specification. "What was the problem?"

When he'd had to leave at four-thirty to make his appointment at The Lemonade Stand before getting back to Darin, they'd had a water flow issue.

"A twist in the main line as it came around the first bend."

"The PVC track should have prevented that from happening."

"Craig missed a piece of the track when he installed it."

How did one miss a piece of a piping apparatus that fit together to make a whole?

"I'm not sure he's going to work out." And Grant didn't have time to hire another new guy. Craig had been with them six months and Grant had had high hopes for the kid.

"He just found out his wife's having a baby," Luke told him.

Luke had two little kids. And he was late getting home to dinner with them. Again.

The guy never complained. And Grant had ridden both of his full-time employees hard that day.

"I should have known that," he said aloud, keeping his voice down as he paced the empty hallway—a twenty-by-ten-foot tiled area that was clearly separate and apart from the mysterious inner sanctum of The Lemonade Stand's main building. "I owe you, man," he told Luke now.

"Buy me a beer sometime," Luke shot back at him.

He'd have to make that a twelve-pack. At the very least. If Grant didn't have Darin… If he'd been able to give the business all of the time and energy Luke brought to it, they could have grown Bishop Landscaping into a lucrative company instead of a highly sought-after, well-booked, small-time operation that supported three families instead of dozens.

Telling Luke that he'd be at the job site at five-thirty the next morning to sign off on the work that had been done and to lay out the next phase of the waterfall garden's installation, Grant rang off. He paced, and then came to rest in front of the glass door leading out to a small, nondescript visitor parking lot that needed shrubbery around it, some perennials for color....

"Mr. Bishop?"

Turning, he recognized the woman approaching him at once. Her long hair was pulled back tightly from her face, but the warm glow in her eyes was just as he'd remembered.

He'd told himself he'd imagined the woman's effect on him the last time Darin had been in the hospital—four years before.

She'd had a wedding ring on back then. She didn't now.

"Lynn," he said, because back then that's all that had been written on her name tag—and that's what he'd called her. She held out her hand. He took it.

And didn't want to let go.

"You don't remember me," he said, quickly shoving his hands into the pockets of his jeans as he faced her in the empty, fluorescent-lit hallway. He'd heard that The Lemonade Stand was beautiful, a haven, resortlike. The commercial beige tile and white walls didn't give him that impression at all.

"I do, actually," she said. "Now that I see you. I recognized your name when you called, but I wasn't sure why. You're the one with the brother. Darin, right?"

"I'm impressed." Grant smiled, in spite of how late he was for his visit with Darin. How late she'd made him. "You were his nurse for one day of a three-day stay, and have to have had hundreds of patients in your years as a nurse. You've got a good memory."

"Darin was memorable."

She didn't say why. He could guess. Darin's brain was damaged, his body wasn't. Grant's older brother had had girls goo-goo eyed over him for as long as Grant could remember. Even after so many years since his accident, Darin's facial expression didn't show his lack of mental coherence. You didn't get that until you'd talked to him for a few minutes and experienced some of his childlike thought processes. Which were interspersed with moments of complete lucidity.

"So what can I do for you?" Lynn asked, that not-quite smile he remembered curving her lips and hitting him where a guy only liked to be hit when he could do something about it. "You said you needed to speak with me in person."

He'd thought maybe they'd be sitting in her office, not standing out in the hall.

He'd thought she'd remember him, too, and she had. But more important, she'd remembered his brother.

With enough affection to pull strings?

The Lemonade Stand was the only option he had. This had to work.

CHAPTER THREE

He had to go.

Facing Grant Bishop in the only section of The Lemonade Stand that was accessible to anyone walking in off the street, she couldn't believe it was *him*. The one man who, in all the years she'd been married, had ever tempted her to think about being unfaithful to Brandon.

Not that either man knew. Or would ever know.

But four years ago, just before she'd become pregnant with Kara, there'd been a bit of an attraction between them. At least, *she'd* been attracted. And she'd been as certain as she could be without verbal confirmation that he was aware of her, as well. There'd been a moment or two of recognition, of something that could've been interesting if she hadn't been married. And if she hadn't been his brother's nurse.

The sexual feelings he'd aroused within her had scared her so badly she'd gone home and made love to her husband like she'd never made love before. Over and over again. For more than a month. Long after Darin Bishop had been discharged and the brothers had left her life forever.

Kara had been the result.

"My brother developed an infection around the portion of stingray barb still lodged in his brain," Grant Bishop was saying.

He wasn't there to see her personally.

Of course not.

"I'm no longer working at the hospital, Mr. Bishop." She could have invited him back to her office. The anonymity of the front hall felt better.

"I know."

He smiled. At her?

Or just to be polite?

"Dr. Zimmer told me this morning that you've been here full-time for the past couple of years. He said there's a physical therapy program here that sometimes accepts nonresident patients. He also said The Lemonade Stand welcomes men into these programs whenever possible—after extensive background checks, of course. That it's part of the overall therapy program for your residents. Something about women needing positive male influences in their environment because it helps build trust, and they'll have to deal with men when they're back in the outside world. Makes sense. I understand you're the chief medical person in charge and thought that maybe, since Darin was once your patient, you might be able to help pave the way for us here. If there is a way."

He wasn't there because he'd remembered her.

Feeling like a bit of a fool, but a relieved one, Lynn kept her face schooled to polite calmness—a talent that she'd developed early on in her nursing career—and said, "Dr. Zimmer sent you?"

The surgeon had been one of her favorites. As busy as he'd been, he'd spent as much time with his patients as they'd needed—emotionally, not just physically. The bodies he worked on weren't just the job. They were attached to people he'd seemed to genuinely care about.

"Darin had surgery yesterday morning to drain the infection. As a result he's displaying partial paralysis on his left side." The look in those brown eyes, a combination of strength and little-boy-lost, tugged at her in a way that was reminiscent of four years before.

No man was ever going to have power over her emotions again.

Her job as live-in certified nurse/midwife at a woman's shelter generally precluded the chance.

"He's going to need physical therapy several times a week over the next few months if he's to have any hope of ever obtaining full mobility again."

Like a flash of lightning, she saw where this was

going. "Dr. Zimmer suggested you apply here for Darin's therapy."

"He also told me that The Lemonade Stand sometimes trades services for services."

"For residents. Or previous residents," she clarified. Many of the services offered at The Lemonade Stand were free to the Stand, donated by former clients. Or by current residents. Some by way of payment. And some just because.

"That's what Dr. Zimmer said." Grant Bishop nodded. "He also said that you have group therapy sessions when patients have similar needs and don't require one-on-one physical touch, and those sessions are less expensive." Grant shrugged as he added, "But he explained that male involvement in group therapy is a sensitive issue and has to be decided on a case-by-case basis."

His hands were still in his pockets. Lynn was still distracted.

"The thing is, I can't afford physical therapy sessions at all."

"Darin's on disability insurance, isn't he?" She'd seen something about it on his paperwork—not that she paid attention or remembered such things about her former patients, but Darin and Grant...they'd been different.

Brothers who were all alone. Devoted. And acting as if their lives were perfect.

"It covers eighty percent of his costs. And I'm

going to be tapped out for a while covering the other twenty percent of yesterday's surgery."

A craniotomy, which was the only way to do the drainage he'd spoken of, could run fifty thousand or more. Just for the procedure. Add in hospital and supply costs...

"I don't know what—"

"Please..." the man interrupted her. "Dr. Zimmer thought you might be able to put a word in for me with Lila McDaniels. I understand she's the managing director of The Lemonade Stand. I'm a landscaper," he continued, almost as though if he didn't stop for air he wouldn't be able to hear the word *no*. "I own a small design business. Darin works with me and I employ a couple of other guys. I don't know what you're currently paying for yard care, but I can already see that that parking lot out there could benefit from some shrubbery." He pointed to the small lot accessible to the public. "I suspect we could make improvements to the rest of the grounds, as well. We'd be willing to take it all on, for free, in exchange for Darin's therapy. Dr. Zimmer said that if there's a session for general motor skill exercise, he'd be fine there."

"And afterward?" Lynn asked, going with the first objection she could voice. "We fire our landscapers, you take over for the couple of months that Darin needs therapy and then what happens?"

"We'll continue to service the clinic indefinitely

at a rate that's ten percent less than you're currently paying."

"You don't know what we're currently paying," she reminded him.

"My brother could be partially paralyzed for the rest of his life if I don't get him this therapy."

If she recommended him, Lila would pay attention. Angelica Morrison, the Stand's physical therapist, would approve the decision, too. As long as both men passed background checks. The Stand's founder was actually a man. A good man. The world was filled with good men. And the residents at The Lemonade Stand needed to be exposed to them.

Grant Bishop's proposal completely fit with their mission statement. Lynn had nothing to do with the Stand's finances, but she was privy to them. Their landscaping bill was exorbitant—and rising.

And landscaping was paramount to the overall healing atmosphere of their center.

"You do realize that the secondhand store and boutique out on the boulevard are part of our center? And the garage on the corner is ours, too," she added. The Lemonade Stand owned a city block.

He'd be responsible for the exterior grounds of all of it.

"I didn't, no. But it doesn't matter. Darin will do what he can. And my boys and I will take care of the rest."

"What about your other jobs?"

"I'll handle them." He was determined. She'd give him that. And she didn't really know much about the landscape business. They took care of yards, she figured. Cleaning up, trimming, cutting grass. Planting. He'd said his business was small. And mentioned design.

Apparently, he was successful enough to support not only him and Darin, but two other men, as well.

"You haven't seen the inner grounds."

He shrugged. "Doesn't matter."

"I think you might change your mind," she said, wishing it were light outside so she could give him a quick, escorted tour of the secured area of The Lemonade Stand—the area where their real work was done. Arms crossed in front of her, she said, "The philosophy here at The Lemonade Stand—when life gives you lemons you make lemonade—is taught by action, not by word." She started in on a speech she'd heard many times before. The rote PR words that every senior staff member at the Stand knew by heart—because they were expected to live by them and up to them.

"We're here to help abused women recover—and to make healthy choices for their futures," she continued. "By nature of what they've come from—being mistreated by someone close to them, someone they trusted to love them—they've mostly learned, often subconsciously, that they don't deserve the best. Abused women, by and large, have low self-concepts. Many of them believe that they're somehow to blame for their abuse. Before they can fully believe in themselves and take charge of broken lives, they have to feel good about who they are. Environment is a huge part of that."

Lynn was leading up to telling him about the grounds at the Stand. The mammoth undertaking that Grant Bishop was offering to absorb without realizing what he was getting himself into. But she stopped speaking for a second when she realized that the speech she was giving was similar to one any prospective employee of the Stand would receive. Like she'd already mentally employed him.

"I understand." His brown-eyed gaze was soft. And she started to speak again.

"Our residents' emotional and mental states are brought on by actions, and we believe that the only way to truly counteract the damage to their psyches is to counteract action with action."

"Absolutely."

"They've been treated horribly and they need to be treated well, not just be told that they deserve to be treated well."

"You don't have to worry about my boys. Luke and I have known each other since college. He's married, has kids, is a great dad. And Craig's wife is expecting their first child. But if you'd rather,

I can make certain that only Darin and I service this facility."

"The women live in bungalows," she said. "Usually four women to a place." Each one had four bedrooms with adjoining bathrooms. Each one was surrounded by beautiful landscaping. "Their living quarters are what they should be able to expect their homes to be—a place that cushions them from the challenges that life will inevitably hand them."

"We'll stay completely away from them."

"First and foremost, these women need to be taught that they are worthy. We treat them like royalty. They are expected to treat one another like royalty and, through action, we hope to replace negative lessons with positive ones."

Grant Bishop leaned forward. "Lynn, I understand. Do any background checks you need to do. I swear to you, your residents have absolutely nothing to fear from any of us, and most particularly not from Darin and me. We will keep our distance from residents at all times, and if we do happen to come into contact with anyone at any time we will show her nothing but respect. You have my word on that."

He smiled. Her stomach flipped.

This was getting way too out of hand.

"Mr. Bishop, what I'm trying to tell you is that, inside the grounds, The Lemonade Stand is resort-like. We're on the ocean, just like most of Santa Raquel. Our facilities, including our landscaping, rival any fine resort on the California coast. The Stand is a safe haven—a place women *want* to be. And the grounds reflect that."

He blinked. Stared for a second, and said, "You're telling me I'm in for a lot of hard work."

"What I'm trying to tell you is that you can't possibly do the job you're promising to do. You have no idea what you're letting yourself in for."

"I will get the work done and do as good a job— or a better job—than the company currently providing the services."

The man was determined.

A characteristic she admired. A lot.

"My brother's quality of life depends on him having that therapy." His gaze spoke directly to her heart.

He wasn't getting it. She couldn't have him around.

"There are only so many hours in a day and you'll still have to earn a living."

"Before he went in for surgery, Darin was experiencing serious bouts of depression," he said. "They were growing increasingly worse, with times of moroseness similar to what we went through about a year after his accident. If he ends up paralyzed for life, I'm going to lose him."

The man's desperation was understandable.

"I'll get the work done," Grant Bishop said again, the words as firm as any promise she'd ever heard.

"I generally do the design work and the guys do the physical labor, which leaves me evenings to focus completely on Darin. If I have to, I'll spend the days out in the yards here, and do my design work at night. Darin needs this therapy more than he needs trips to baseball games with me. And I swear to you, your residents will have nothing to fear from either me or Darin. He's like he is because he was protecting a woman."

The cause of Darin's condition, the stingray barb lodged in his brain, had been in his file. The circumstances that had caused that barb to be there were not.

She couldn't help herself. "What happened?" she asked.

Boundaries! The word screamed in her brain. Vital rule of health care—keep your boundaries.

But things were different at the Stand.

"He and his wife were scuba diving. She got tangled in her line and was losing all of her air. He got her untangled but was attacked by the stingray during the process so it took him longer than it should have. Badly bleeding and half out of his mind, he still got her up to the surface."

"Darin's married?"

"Was."

"She left him? After he saved her life?" Because he was brain damaged. Some people were that selfish.

"She died. She was gone by the time they got her out of the water."

"After he went through all that she didn't make it?"

Grant swallowed, and that told her more than any words he could have said.

"If there was anywhere else I could afford to get the quality of therapy he needs, I'd be pounding on their door, too." Grant Bishop's quiet words fell into the silence. "Dr. Zimmer said that The Lemonade Stand is Darin's best hope. Apparently, your therapist has a group session for the mentally handicapped."

"Yes," Lynn said. "She specializes in working with emotionally—and mentally—handicapped patients who are also physically injured." The group session for the mentally handicapped had only one patient at the moment.

"Dr. Zimmer indicated that she's good at encouraging the hopeless to find hope," Grant Bishop said, looking her straight in the eye.

They were her own words to Dr. Zimmer the last time she'd seen him.

Grant said Darin had been suffering from depression even before the surgery. Lynn surmised that without sensitivity to Darin's emotional issues, physical therapy might do him no good at all.

The Lemonade Stand, founded by a young man who'd grown up in an abusive household, existed to help save and protect human life. In a very real sense, Darin's life depended on them. If the landscaping work was too much for Grant's small company, they could hire out half of the landscaping, help Darin and still save the Stand some money.

"I'll make a recommendation," Lynn told the man. "Talk to your brother to make certain that you'll have his cooperation with your plan, and call me in the morning."

Call me in the morning. The words were a medical cliché, and in this case, they were a promise, too.

CHAPTER FOUR

"TELL ME AGAIN what this woman's name is." Sitting straight up, looking as handsome as ever in jeans and a button-down shirt with the sleeves rolled up to just beneath his elbows, Darin spoke with the authority of one who was in complete control. He was using his "normal" voice, as Grant had somewhere along the way begun to catalog it. "Normal" as opposed to his "child" voice—the one that was a repercussion of the brain damage he'd received during his attempt to save his wife's life.

"Lynn Duncan."

"And she was my nurse."

"Four years ago, yes."

"I don't remember her."

"You might when you see her."

With his chin jutting slightly forward, Darin nodded, his gaze toward the highway visible through the front windshield.

"You know what I miss most?" Darin asked.

"Besides your memory, you mean?" Grant quipped lightly. Because that was what the brothers did in these moments when Darin could focus clearly.

"I miss driving," Darin said. "How come you don't ever let me drive, Grant?"

Just like that, the child was back, the last words ending on a near-whine.

"You can drive sometime," Grant said just as easily as he'd named the nurse they were on their way to see. "I'll take you out to the desert this weekend."

To the vast expanse of land they visited on occasion, just to let Darin get behind the wheel of a vehicle again.

His older brother turned to stare at him. "You promise?"

He'd hoped to have the weekend to tend to landscaping at the women's shelter. Hoped to be able to do the job in his spare time. To spare Luke and Craig any additional work. "Yeah, I promise," he said, because he had to.

And because he hadn't even seen the women's shelter landscaping. Maybe Lynn had been exaggerating. Seeing the job from a layman's eyes. He and his guys had designed and installed a block's worth of new landscaping in a day. Surely it couldn't take Darin and Grant more than that to keep it up.

"But today is only Monday so we have to get a week's worth of work done first," he said now as they pulled into the parking lot outside the The Lemonade Stand.

"They make lemonade here?" Darin asked. "I like lemonade. Do you think they'll let me have some?"

"There's a cafeteria," Grant said, information gleaned from his recent conversation with Lynn, Angelica and Lila McDaniels to finalize their plans and schedule Darin's first therapy session. "We'll see if they have lemonade. And you remember what I told you about the ladies, right?"

They'd been over this every day for the past week. Morning and night.

"They've been hurt and need me to stay away."

It was the childish version, but at least the message was clear.

"That's right."

"I've never hurt anyone, have I, Grant?"

"Nope. As long as you don't count those times you got me in a headlock and knuckle brushed my head."

"Yeah," Darin snorted as he grinned. "But you deserved it."

"What did I ever do to deserve that? It hurt like hell."

"One time you put my leather baseball glove in the bathtub."

"It was dirty. I wanted to clean it for you."

"You ruined it, Grant."

"I know." But he hadn't meant to. He'd been four at the time.

"It was my first real glove and Mom and Dad didn't have the money to buy me another one."

Funny how things worked. Darin had damaged

crucial parts of his brain attempting to save his wife. But he could still remember an event like this, which had happened more than thirty years before, as if it'd been yesterday.

"I'm sorry."

Darin nodded. And gazed out at the nondescript parking lot.

"I'm afraid, Grant." His tone was back to preaccident Darin. The admission was nothing he'd ever have expected to hear from his big brother.

"What if therapy doesn't work?" he went on. "What if I never get the use of my arm back? I'm burden enough to you."

Shoving the truck's automatic gearshift into Park, Grant gave Darin a light punch on the shoulder. "It's going to work, bro. And in the meantime, you're going to be pushing a lawn mower with one hand. Just be glad it's your right one that works."

With one capable movement, Darin unfastened his seat belt and opened the door to the truck. Grant read the tension in the stiffness of his brother's upper lip.

"Hey," he said, a hand on Darin's paralyzed limb. "We're in this together, right?"

As long as Darin believed that, they'd be fine. Because Grant wasn't going to let go. Or give up. Ever.

Darin took a long moment to answer. Grant waited.

"Right." The answer finally came.

With that, Grant led his slightly taller and broader brother into the front hallway of The Lemonade Stand.

"LYNN!" THE CRY was a harried whisper. "That man is back."

Sitting in her office close to the public access door at the Stand, Lynn glanced up from charting a twenty-eight-year-old pregnant woman who'd just been in for a checkup to see Maddie hovering in the doorway.

She frowned. "What man?"

A lot of men wanted access to their residents. The Stand's job was to keep them away.

"The one who was here before, the baseball-cap-slapping-when-he-walked-in-the-hallway one."

Ah. Grant Bishop. He was fifteen minutes early.

"It's okay, Maddie, we're expecting him. Lila was supposed to tell you."

Lila McDaniels, The Lemonade Stand's managing director, made it a point to give Maddie her duties every single morning.

"Oh, that's right. I just saw that baseball cap and freaked out, didn't I?" the woman said. "And he's got someone with him, too. Lynn, is that okay? Does Lila know about him?"

Standing, Lynn wrapped an arm around the pretty woman's slim shoulders; this morning Maddie wore a yellow Lemonade Stand oxford shirt with their white logo stitched above the breast pocket. "His name's Darin," Lynn said as she led the woman out to the hallway. "He's going to be doing therapy with you during your session and…he's…special, Maddie. I was hoping you'd spin some of your Maddie magic on him and help him feel welcome."

"I just like to be around women."

"I know, but he's a nice man. He's been approved to be here, and I'm asking as a special favor," Lynn said, praying that her assessment of Darin hadn't been wrong four years before. And that it wasn't wrong to trust that assessment a little bit now. "You won't have to be alone with him at all, and if he makes you afraid, you're to stop Angelica immediately and she'll get you out of there."

She could have told Maddie about the newest patient in what was scheduled as a group therapy session but most often consisted of just Maddie. But she hadn't wanted her to fret—and blow the situation so far out of proportion that she wouldn't be capable of trying.

Lynn, stopping on the private side of the door leading out to the lobby, put both her hands on Maddie's shoulders. "You know we've all talked about the fact that you don't want to live your whole life afraid of men," she said.

Maddie nodded.

"You and Sara have talked about this a lot and you told her that you understood and would try."

Maddie was frowning. "But I didn't know it meant now, Lynn," she said, her voice trembling. "Sara didn't say it was now. Does Lila know?"

"Yes." Maddie's cooperation wasn't critical to Darin's opportunity at the Stand, but it was vital to Maddie's mental and emotional health. "I believe what Sara explained to you was that you can't continue to live here forever if you don't try your best to be healthy. We aren't a hideout, Maddie, and we don't want the women who come to us to think that we are. As a resident here, you're an example to them, so you can't be hiding out, either. That means you have to be able to be around men occasionally."

"I know, but—"

"Maddie? Look at me." Lynn waited.

The pretty blue eyes eventually focused on her. "What Alan did, I don't want that anymore, Lynn," she said, her eyes filling with tears. "And I…you know…I'm…well…I wasn't smart enough to stop him."

All the air left Lynn's lungs. She'd never heard Maddie acknowledge her challenges. Wasn't even sure how much she was aware of them.

"Alan abused you because he was a bad person, Maddie, and for no other reason. You stayed because you loved him. Just like lots of the other women here. Think of Jennifer. She's practically a genius and she stayed."

"She's an animal doctor."

"I know," Lynn said. "I've met Darin, Maddie. He's a good person, I promise."

Maddie nodded, but looked at the door in front of them as though she was facing a guillotine.

Grant Bishop had signed all of the necessary waivers on Darin's behalf, allowing those within the shelter to share his information.

"Darin had a brain injury, Maddie. He...struggles."

The slender woman's brows drew farther together as she alternated between biting and licking her lower lip. "Is he retarded?"

"No. And you know we don't like that word. But sometimes things don't come together for him like they used to."

"He's dumb like me?"

What was this? She'd never heard Maddie sound so derogatory about herself. But then, they'd only been close for a little over a year.

"You aren't dumb, Maddie."

"I am, too, Lynn. And Sara says that I have to be strong and face my life, not run from it."

"Did you tell Sara you were dumb?" There was no way the counselor would have promoted such thinking. Or allowed it if she could help put a stop to it.

Maddie looked down.

And Lynn got a sick feeling. "Who told you you were dumb?"

Maddie shrugged. And mumbled, "No one."

With a finger under the woman's chin, Lynn lifted Maddie's face until she looked her straight in the eye.

"Maddie? You know my rule. It's okay if you make a million mistakes a day, you just don't lie to me."

Her eyes widening in horror, Maddie said, "I don't, Lynn, I swear I don't and—"

"It's okay, I know you don't." Lynn gave Maddie's shoulders a squeeze. "And I need you to tell me who told you you were dumb."

"I don't want to get anybody in trouble, and besides, she didn't tell *me*."

"Who did she tell?"

"Regina Cooper with the stitches in her face."

"And what did Regina say?"

"She told her to shut up because she saw me standing there."

"She told her not to talk like that because it's not true," Lynn said now, letting Maddie off the hook, while making a mental note to prepare Sara for her next session with Maddie. And to mention the incident at their staff meeting later that morning, too.

They'd know who was talking to Regina about Maddie by the end of the day. And if it happened again, the mystery woman would be asked to leave.

"Maddie? Darin Bishop got hurt trying to save his wife," she said. "I'm trusting you with that information because I know you're smart enough to know what to do with it."

Maddie stared at her, blinking a couple of times while she chewed her lip, and then took Lynn's hand from off her shoulder and clutched it tightly. "Okay, Lynn, let's go. I'll be friends with him," she said.

And for Maddie, that appeared to be that.

In that moment, as she pushed through the door to greet Grant and Darin Bishop, Lynn almost envied the other woman's simplicity.

CHAPTER FIVE

"I REMEMBER YOU." Darin's wide-faced grin matched his five-year-old tone and Grant stiffened, a natural reaction to exposing his older brother to people who might not expect to hear near–baby talk coming from a grown man.

Because if they reacted adversely, Darin would be able to tell and it would upset him.

"You do?" Lynn's smile appeared genuine as she approached, her gaze meeting Darin's. She held out her hand. "I'm glad because I've never forgotten you."

"I'm pretty memorable." Darin shook Lynn's hand as his voice reverted to that of a grown man. A completely harmless, charming grown man.

"I'm glad you're here."

"I'm going to work hard because I want to use my arm and because I promised Grant. Who's that?" Like Grant, Darin had noticed the slender blonde woman in jeans and a staff blouse who was hovering behind Lynn.

Unlike Grant, his older brother had the tact of a child.

"Darin, Grant, this is Maddie," Lynn said, turning to take the other woman's hand and pull her forward.

"You're pretty." Darin smiled the killer smile that had been unwittingly stealing hearts from good men for most of his life.

"It's good to meet you," Maddie said, her words a tad slow and thick sounding. After a quick glance at each of them, her gaze returned to the floor.

"Do you see a spider?" Darin asked. "I could kill it for you. I can step on him. Both of my feet still work."

"I don't see a spider." With a sideways glance, Maddie seemed to send Lynn some kind of message.

"Maddie's in physical therapy, too," Lynn said. "She and Darin will be sharing this morning's session."

"And maybe more," Maddie said. "Angelica mostly works with groups unless someone needs her to stand right there next to them the whole time. I don't need that. I know my exercises and don't need help with the machines anymore. She just has to check and make sure that I'm using my muscles right."

Grant studied the other woman. She was…way above average in the looks department. Her blue gaze was clear. And yet…she reminded him of Darin. Postaccident Darin.

"Maddie works here," Lynn told the two men.

"I'm a good Friday."

"A girl Friday," Lynn said quickly, and Grant took a mental step back. He'd been so busy taking care of his own business and finding help for Darin that he hadn't really considered the day-to-day business of The Lemonade Stand.

Lynn had mentioned residents. She'd been referring to abused and battered women.

Like Maddie?

Was she in therapy to recover from injuries caused by physical abuse?

Had she been hit in the head?

"I saw a movie called *His Girl Friday*," Darin inserted into the conversation. "It's a Cary Grant film that's part of the National Film Registry's catalog and ranks number nineteen on the American Film Institute's 100 Years...100 Laughs," the man who'd once been headed toward a top position on Wall Street finished.

"That was a funny movie," Maddie said. "That guy kept getting arrested. But I didn't like it that the main guy yelled all the time. If you'd like to come with me, I'll show you where we do therapy...."

Darin stepped forward, took Maddie's elbow and Lynn started. She looked as though she was going to step in.

"Okay, but I'm a little scared." Darin's childlike voice could be heard as the two walked through the door that Darin opened after letting go of Maddie while she typed a code into the box on the wall. "I can't use my left arm at all, you know...."

Lynn followed, looking like a mother hen as her gaze darted back and forth between Maddie and Darin.

"He won't hurt her," Grant whispered, leaning in close as he fell into step beside her.

Lynn put visible and immediate distance between them, saying nothing. And Grant cursed himself silently for not being more aware, more in tune, with the fact that he and his brother had just entered a very sensitive culture.

It wasn't going to be enough just to make certain that he and Darin didn't do anything to hurt these women; they were going to have to be aware that every move they made, every look they gave, every sentence they spoke, could potentially scare any one of them.

Lynn Duncan included—apparently.

"WE CAN WATCH through here." Avoiding eye contact with the man she'd been schooling herself not to think about for a week now, Lynn walked toward the large window in the hallway outside the physical therapy room where Maddie had led Darrin. "Angelica keeps the blinds closed when she has to, but if she can keep them open, she does. A lot of battered women suffer from PTSD—post-traumatic stress disorder—and often that's accompanied by bouts of claustrophobia." Keeping it professional. Aside from the warmth that suffused her body as it came, once again, in close contact with Grant Bishop.

What in the hell was the matter with her?

Darin looked up, saw them and waved. With a tap on his shoulder, Angelica called his attention back to her and the bar she'd placed within his brother's left grasp.

"If you want to hand me over to whoever's going to show me the grounds, we can move on," Grant said. "He'll do better if I'm not here distracting him."

"Lila, our managing director, was going to go over things with you, but she's…busy…this morning." Their newest resident, a middle-aged woman named Melanie Zoyne, had appeared on the doorstep in the middle of the night with no broken bones or cuts that needed stitching, but bruising on every bruisable part of her body. "My next appointment isn't until after lunch, so as long as there aren't any emergencies, I've been elected to do the honors."

She'd been up with Melanie since three—thankfully there'd been no indication of internal injuries to accompany the varying stages of bruising the woman's brother had left in his wake—and was running on adrenaline.

Which might explain the weakened state that was

allowing for inappropriate reactions to the jeans-clad man standing beside her.

He was just a man. Like any other.

"Darin's eager to please you." It was one of the things she'd noticed about the brothers four years before. Rather than being cantankerous or resentful, as many injury patients were, Darin just seemed to want to keep his brother happy.

Did Grant have that effect on everyone?

"He's eager to get the use of his arm back," the man at her side said, his gaze trained on his brother. And then he glanced at her. "Dr. Zimmer says that the location of the injury, the part of the brain affected by the surgery, is retrainable. With hard work Darin will be as good as new."

As good as he'd ever be with an incurable brain injury. Grant was still watching her. Waiting?

"I know, he told me," she said. "And while I'm not a surgeon, I dealt with a lot of brain injury patients during my years on the neurosurgery ward, and from everything I've studied, seen and learned, I completely believe that Darin can recover from this latest setback." She sounded like the consummate professional. With a last glance in the therapy room, not at Grant's brother, but to make certain that Maddie was fine, Lynn headed down the wide hallway, stopping to straighten a magazine on one of the cherrywood end tables in one of the conversation nooks stationed along the wall.

She'd take him to Lila's outer office. Show him the large map of the grounds on the wall across from Lila's desk. Take him out to the garage that housed the lawn equipment and fertilizer they already owned—collected through donations. Then give him a brief tour of the private beach and the bungalows because he couldn't explore those unescorted—and finally get back to real life.

Lunch with Kara, whom she hadn't seen since Maddie had brought the little girl to her office on the way to the preschool housed on the property. This was the private preschool for residents at the Stand, not the preschool run by current and former residents that was attended by neighboring children and—like the other businesses—helped support the Stand.

She'd get through these next moments and then get her mind back on the things that mattered most.

"YOU AND DARIN have the biggest part of the battle won," Lynn Duncan said as she guided him through a maze of hallways that were wide enough to be rooms. "He's willing to work hard."

"Darin's always been willing to go the extra mile."

"But his attitude is good," she said, turning another corner closely enough that he bumped into her.

And moved away immediately.

"After what you said about his depression, I expected him to be at least minimally resistant. In my experience, patients with a brain injury like his, one that allows moments of complete lucidity, tend to battle with frustration, resentment and even bitterness as they experience awareness of their loss again and again."

She didn't seem bothered by his accidental touch. Grant filed the knowledge away. Yet she'd shied away earlier, when he leaned in too close. He'd never dealt firsthand with a battered woman before, and while he'd assured the gorgeous nurse that he and Darin would behave with impeccable decorum, while his brother's future depended on them doing so, he'd just realized that he had no idea what that decorum required.

"Darin has his moments, but overall he handles his situation with the dignity and class that I've always associated with him," he said, keeping his voice level down, his tone easy.

One hall led to another and they entered a large, upscale lobby complete with a shiny black baby grand piano set on a dais that dominated about a quarter of the room.

"It's great when situations like these bring out the best in people. It could just as easily have brought out the worst." Lynn sounded like a doctor on rounds with med students. Or at least what Grant imagined one would sound like.

"I can't honestly tell you what Darin's worst is. Except maybe taking too much on himself. Which, I'm told, brings on the depression. He can't stand being a burden to me. Or anyone."

The look she gave him was a bit unsettling, as though she was reading more into his words than he'd put there.

"So you take him to work with you so he feels like he's contributing," she said. "That can't be easy, trying to run a business and watching out for Darin at the same time."

He didn't like the way her statement made him feel. As if he had a problem. "Darin's a big help." He set her straight on that one. "Even in his childlike moments he can perform the simple tasks accurately."

As he spoke, his voice rose a bit, and Grant noticed the women milling in the areas around them. Some stared. A couple bowed their heads. One faded away down a hall, giving real meaning to the phrase "fading into the woodwork."

"I'm sorry," he said more softly. "Was I too loud?"

"You're fine." Her smile made him uncomfortable again. In an entirely different fashion. Grant didn't have a lot of opportunity for sex in his life, or women in general. But he liked them.

And he liked this particular woman a lot.

"You're with me," she said, as though that explained everything.

Maybe it did. These women trusted her.

"That's why we're walking all these hallways, isn't it?" he asked, eyeing her with new respect. "You're showing them that I'm trustworthy."

"Yes. But that doesn't mean they won't be afraid."

He nodded. And frowned, too, feeling as if he should be able to do something to help.

He was there to do landscaping. Nothing more.

"I'll keep my distance," he assured his companion as they entered yet another hallway, this one a bit narrower but still oversized, with closed doors lining both sides.

Lynn stopped before one and knocked. "It's okay to talk to anyone here," she told him. "As long as they speak with you first. Our residents need to feel safe, but they also need to be able to interact with men. The world they'll be going back to is full of them."

She smiled and, when her knock wasn't answered, opened the door.

"You know we did background checks on you and your brother this week," she was saying, reminding him of the permission he'd granted several days before when he'd stopped in to finalize details and paperwork for the day's appointments. "And Dr. Zimmer vouched for you, as well. You wouldn't be here if the staff had concerns about our residents being exposed to either one of you. We have four full-time security guards, all women, and three part-timers, two of whom are men. So there's someone here twenty-four hours a day, seven days a week. The bungalows all have panic buttons in them and everyone has Security on their speed dial."

Made sense.

They were in an office—of sorts. There was a desk in one section, but it didn't dominate the room.

"This is Lila's office," Lynn said, brushing a strand of hair back over her shoulder in a movement that was completely feminine—and drew his attention to her...womanliness.

The rest of the place looked like a formal living room in a wonderfully kept, warm and inviting home, with off-white couches, maroon pillows, a vase of roses on the glass coffee table and mirrors with gilded accents on the walls.

Grant was wearing leather work boots and the jeans he'd had on when he'd dug holes at six that morning to mark where a brick fence would be going.

If she was planning to ask him to have a seat, he'd have to come up with a tactful way to decline.

She turned to face the wall, holding the door they'd come through. "This map shows you The Lemonade Stand premises in its entirety," she said, walking up to a framed three-dimensional aerial photograph that was taller than he was and almost the width of the office.

Grant studied the scaled-to-size model of a complex that was twice as massive as he'd imagined.

And exquisitely laid out.

At one time, he'd had dreams of designing properties just like this one, and he was kind of jazzed at the thought of working on one again. Getting his hands dirty.

And maybe updating and making improvements, too, if…

He was getting ahead of himself. He mentioned flower beds, underground irrigation, fruit trees, all things that he imagined he was looking at but couldn't be sure.

"I'm sorry, I—"

"It's not a problem," Grant assured her, realizing that while Lynn understood the aesthetics of the grounds, she knew absolutely nothing about the technicalities of the job he had in store for him. "All I need is a walk around the place and I'll find my answers." He felt like grinning when the frown cleared from her brow.

She wasn't wearing any makeup.

He couldn't remember if she'd had makeup on the day he'd spent with her in the hospital four years before. But he thought so.

Her hair had been curled then, too, now that he thought about it. Gathered loosely in the back by some kind of clip. Darin had pulled on a curl, laughing when it sprang back, and Grant had stepped up, preparing to take accountability for his brother if the nurse had been offended. Instead, she'd let Darin pull the curl again and laughed with him this time.

Today her hair was as it had been when he'd seen her the week before. Pulled back tight into a ponytail, with the exception of that one small piece that had escaped and kept falling over her shoulder.

The change, between four years ago and now, made him curious, but no less attracted to her.

CHAPTER SIX

"DADDY GIVED ME this and I named him Sammy and then Daddy taked me to see el'phants but he spit and I got scared and Daddy picked me up and then he sucked water up his nooosse...." Kara's sweet little voice erupted in giggles. It was the following Saturday afternoon, almost a week since Darin and Grant Bishop had descended on The Lemonade Stand with their charm and kindness. A long week.

Brandon's gaze met Lynn's as she took the teddy bear her daughter handed her and stood back to let the two inside the bungalow Kara and Lynn shared. She looked away first. Quickly.

She'd just gotten off the phone with her folks, who lived in Denver to be close to Katie and her kids. Her mom didn't blame Brandon for his sexual preferences but didn't understand why he'd chosen to leave his family rather than ignore his gay tendencies. She'd been after Lynn to start dating again.

It was a continuous go-nowhere conversation.

"I took her to the zoo," Brandon said.

"You said you were going to the beach. She was

dressed for the beach and had flip-flops instead of tennis shoes."

"Can I take Sammy to show him our room?" The lispy voice piped up between them.

"Of course you can." Lynn smiled at her daughter and, bending down, added, "as soon as you give Mama a hug. I missed you, squirt."

"I miss you, too, Mama," Kara said, her pudgy little mouth pouty for a second as she leaned forward to give Lynn a wet kiss. Then, grabbing Sammy from Lynn's fingers, she tripped over her feet as she ran through the little living area toward her bedroom, stopping before she left them. "Bye, Daddy, see you soon I love you," she said, the words slurring together in a rush of baby talk that was their rote goodbye phrase, and was gone.

Lynn stood and took the day bag she'd packed that morning from Brandon's outstretched hand, avoiding eye contact. "You said you were taking her to the beach."

She sounded petulant. And hated that.

"Lynnie." Brandon took hold of her shoulders, turning her to face him. "I'm sorry," he said when, by rights, he could have been telling her to mind her own damned business. While she had full custody and he paid child support, Brandon also had full visiting privileges and didn't have to tell her anything about his time with Kara. Just like she didn't have to report to him every time she did something with her daughter.

He also didn't have to travel to Santa Raquel for every visit. He would be well within his rights to take the child to San Francisco where he'd moved after the divorce.

"I should have called."

She nodded. "Where's Douglas?"

"He had to work and couldn't make it down with me, which is why we didn't go to the beach. I couldn't prepare the picnic and keep an eagle eye on her by the water at the same time."

"I take her to the beach by myself."

"And you live with her, too. You know every move she's going to make practically before she makes it. I don't. I have to rely on my eyes and ears and I'm not going to risk her life on the chance that they'd fail me."

She was making a big deal out of nothing. And...

"It's just...her life is so unusual," she said. "It's not a bad thing, but because she doesn't have a traditional home I think it's important that she is at least able to rely on us to do what we say we're going to do."

"I know." His hand was on her arm again. Rubbing gently. Like he'd done countless times in the past. The touch used to remind her of the physical bond they shared.

Now it just offered support.

She covered his hand with hers and squeezed. "Thank you," she said, glancing up at him. "I know I'm being an idiot. You couldn't help your change of plans, and obviously you told Kara about them."

"You're not an idiot, my dear. Anything but. And as soon as I knew that plans had changed I should have called you and let you know. If anything had happened to us, you wouldn't have known where to tell people to start looking."

Their gazes met and she relaxed. Again. With a smile she asked, "So you had a good time?"

She invited Brandon to stay for dinner, but he had to get to the airport to catch his flight back to San Francisco. He and Douglas had tickets to a jazz festival the next afternoon.

And Lynn had a couple of women to see. One who'd checked in the day before with a concussion, and a twenty-seven weeks pregnant woman, Missy, who'd been spotting earlier in the week.

Knowing that Maddie was due over to feed Kara as soon as Maddie finished her afternoon therapy session, Lynn said goodbye to her ex-husband—but still best friend—and went in to spend a few minutes of quality time with her little girl.

BY FIVE-THIRTY MONDAY evening, Darin's therapy was done for the day. Grant's job wasn't. Finishing up a weeklong venture of trimming, shaping and adjusting irrigation spray heads, he still had piles to load into the trailer hitched to the back of his truck.

"I can't do my job," Darin's little-boy voice came from just behind him. "Not until four more weeks."

"That's right." Grunting, Grant lifted a rake full of thorn-filled branches and, with thick-gloved hands, carried it over to the already heaping trailer.

"No lifting and bending," Darin said, following at his heels. "I told Angelica, but she already knew."

"She's in touch with Dr. Zimmer," Grant reminded him. "That's how she knows how to help you."

"Yeah…" Darin's voice trailed off. And then he said, "I'd like to go for a little walk, Grant. Not far, just over to the park area. I won't disturb any of the women, I promise."

"I'll bet one or two of them'll notice your good looks, though, bro," Grant said, standing to grin at his big brother. "You could've shared a little of that charisma with me, you know."

"Right." Hands in his pockets, Darin gave him a teasing smirk. "I almost missed my physics final my senior year in college because I was busy rescuing you from a bunch of beauties."

Darin was teasing. And there was truth in his words, too. Grant, an orphan at seventeen, had given his brother some rough nights.

"Anyway, can I go for a walk?"

Grant studied the other man, thrilled, and a bit

cautious, too. Darin almost never left his sight—by choice. If being in therapy, being at the Stand, was going to have this kind of effect on him, the grueling hours were worth every single minute.

Reaching for another pile of brush, he scooped it up between his hands and stood. "Show me which direction you want to go."

"Over there." Darin pointed. With his right hand.

"I'm not looking at your right hand, bro."

Frowning, the older man turned his left side toward the direction he'd been pointing. His tongue rolled inward while the rest of his body remained still. Grant stood, holding the brush. One minute. Two. Sweat beaded on Darin's upper lip. The injured man's brow was creased and his gaze trained on his left arm. He took a couple of deep breaths.

And the arm moved. Just like that. Not much. An inch at most. But…

Throwing the brush up in the air, Grant said, "You did it!" and rushed over to grab Darin's arms. "You did it, bro!"

Darin smiled, but looked off to the distance. "Can I go for my walk now?" he asked, seemingly more harried than happy.

"Of course. No farther than the park, though, okay?"

"Just the park," Darin said, his voice lifting a bit as he strode off.

And Grant wondered if this was what it felt like when a man sent his kid off for his first campout without him.

HER CONCUSSION PATIENT was progressing nicely. Not even a headache to speak of. Lynn had a call just before she'd left the office on Monday saying that the woman had attended her first group counseling session and, it was discovered, was an incredible seamstress. She was already at work stitching up some tank-style summer dresses from patterns and fabric that had been donated to the Stand.

Missy, the twenty-seven weeks pregnant resident whose husband had thought a wedding ring gave him the right to take his panic and frustration out on his wife's body, was doing better, as well. No more signs of spotting. And an examination showed that everything was as it should be. She'd released Missy to normal activity and was eager to get home to Kara. It had been a long day.

She heard the squeal and recognized her daughter's voice before she saw them. Maddie was sliding down the slide at the park with Kara settled securely between her knees. The playground had been designed for the underage residents at the Stand, most of whom were there with their mothers, many of whom had suffered physical abuse as well as the trauma of living in a fear-based home. "Again!" The curly-haired charmer clapped when they reached the bottom.

Just as Lynn was about to approach, to put an end to the day's fun and get her little one home for her bath and a quick story before bed, she noticed the man who appeared from the other side of the slide.

"I'll take her over to you again," the voice said, a strange combination of masculine capability and little-boy tone. Darin Bishop. The man held Maddie's hand with his good one, and walked her to the back of the slide. He waited while Maddie climbed the steps and sat. Then he stood with his hands an inch from Kara as she climbed up to where Maddie could reach her.

Ducking behind a tree, Lynn watched for another couple of seconds. She could go back to her house, meet Maddie there as planned.

"You should count." Darin's voice carried easily. "One…two…three…go!"

"One…two…three…go!" Maddie repeated, and Kara squealed.

The same sound that had attracted Lynn's attention in the first place. She wasn't needed here. Which left her with a rare few moments to herself.

Heading toward her bungalow about a block away across perfectly manicured grounds, Lynn walked the sidewalk that trailed through the grounds, saying hello as she passed a couple of residents, waving to a mother and her two children who'd checked in the week before and thanking the fates that had allowed her to meet a man like Brandon—one who was still kind and protective, even after they were no longer a couple.

Her sister, Katie, her aunt Evelyn, who'd been killed by an abusive husband before Lynn had been born...they hadn't been so lucky.

And they were the reason Lynn had originally begun volunteering at the Stand. Dr. Zimmer had told her about the place after she'd taken personal leave to fly to Denver and help her mom and dad move Katie's things out of the five-bedroom home her sister had owned with her ex-husband.

Brandon had been the exact opposite of her brother-in-law. Instead of looking to Lynn for what she could do for him, he'd given her everything that he could give. He'd given her Kara. And the chance to go to grad school and get her certified midwife certificate so she could spend her life exactly as she wanted to spend it—giving to others.

It wasn't his fault that she'd lost her sexual allure where he was concerned....

"Hey! I was beginning to wonder if you'd left the planet!"

Spinning around, her heart beating a rapid tattoo, Lynn faced the man she'd been trying not to think about. She'd been succeeding, too.

Sort of.

"Grant!" she said, waiting for him to catch up to

her. "I just saw Darin over at the park. I wondered where you were." Or rather, had avoided letting herself wonder by focusing on what mattered. Kara. Their good luck. Their lives.

"Just finished my first round of the grounds," he said, facing her on the sidewalk as he motioned toward the trailer in the grass, barely visible through the island of trees just behind him. "I've got to haul that stuff to the dump still tonight, but was waiting for Darin to show up. He went for a walk."

"He's over at the park," she said. "With Maddie and Kara. I can take you there…."

"I know where the park is," Grant said, grinning at her. "I spent two days this week getting to know it intimately."

Was that innuendo intentional? "Of course," she said, choosing to avoid any possible flirtation. "I'm sorry, I… I've been busy," she improvised. Busy avoiding him.

"It's certainly busy around here," he said, his gloves in one hand tapping against his leg. "I had no idea."

"Most people don't." Lynn glanced around them, looking for escape.

"If you've got a minute, I'd like to tell you about an idea I had for the Garden of Renewal."

Maddie and Kara were still playing, enjoying themselves, thinking she'd be with her patients a while longer. Even if they went back to the house,

Maddie would stay with Kara until Lynn got home. And if it was past her bedtime, she'd call to make sure someone else was with them. Maddie didn't spend the night unsupervised. Meanwhile, Grant was talking about removing the gazebo from the Garden of Renewal and replacing it with benches interspersed throughout the three-acre haven of beautiful growth.

"That way women can have alone time if they need to find renewal from within, or have more personal one-on-one conversations if they're there with someone else."

She stared at him. He'd only been there a week. And he understood.

"I never liked the gazebo," she said. But it had been donated. And there before she'd arrived.

"I think it would be put to better use in the park area," he said. "That's a more public gathering place. Unless I've misunderstood. But the garden area, it seems to be more of a place to find peace, quiet. Not to gather socially."

"That's right."

He started toward the area visible across the grassy commons. She walked with him—and noticed the perusal he gave her. Which she then told herself she'd imagined.

She spent the next five minutes listening as he talked about a large rock fountain in the center of the garden in place of the gazebo. About flowering shrubs and blooms that would appear at different times throughout the year, giving the garden a sense of new life year-round. Endings and new beginnings, no matter what time of year it was.

She was trying not to think about a new beginning for herself. With him in the picture somewhere.

"What?" He was smiling at her again, but it was a more personal smile.

"What, what?"

"I don't know. You just looked like you had something to say."

They weren't talking about flowers. And she wasn't imagining anything.

"I appreciate what you're doing here," she said, opting for what she knew to be true, not hoping for what couldn't be. "You've captured the essence of what we're trying to create and devised a plan that would bring it to life much better than anything we've accomplished so far."

He paused, watched her for a moment and then said, "It's my business."

"Our agreement only requires you to keep up the premises, not enhance it."

"Do you always only give what's expected of you? What you're required to give?"

They weren't talking about landscaping. Or jobs.

"Of course not."

"I didn't think so." His expression serious, he

moved farther into the garden, with occasional glances back toward where they'd come.

"You can go get him," Lynn said, understanding the burden of being solely responsible for the welfare of another human being—the senses that had to be tuned in every hour of every day, whether you were physically with that person or not.

Grant shook his head. "No, as much as I'd like to, I can't."

"Why not?"

"For the first time in longer than I can remember, Darin reached out for freedom today. It makes me nervous, but from what I'm told, he has to form some kind of life for himself or risk falling into a depression that could eventually kill him."

And she only had to watch over Kara while she grew up and could take responsibility for herself....

"He moved his arm a little bit ago." Grant's tone reminded her of Brandon when he'd called her in between her university classes to tell her he'd seen Kara take her first step. "He's only had six days of therapy and already there's improvement."

"That's great!" she said, meaning it. "I expected it to take a couple of weeks, at least, before there was any noticeable change."

"Don't get me wrong. It wasn't much. Just an inch or so. But I saw it with my own eyes. He moved his arm."

"I'm not surprised, Grant," she said when he started to sound defensive. "Darin's determined. And the damage the surgery did was to a portion of the brain that is retrainable, as you know. I'm just surprised at the speed with which we've seen progress!"

"That's my brother for you. Once he's made his mind up about something, there's no going back."

The way he was looking at her seemed to be sending some kind of personal message—beyond the perfectly circumspect conversation they were having. Had Grant made up his mind about something, too?

Something to do with her?

And him?

CHAPTER SEVEN

"I REMEMBER WHEN Darin decided he was going to play ball for the high school team." Grant was heading for the middle of the garden, and Lynn kept pace beside him, trying to follow his conversation while she recovered her breath and wondered if she'd imagined the double meaning behind his words. "He'd been a star in Little League. I'd gone to all his games. But his high school…they had guys playing for them that were expected to go straight to Triple-A. That didn't stop Darin, though. He wasn't just going to play ball, he was going to play first base. I didn't doubt him for a second."

"You two were close growing up." She had herself fully back in control.

"Yeah."

"That's kind of unusual, given your age difference." They'd reached the gazebo and were standing inside of it. Out of the setting sun. Glad that she'd brought her sweater with her, Lynn rubbed her arms to stave off the chill of the February evening air.

She tried not to notice the way Grant Bishop's

jeans fit thighs that were proportioned perfectly enough to be etched in stone and gawked at for eternity.

Or to be aware of the fact that they were in the private gazebo all alone.

"Our father was an officer with the LAPD, killed in the line of duty when I was eight," Grant said, and somehow they were sitting together on a bench of one of the three wooden picnic tables set in the gazebo. His long legs were stretched out in front of him, his work gloves on his thigh, as he sat with his back to the table, facing the direction of the park across the commons. She was facing out, as well, with several inches between them.

"Darin was fourteen at the time. Somewhere along the way someone told him he was the man of the house, and he took his responsibility seriously."

"Was this before or after his resolve to try out for high school baseball?"

She could see the writing on the wall. Darin giving up his dreams to care for his little brother…and after Darin's accident, Grant returning the favor for the rest of his life.

"Dad was killed the summer before Darin started high school."

"So he didn't have a chance to make the team?"

"He made the team. As a freshman. And by the time he was a junior he was starting at first. I'm telling you, my brother has what it takes to get it done."

Considering the Bishop brothers' current circumstances, the near–hero worship choked her up.

"You're a lot like him." Softly, she told him what she was thinking. His gaze met hers again. And held. Long enough for her to read the appreciation in his eyes.

Her comment had been personal.

But so was the connection between them.

And while she wasn't married anymore, she wasn't any more open to a romantic relationship between them than she'd been four years before.

Everyone had their gift to give the world, their own particular difference to make. Hers was here. With these women. And raising Kara.

Their life was unusual. And didn't leave room for another personal partnership.

"I'm not like him," Grant was saying, while Lynn, suffering from a heavy dose of sexual attraction, busily disavowed herself of a relationship he hadn't offered. "He was able to do it all and stay kind and considerate. I get irritable just keeping up my half."

"He had help. Your mother was there to help shoulder the responsibility of raising you. And, based on normal childhood development, you got more independent every year, too."

He was facing a life sentence without parole. Not that she'd ever tell him so. He didn't need her reminding him of the burden he'd undertaken.

But as a medical professional, she was completely aware of it. And knew all about the stresses common to family members of terminally ill or injured patients.

She admired those family members so much—admired their ability to face the burden that had been given to their loved one—and consequently to them.

Grant was shaking his head.

"Our mother died of a rare form of leukemia when I was a junior in high school. Grant was married by then, and he and Shelley took me in and not only gave me a home, they helped put me through college."

Her heart caught again. "I'm sorry. I had no idea...."

She felt as if she had to do something. To help somehow. More than just as a facilitator of Darin's therapy at The Lemonade Stand.

Except that his problems weren't hers.

With his elbows leaning on his knees, Grant's gaze was pointed out toward the direction they'd come—across the grassy expanse. She had a feeling that the second his brother appeared, he'd be up and out of there, shooting across the yard like a torpedo.

"You know, through all of that, I can only remember my brother losing his temper twice."

Curious, she glanced at him. "When?"

"The first time was the one time I came home drunk. He half carried me to the bathroom and stood there while I threw up. He handed me an aspirin and stood over me while I drank it down. And then he put me to bed, all without saying a word or offering an ounce of sympathy. The next morning, in a very cold voice he let me know that he was not going to ask his wife to live with a young man who was so selfish, immature and weak as to lose control of himself to that extent. That's all he said, but I knew he'd given me warning. If I ever came home drunk again, I would have to find another place to live."

A bit extreme, maybe. For a first drinking experience.

And yet…

"I'm guessing you never came home drunk again."

"More to the point, I never got drunk again. At least, not until I was of age and in my own living room."

Which made her wonder when and why he'd done that. What had driven him to the point, as an adult, to sit in his own home and drink himself into a stupor?

Just with the little she knew of him, she could pinpoint a time or two that could prompt such an act.

"When was the second time you saw him angry?"

"When Shelley was fired from her job as a paralegal for filing a written complaint against one of the attorneys in the firm for sexual impropriety." He stood up. "We should head back. I don't want him confused if he gets back and I'm not there."

"He can't leave the grounds. Not without going through the main hallway, and the staff know to redirect him."

"I'm not worried about him getting lost," Grant said. "Darin wears his phone on his belt at all times. I'm the first speed dial, and also a speed dial picture on his front screen. He knows to call it if he needs me." They were walking at a brisker pace now. "But if I'm not there he could get confused, which makes him feel…less than whole. Which depresses him."

She wondered who looked out for Grant's emotional well-being.

Keeping up with him, she said, "It's a good thing you're doing, Grant. Not only caring for him, but protecting his confidence in himself, as well."

"He's still my big brother. So do you want to check with Lila and the board and see if we can get the go-ahead to remodel the Garden of Renewal?"

They were done talking about Darin. She got the point.

"Based on how you described things, I know they'd love the idea," Lynn said, attempting to switch gears as rapidly as he did. "But I'm afraid

the cost of such a thing is out of our league right
now. The initial design work on the grounds was
donated several years ago when the concept of The
Lemonade Stand was first devised. It takes everything we have budget-wise just to keep it all up."

"I wasn't planning on charging you," Grant said
with a sideways look at her that made her insides
dance as they walked toward the park. "I work in
exchange for Darin's time here, remember? In case
you hadn't noticed, my brother is practically living
here during the day."

Darin had already progressed to therapy twice
a day but had been helping out in the kitchen—of
his own volition—during the lunch hour.

"We can't even afford the supplies…." Which
was a shame. The rock fountain, the ambiance he'd
described…Lynn could even see herself gravitat-
ing toward the area for an occasional respite from
the emotional traumas of life.

"Darin and I can build the benches ourselves.
And, with your permission, I'd like to hit my suppliers up to donate the plants and the rest of the
materials. I bring them more than a million dollars of business a year—I think they'll carry me
on this one. But for the initial rock work, I'll need
to bring in Luke and Craig—my two full-timers.
They're good guys, as your background check will
show you. As I said before, Luke's been with me

since college and Craig's someone he met working at Habitat for Humanity."

Very familiar with the volunteer organization that built homes for needy families, Lynn's mind was reeling. She was used to being the one most on top of things, of taking control and making things happen.

Grant was...impressive.

The oasis he was describing would be a godsend to their work. Grant was talking about providing a place of serene beauty, of aesthetic wonder. A place that could help heal the soul. And that was the part of these women that was damaged most of all.

They'd made it back to the area where Darin had left Grant.

"I'll talk to Lila tonight," she told him. "But I can pretty much guarantee she'll be delighted."

"As soon as you get an official go-ahead, let me know and we'll get started."

Just like that.

He was watching her watch him. She moistened her lips with her tongue, and his gaze lowered to them, then rose back up to meet hers.

What were they doing here?

"How long do you think it will take?" Her words were a little too slow. Too soft.

"A week. Tops."

She said something appropriate. Told him she had to get going. He glanced at her mouth again.

And Lynn fled.

LATE THE FOLLOWING Monday, after putting in a full day as owner and CEO of Bishop Landscaping, Grant was in the Garden of Renewal with design software opened on his tablet, measuring off distances and envisioning finished results. With the help of the software, which would take his inputted measurements and choices and display outcomes, his idea would materialize into a working plan.

"Darin said I'd find you here." The voice startled him. Turning, Grant almost dropped his tablet.

"Wow!" He'd said the word out loud before realizing he was doing so. In a pair of tight black jeans, high-heeled black leather sandals and a button-down, tapered white blouse, Lynn looked... nothing like a nurse. Her hair, loose and curling around her shoulders, was longer than he'd suspected. She was wearing makeup.

And not meeting his eyes as she handed him a manila folder. "This is the signed letter with our nonprofit tax ID that should be all your vendors need for their donations," she said, her tone unusually subdued.

She seemed to be looking right through him. Or over him.

Taking the folder, Grant wanted to touch her hand. Her face. To bring her back to him. She was at the Stand for a reason. Had left her job at the hospital to live here.

Because she'd been abused? He knew for certain

she'd been wearing a wedding ring four years before. He'd checked. He didn't ever flirt or even think about flirting with another man's wife.

Her fingers were unadorned now.

"I'm sorry, I shouldn't have sounded so surprised," he said, making certain that he didn't touch her at all. "I've just never seen you out of uniform."

He'd begun to picture her wearing her various colored and designed scrubs to bed. Only the top. With nothing on beneath it.

Because he was certain he hadn't misread those looks—the way she'd licked her lips…the softer, sexy tone she used a time or two….

"I had a fundraising lunch," she said. "It was outdoors, on a patio at a country club, and part of the program was a fashion show. I agreed to be a model and they gifted me the clothes as long as I wore them through lunch. We not only raised enough money to keep us going here for a month, but the fashion designer donated makeup and an outfit for each one of our residents."

Noticing that it was almost time for Darin's therapy session to end, he closed his tablet, latched his tape measure back onto his black leather belt and tucked the folder she'd walked all the way out there to give him under his arm.

She'd walked all the way out here, dressed like that, to give him a folder she could have left for him someplace. She could have texted or called to tell him to pick it up at the front office.

She'd wanted him to see her.

"How many residents are currently living at the Stand?" he asked, treading carefully as he walked with her back toward the main house.

She was attracted. And afraid? Not a combination he'd ever dealt with before.

"Two hundred and forty-two. We're almost maxed out at the moment. But Lila's working on a deal that would include enough new bungalows to allow us to take in another fifty." The voice of a woman who didn't sound the least bit fearful.

Because when she was a nurse, she was in her element? Secure and confident?

Living with Darin had made him more sensitive to the fact that people behaved differently in different circumstances.

"Is there some kind of a time limit for how long someone can live here?" he asked, partially to keep her comfortable, but also because he was growing more and more curious about this aspect of life that he'd, thankfully, never been exposed to before.

His dad had adored his mother. He'd revered her. And so had her sons.

Apparently, the world was also filled with jackasses who didn't cherish the women in their lives. He'd known there were some...but two hundred and forty-two right here in Santa Raquel? The town wasn't that big.

"Not in terms of a number of days or weeks or months," she said, answering his question. "A few of us, like Maddie and me, are paid employees and live here full-time as part of our jobs," she said.

"I thought Maddie was a resident who donated her skills while she was here." She'd told him before that much of the general running of the place—the cooking, cleaning, laundry and even a lot of the computer and office work—was handled by residents.

"She was, when she originally came to us," Lynn said. "Maddie's situation was different, and it suited everyone best if she stayed on. But the idea here is to help these women heal, inside and out, to prepare them for happy healthy futures as they resume their lives. We're a hideaway, but the only thing we hide our residents from is the wrongful abuse. Otherwise, our goal is to prepare them to face the world, not hide from it. These women and their children have loved ones. Jobs and schools and friends and lives. We want them to be able to live those lives. Or, if they choose, to start new ones."

So had she been healed? Had Maddie?

They'd reached the main building and were standing in one of the extrawide, fancily decorated hallways so he lowered his voice. "But there's no time limit attached to it."

Lynn smiled at a couple of residents. Handed a toy back to a toddler who'd dropped it. Said hello a few times. They went through a door and reached the more private hallway that led to the therapy rooms.

Grant, walking beside her the entire time, smiling and trying to appear as unthreatening as possible, had the crazy urge to hold her hand.

"We run on a tiered system," she said, stopping inside the door to lean back against the wall, and it took him a minute to realize she was answering his earlier question. Her arms were crossed. "Our residents have objectives based on their personal circumstances. There are measurements for each objective and they have to show a certain amount of progress toward meeting those objectives, and reaching the next tier in their own personalized plan, in order to remain a part of the program."

Her tongue peeked out between her lips as she met his eyes. He wanted to promise her something, but had no idea what it would be.

He wanted to sleep with her. But had absolutely no room in his life for another commitment.

There hadn't been time or opportunity for a committed relationship in his life since Darin's accident.

"I wondered," he said now. "This place is so nice, who wouldn't want to stay here forever?"

"People who want to get back to their families. To their friends and jobs. To have their own homes where they can decorate as they please, cook when they please, leave as much of a mess or not as they please."

"What about you?"

He knew he shouldn't have asked the question. But Grant had never been known to have a lot of finesse. He was more the bull-in-a-china-shop type.

"I have my own home here on the premises. And this *is* my job."

He wanted to ask about family. Friends. And thought better of it.

"So what happens when a resident doesn't show progress?"

He'd kept his distance at the Stand. Hadn't had more than cursory and very polite conversations with Darin's therapist, with Lila, the managing director and with Maddie on one occasion when she was still in the room when he'd come to collect Darin. But he knew enough to know that the people here would not just throw a woman out on the street.

"Anyone who doesn't try to help herself is given special counseling," Lynn was saying, still leaning against the wall a couple of closed doors down from the therapy room. "She's assigned a one-on-one mentor. If she still doesn't help herself, we help her find some kind of job and a place to stay that she can afford with the money she has, and we help her move. We help her unpack in her new place, have a little housewarming for her. And invite her back to the Stand for any counseling she wants and for dinner once a week."

"What's the success rate on that?"

"Better than average." Lynn stood, shrugged. "Some people just don't want to help themselves. But the majority do. Our overall success rate here is better than anyone imagined," she added.

Anyone imagined. "Who's anyone?" he asked, growing more and more connected to a place that he'd never known existed and probably wouldn't have given more than a cursory thought if he had. Who had the wherewithal, or the need or the foresight, to conjure up The Lemonade Stand?

"Our founder is a thirty-six-year-old man who grew up in an abusive household. His mother had left with him and his sister a couple of times before she got pregnant again. They'd spend a week or more in a seedy motel while she tried to keep them safe and find a means of supporting them, and each time, they'd end up having to go back. Until one night after their little sister was born, when he and his other sister saw his father knock his mother unconscious and then shake the crying toddler to death. He hurled himself at the man and doesn't remember much after that until he woke up in a hospital. But they say he hit his father in the head with his own beer bottle."

And he thought he'd had it rough.

"How old was he?"

"Twelve. His old man survived but was sentenced to life in prison for killing his own daughter."

"And his mother?"

"She survived, too. And is doing well."

"Did his father have money that your founder used to build The Lemonade Stand?" It was fitting.

"There was some money, enough for his mom to provide a home for herself and her two remaining children, to provide them all with college educations, including herself. Our founder started a dot-com business when he was at university, which he sold upon graduation for a hefty sum and that's what he used to set up The Lemonade Stand. He was twenty-four at the time. Originally there were four bungalows on a couple of acres that housed sixteen victims. He spent the next year crusading for investors and grants and government funding. That was twelve years ago."

"Is he still around?"

"He sits on our board."

"And his mother?"

She straightened, standing free of the wall. "She's around."

He had to collect Darin and get in a couple of hours of mowing and trimming before the sun went down.

"You were married," he said instead of "Thank you for the tax papers."

Her eyebrows rose but she didn't say anything.

"Before…that day at the hospital. You were wearing a wedding ring."

She nodded.

"Now you aren't."

Her husband could have died.

She didn't have the demeanor of a widow. Maura, his next-door neighbor who helped out with Darin, had the demeanor of a widow.

"I'm divorced."

Grant didn't ask any more questions. The shadow that had immediately fallen over her face at the words was answer enough.

The bastard had hurt her.

Bad.

It was also clear, from her tone, her changed and distant demeanor, that Lynn wasn't open to discussing the topic.

Hopefully, someday, she would be.

CHAPTER EIGHT

LYNN WAS COMING from her office on Wednesday afternoon and took the long way around, passing through the grassy commons. The February weather was perfect. A sunny and balmy seventy degrees. She wanted to take a couple of minutes to enjoy it.

She wanted to see if Grant was still there. Not for any reason. Just to see.

When she noticed him and Darin at the edge of the Garden of Renewal unloading stones one by one from a cart, she picked up her pace toward home, taking a couple of shortcuts and making it there in record time.

"She's still asleep." Maddie met her at the door, her finger to her lips, although Kara would sleep through an earthquake. "She had swimming lessons this afternoon," Maddie reminded her. "With LaQueisha." An ex-Olympic-bound swimmer whose older brother had used her to practice his boxing skills and irreparably damaged her left shoulder in the process, killing her chances to swim competitively ever again. Her divorced father, who'd been unaware of his son's anger issues, was prepared to take LaQueisha to live with him, to put her through college, as soon as she was ready to leave the Stand.

"Then I'm going to go help unload some rock," Lynn whispered, heading into her room to change into jeans, a T-shirt and tennis shoes. "I'll be back in an hour, and if she's not up yet, we can wake her for dinner."

Dinner was always at six. Whether Lynn was home to eat with Kara or not.

Kara had her bath between 7:30 and 7:45 and was in bed by eight. Story time was Lynn's time. She'd lie in bed with her little girl and read to her. Sometimes long after Kara had fallen asleep.

Five minutes later, Lynn arrived at the cordoned-off site. "I'm here to help," she announced, not singling out either brother as she directed her words.

"Hi, Lynn, you look different in a T-shirt," Darin said as he knelt by a section of neatly stacked rock.

"He means cute," Grant said, standing, his gloved hands empty as he smiled at her.

"No, I meant different." Darin's tone was slightly petulant. "But she is cute," he finished, with a grin that was all male.

Hot inside, and feeling suddenly uncomfortable, Lynn asked, "What can I do to help?"

"I'm stacking the rock," Darin said. "Normally

I lift, but I can't because of my surgery. Another three weeks, huh, Grant?"

"Yep." Grant grunted as he lifted a stack of about ten stones and carried them over to Darin, who took them one at a time and placed them, at different angles, on top of one another.

"This is how we'll place them when we build the wall," Darin said. "See how they form this circle…?"

Pointing with his right hand to the more defined edges of the somewhat flattened stones, Darin gave her a brief rundown of the job ahead.

"Looks like you've got that part covered," she told him, and then moved toward the loaded-down trailer in the yard beyond the garden. "I'll help carry," she said.

Grant stopped, hands on his hips, and stared at her. "You are not going to lift river rock."

"Not as many of them at a time as you are," she agreed. "But I want to help. This garden, it's over and beyond our agreement. And I have a free hour."

She wanted to spend time with Grant. It didn't make sense. She didn't want a relationship with him. Or anyone, in a partnership sense. But knowing he was there…

His presence drew her.

And so, ignoring his objections, she spent the next forty-five minutes carrying rock.

GRANT WAS PULLING weeds from a flowered border along the sidewalks between the bungalows later that week when he heard someone behind him. Darin was due out of therapy soon and they were going to put in an hour on the garden before heading home to an increasingly rare night of pizza, beer and college basketball.

They both had twenty bucks in a pool of tiered picks, a fantasy game set up by a buddy of Darin's from college.

A buddy who still included them in sports pools but rarely came around anymore.

Maddie stood there, holding the hand of the cutest little kid he'd ever seen.

"Why you pullin' flowers, Mister?" All curly hair, chubby cheeks and questions, the child had a babyish lisp that made her a little hard to understand.

"I'm not pulling flowers," he told the toddler with a nod and a grin at Maddie—the woman Lynn had introduced them to that first day. The woman who shared her morning therapy sessions with Darin.

The woman who'd been abused but was now a full-time paid employee of the Stand.

Lynn hadn't mentioned that the woman had a daughter.

But then Lynn hadn't talked about any of the Stand's residents on a personal basis. Or former residents, either. Other than to mention that Maddie was a full-time employee.

"See these flowers—" with one finger, Grant touched a fragile yet velvety yellow petal "—they're colorful. They were planted on purpose to be here because they're so pretty to look at."

Letting go of Maddie's hand, the little girl bent at the knees to put her face within six inches of the flower. As though she was studying it.

"Preetty," she said, clearly mimicking something she'd heard before.

"These things—" he picked up a couple of stalks from the pile he'd been amassing on a small tarp at the edge of the sidewalk "—are not pretty," he said. "See how it's kind of prickly on the edges? It wasn't planted here. Its seeds blew in the wind and if we let it stay it will use up all of the food and the water that the pretty flowers need to grow and then there would only be these ugly things and no pretty flowers."

He was no more used to children than he was to battered women. But she was such a serious, cute little thing.

And then she giggled and looked up at Maddie. "Mister said the pretty flowers eat food." She sprayed spit as she said the words, laughing.

"They do eat food," Maddie said, her words a bit forced, as if she'd had to work hard to make them come out.

He wondered again if Maddie might have suffered some kind of brain injury. It was discomfiting, being around so many women who were there because they'd been injured, and yet not knowing, or being in a position to ask, what specific damage had been done to any of them.

Maddie seemed to have come off worse than most.

And she had a daughter? That was rough.

"Do pretty flowers eat macaroni?" the little girl said with another chuckle as she continued to squat next to him.

"No, it's not like food we eat," Maddie explained, her words slow, but seemingly just right for the child who looked so trustingly to her for guidance. As a child would a mother. The toddler wouldn't understand yet that her mother struggled more than normal. "It's called *nutrients* and I don't know all what's in it but ground comes with nutrients."

The little girl looked back at him. "What's that?" she asked, pointing at the hairy stalk he still held.

"This is called a weed." He could give the child the scientific name. Could lecture her about wildflowers, those which weren't cultivated, that most gardeners considered weeds because they came uninvited and took over. He could also give her many instances when these so-called weeds were used to create exquisite beauty.

"Weed bad, hurt pretty flower," the little girl said.

"That's right," Grant told her, glad he'd kept his lecture to himself. "What's your name?"

"Kara."

Her short legs, dressed in jeans with a design on the pockets that matched the pink design on her short-sleeved white top and the pink in her little white tennis shoes, didn't seem to tire from her position.

And her mother wasn't calling her away from bothering him.

Or acting bothered by him, either.

"How old are you, Kara?"

"Three."

She was rocking back and forth, still squatting, and then just as suddenly as she'd been there, she was standing, putting her hand back in Maddie's.

"Bye, Mister, see you soon I love you."

The words came out so fast, and with babyish garble, and he wasn't sure he'd heard them right. And then she was gone.

It took Grant a couple of seconds to realize that he was pulling weeds with a grin on his face.

"LYNN, CAN I talk to you for a minute?" Maddie's words were enunciated as slowly as always, her pretty face marred with anxiety, about half an hour before her therapy session Friday morning.

"Of course. Close the door," she told the woman who looked great in her leggings and lightweight

T-shirt. Maddie's short blond hair was curled this morning, and sprayed. She was wearing makeup.

Not a first, but not usual, either. Makeup on Maddie usually meant she'd been spending time at a bungalow that housed some of their younger residents. One in particular, Katrina, had been with them for several months and was good with Maddie. She also had dreams of being a cosmetologist.

"I'm prettier with makeup," Maddie said, sitting down on the edge of a chair across from Lynn's desk. Maddie's hands were clasped tightly in her lap. Her knees bobbed up and down.

"You're pretty either way," Lynn told her. "Pretty comes from the inside out."

The cliché rolled off her tongue with very little thought—or emotion, either, for that matter. Because she was starting to take the job for granted?

God, she hoped not.

"If I want boys to notice me, I have to take care of myself."

Lynn leaned forward. "Who told you that?"

"I'd rather not say." Maddie seemed irritated by the question, not agitated. A difference Lynn had learned to ascertain.

"Have you talked to Sara?"

Maddie was fond of her counselor, but seemed to have bonded more with Lynn. Lynn and Sara had discussed the situation with Lila, who guessed that Maddie probably felt closer to Lynn because of Kara, and wasn't concerned.

It didn't really matter which of them helped Maddie as long as they helped her.

"No."

"Okay, what's up?"

"I like someone." There was no glee in the words. No excitement. Only… Yes, there it was now, agitation.

"Who?"

"I don't want to say."

There was a time to accept that answer, and a time when she couldn't.

"I can't help you unless I know who we're talking about."

"I just… Do you think it's wrong for me to like someone?"

"Absolutely not. But it's always good to get the opinion of a trusted source before you pursue a relationship."

Most particularly in Maddie's case. She couldn't read people, was an easy target and…

Lynn's senses were on full alert. As far as she knew, Maddie hadn't left the grounds in over a month. But she wasn't aware of the outside workings at the Stand a lot of the days when she was in her office with patients. Or tending to new arrivals.

"I just like him," Maddie said now, looking down.

"And he might like me." The words were nearly a whisper, aimed at Maddie's rib cage.

"Who is he, Maddie?" Lynn wasn't joking around. Period.

"Darin."

The response sent Lynn backward in her chair with a whoosh. Of course. She should have seen it. Expected it. Known. Maddie and Darin, alike in some ways, pushing themselves through the rigors of therapy together...

They'd been at the park together, with Kara.

But...

"You haven't ever liked anyone but Alan," she said out loud.

"I know."

They all should have seen this coming, but Lynn hadn't. And as far as she knew, Sara hadn't, either. Just the opposite, in fact. Maddie was deathly afraid of men. She was the last resident they'd have thought would be in danger of some kind of transference or neediness with the Bishop men on campus.

To the contrary, they'd hoped an association with someone as harmless as Darin would help ease Maddie back into an ability to be more comfortable around men.

"Maybe Darin just seems like a good Alan to you. Someone who will take care of you."

The man had that air about him. Like he'd right wrongs, fix that which was broken. In spite of his injury.

Maddie shook her head. "He...looks at me. And I get all rubbery inside."

Oh, boy.

"Has he ever touched you, Maddie?" She kept her voice soft, calm.

"No! Darin, he wouldn't hurt anything. Except a spider. He stepped on it."

Apparently, there'd been a spider during therapy....

"Is it wrong for me to like him, Lynn?"

"No! Of course not." It wasn't. In theory. But, oh, boy. Lynn's insides were churning now, too.

And not in a rubbery way.

CHAPTER NINE

GRANT GAVE LUKE and Craig the whole weekend off. He was going to need them to work overtime the following week, just long enough to set the big boulders in the rock fountain and help with the trenching and plumbing. He'd already purchased treated cedar and metal joists for the benches that he and Darin were going to build on Sunday. And Saturday, he was going to get caught up with all of the regular mowing, irrigation checks, trimming and spraying for weeds so that he could devote the beginning of the next week, after his Bishop Landscaping work, completely to the Garden of Renewal.

The women at The Lemonade Stand needed their garden. He didn't want to keep them waiting any longer.

Lynn, dressed in scrubs, was walking from the main building, where she had her office and saw her patients, toward the cluster of bungalows at the back of the property. He'd mowed her yard. At least twice since he'd been there.

He just didn't know which one it was.

But he knew she had a cute ass. A distraction

on this Saturday morning. He watched until it was out of sight.

"Hey, Mister…" The voice was close.

He'd been alone. Had just mowed around a small pond in one of the landscaped atriums between buildings, and had noticed that the intake line had not been flowing smoothly. He'd taken the metal cover off the grass-covered hole in the ground that housed the pond's motorized equipment.

"Kara, no!" He shouted the words as he lunged for the little girl, scooping her up just before she ran right into that hole in her eagerness to get to him.

Maddie…and *Darin?*…who obviously had no idea the cover was off the access hole, were walking not far behind, watching Kara, but Darin's head was bent toward something Maddie was saying.

Kara's shriek was cut off as her body slammed into his chest, probably knocking the air half out of her. And then little arms slapped him on both sides of his neck as the tiny body clung to him. Kara shook and it didn't take a genius to figure out that the child was sobbing. The arms that had clutched him were pushing against him.

He'd scared the crap out of her.

"It's all right," he said, the words coming from somewhere he didn't know existed within him, trying not to drop the squirming little body, but not wanting to hurt her, either. "It's all right. I didn't want you to fall in the hole in the ground. See?"

Turning, he tilted so that her gaze was facing the hole. "It's supposed to be covered, but it wasn't because there was a boo-boo on that machine down there and I had to fix it."

A *boo-boo?* Where in the hell had he come up with that?

"Bwoken." Kara hiccupped. And just as quickly as her emotional storm had started, it was over. Tears hung on her lashes. Her breathing still hitched. But she was looking at him with questions in those big hazel eyes, not fear. Her red-gold curls bobbed as she threw her body downward, trying to get a closer look at the hole—he presumed.

Thankfully, he had a secure enough hold on her.

"What happened, Grant?" Darin came running over with Maddie, her legs seeming to stumble over themselves a bit, not far behind him. And Grant wanted to ask his brother what he was doing with Maddie and her little girl again.

"Bwoken," Kara repeated, sounding important now as she showed the new arrivals what she'd discovered.

"I'm sorry, Mr. Bishop." Maddie reached for the little girl, who went to her willingly. Putting Kara down, Maddie took the child's hand. "This is why you don't run ahead," she said. "Because we don't know what's in the grass."

True. Though not quite what he'd have said. All

kids should be able to run through the grass bare-foot. Shouldn't they?

"Maddie and I just finished therapy and she picked up Kara from the day care and I was walking them partway home," Darin explained, almost no child in his voice at all. "It's my fault, Grant. I distracted Maddie and put the little girl at risk and I'm sorry."

"It's not your fault." Grant saw a bad evening coming on. "If anyone's at fault it's me," he said. "I left the cover off and turned my back. You know it's a rule never to do that."

He'd turned to watch a beautiful woman who turned him on. Watched her until she'd completely disappeared from view.

"It was an accident, Darin," he said.

"Are you hungry, Kara?" Maddie, looking college-campus cute in black leggings and a short T-shirt, her slim body almost perfectly proportioned, hadn't taken her gaze from the little girl since she took her out of Grant's arms. Her weight shifted from foot to foot and she was biting on her lower lip.

Grant had no idea what she was thinking. Or feeling.

But like a good mother, she was focused on her child.

"Yes!" Kara chortled with childish glee.

"We have peanut butter and jelly sandwiches for lunch today," Maddie said, her expression so serious it almost hurt to watch her. Because she had to concentrate so hard to complete the simple mothering tasks?

Was that why Maddie lived at The Lemonade Stand? So the ladies there could help her watch Kara? Help raise Kara?

"It's not your fault, Maddie." Darin's voice came out soft and slow. "You take excellent care of her, you know." Innocence shone through every word. An inability to adjust his words to fit adult social mores, but an adult awareness of his surroundings.

Or something like that. "He's right," Grant said, taking his cue from Darin as he saw the look of guilt cross over his brother's face. "The only big deal here is that I didn't follow safety protocol when I turned my back on the opened hole. Kara should be allowed to run in the grass and there's no way either of you could have known that the hole was uncovered."

"Yeah, Maddie, Grant's right. You couldn't have known."

Still watching Kara, Maddie nodded. "We have to go," she said. "Come on, Kara."

"Bye, Mister, and Dawin, see you soon I love you...." The little girl pulled Maddie toward the bungalows.

Maddie glanced up then. Once. At Darin. "Bye," she said.

But never cracked a smile.

"I think she's mad at me." Darin's gaze followed the other woman.

Grant, kissing extra work on his lunch hour goodbye as he realized he was going to have to accompany his brother to the cafeteria where he'd expected Darin to be already, bent to the grate and said, "She's not mad at you, bro. She's scared. Women get scared in times of crisis. You taught me that."

The time he'd crashed his motorcycle out in front of their house, barely scratching either it or himself, and Shelley had come running out of the house, screaming, embarrassing the heck out of him in front of his friends.

"I guess," Darin said.

And Grant was happy to let the entire incident pass.

ALL THROUGH LUNCH Lynn heard about the incident with Grant and Kara. Her three-year-old, apparently, was quite taken with "Mister," pronounced with *r*s that sounded like *w*s.

Maddie was too sick to eat, and it took Lynn a good twenty minutes to get the other woman to agree to stay alone with Kara while she napped and Lynn went back to the clinic. She had only a couple of afternoon appointments, but needed to get her charting done.

"What if I screw up again, Lynn?" the woman

asked, her eyes wide and filled with pain. She'd chewed her lip so much in the past hour Lynn was surprised it wasn't bleeding. "What if she gets hurt? I'd rather die than that."

"So would I." Lynn turned from the sink where she'd been rinsing her glass and the knife she'd used to make sandwiches. "I also trust you with Kara. And we do our very, very best to see that she's safe and healthy and happy."

Sitting at the table, watching Kara finish her last bit of goo-smeared bread on her paper plate, Maddie gnawed at her lip, her knees bobbing up and down.

"Watch this!" Kara grabbed a handful of bread and put her fist up to her mouth.

"Uh-uh, little girl," Maddie said, reaching out to pull Kara's hand down. "You know we don't put too much in our mouths at once or we'll choke," she said. She gently pried Kara's fingers apart to take away half of the bread.

"You see," Lynn said softly, hanging the towel she'd just used to dry her hands. "You take very good care of her, Maddie. Accidents happen. To moms and dads and babysitters. They wouldn't let you help in the day care if anyone thought the kids weren't safe with you."

"But I got distracted and…"

They went around and around the issue for the next hour. But by the time Lynn left, assuring Maddie that she wouldn't be doing so if she thought for one second that her daughter was in any danger, Maddie was smiling again.

But Lynn couldn't get the incident out of her mind. As soon as she finished with her patient, she called Maddie's cell to make certain that everything was fine.

Maddie, answering on the first ring, assured her that all was well. Kara had gone down for her nap right on schedule and was still asleep.

"I'm just worried that you're mad at me," Maddie tacked on in a rush at the end of the report.

"I'm not mad." But she called Sara as soon as she hung up the phone, asking the other woman to find time for a talk with the upset woman. Maddie's biggest challenge was learning how to rein in her agitation and she was afraid that the morning's incident could cause a setback from the several months' worth of progress Maddie had made.

She also told Sara about Maddie's interest in Darin.

She was just hanging up the phone when her emergency pager went off. A 9-1-1 from Angelica, the Stand's physical therapist. She'd turned to grab a towel for Darin and he'd picked up a heavier weight than she'd instructed, apparently determined that she wasn't moving him along quickly enough. He'd dropped the weight, which hit his shin and split the skin wide open.

"It looks bad...."

Her bag of emergency supplies sat by her office door and, grabbing them, Lynn was on her way before Angelica finished that last sentence.

DAYS WERE SUPPOSED to go as planned. It was one thing Grant could usually count on. Because he thought ahead, planned for eventualities, left margin for plan's error. And other than Luke, and in a small way Maura occasionally, Grant didn't rely on anyone but himself. He didn't open his life to outside sources that could waylay him.

And that Saturday was waylaying him all over the place. First the pond's irrigation system had been clogged. He'd just done maintenance on all the water features the week before and everything had tested fine.

Then there'd been the incident with Maddie's little girl, Kara, which had upset Darin to the point that Grant had to accompany his brother to lunch when he'd planned to eat granola bars and keep working through the hour or two Darin normally spent at the Stand's cafeteria.

Darin had been different, strangely upset, not *predictably* upset, all through lunch. Over such an apparently simple thing.

Maybe because in the past seventeen years he'd had very little contact with strangers, other than medical personnel. He knew Luke well, and now Craig. Maura was like family to him.

And that was all.

Grant didn't have time to think on it any further at the moment.

After lunch, his lawn mower had run out of gas—a stupid lapse of paying attention on his part because he'd been distracted by Darin's distress over a woman he hardly knew—and he'd had to walk the two blocks to his fuel source, load up and walk back.

And he'd spent the entire time looking for any sign of the beautiful nurse who'd taken up residence in his subconscious and who tortured him with fantastic odysseys every night in his dreams.

Waking up wasn't quite as great as it used to be.

And then later, when he was wheeling a load of debris to the trailer, the star of his nighttime fantasies called just as he was contemplating a particularly athletic move she'd made in his dreams the night before. He'd actually been trying to figure out if there was a way to actually physically do what his mind had conjured up. So when he heard her voice on the phone he got instantly hard.

Which embarrassed the shit out of him.

"Your brother asked me to call you." Her words stopped him in his tracks. Literally. Wheelbarrow balanced in the grasp of one hand he stood in the middle of the front commons, his phone to his ear.

"You're with Darin? What's wrong?" He shouldn't have gone back to work. He'd known Darin was agitated over the morning's incident with Maddie's little girl.

His brother had as little experience with children as Grant did. Maybe that was it.

"He's fine." Lynn's tone was reassuring. "I'm taking him to my house."

Oh. Well, he wasn't entirely displeased by the knowledge. A little jealous, maybe. He'd been wanting to know which place was hers for over a week, and Darin was just going to stroll right on over with her.

"Why?" He asked the question that hadn't occurred to him immediately. It should have.

"He dropped a weight during therapy. It hit his shin and broke the skin. Angelica called me." Her tone was reticent.

"Why would his therapist call you because of a little broken skin?"

"It wasn't actually a little." Lynn's reply didn't surprise him as much as it might have. "I had to stitch it."

Wheeling the barrow with one hand because he had to get the thing over to the trailer and get his ass over to his brother, he said, "How many stitches?"

"Eight. He'll need to have them for a week to ten days."

"Let me talk to him."

There was a pause on the line. He heard rustling, her voice murmuring something unintelligible in the background. And then she was talking to him again. "He's shaking his head."

Grant pushed faster, swerving as the unwieldy cart almost tipped over. He knew better than to wheel a barrow with one hand.

He also knew better than to run out of gas or fantasize about any one woman.

"You still there?" Lynn's tone had softened.

"Yeah. My brother doesn't want to talk to me?"

"He knows you aren't going to be pleased."

"Because he had an accident? That's ridiculous. Darin knows me better than that."

What, he was some kind of ogre caregiver now?

He thought about what she'd told him about the incident. "How did a three-pound weight cause that much damage?" he asked now, getting away from his own issues and back with the program.

"It was a twenty-pound weight."

"What? Are you kidding me? He's progressed from three to twenty pounds in a few days?" That inch of arm movement must have been the beginning...

Relief flooded him.

"No. Angelica handed him the three-pound weight, which he was supposed to be holding while she got a warm compress. He put it down and picked up a twenty-pound weight."

"Attempted to pick it up." He heard Darin's voice in the background.

"He managed to get it off the rack, but immediately dropped it."

"On his shin."

"Yes."

"And no bones were broken?"

"Nope. His bone health is just fine. Though he's going to have some pretty painful bruising by morning."

"Where are you now?"

"In front of my house, getting ready to go inside."

"Which bungalow is it?"

She told him. And he knew it immediately. Set back in the corner of the commons farthest from the main house, the bungalow was one of the nicest, in terms of size and setting. But he wouldn't have figured she'd be located so far back on the property. Not only did it mean a bit of a hike anytime she got a call, but she'd have to make that walk from any of the parking lots across the grounds with groceries and anything else she brought home, too. Not convenient for when she was off work, to be sure.

"I'm on my way." As soon as he emptied the wheelbarrow and stashed it in the back of the trailer.

"Wait."

He heard voices, but couldn't make out what they were saying.

"Darin wants to know how angry you are."

"I'm not angry at all." He wasn't. "I trust my brother to push himself as far as he thinks he should. And if he pushes too far, he'll learn. Hell, I'm thrilled he's pushing at all. It's been a while."

Truth be told, he was relieved. A few stitches were a small price to pay to have what was left of his brother back.

CHAPTER TEN

LYNN HAD DEBATED the advisability of bringing Darin back to her bungalow, knowing that Maddie was there. Sara had warned that she shouldn't try to stop Maddie's budding interest in Grant's older brother. Maddie was slow, not incapacitated. Although she'd probably never be able to live completely alone, she still needed relationships in her life and had to learn how to have healthy ones.

Sara was concerned, but said she'd talk to Maddie.

And in the meantime, the more Lynn and the rest of them could watch over Maddie's time with Darin, the more they could help the other woman through this stage of her recovery.

It wasn't like Maddie and Darin would ever have a chance to be on their own, other than for perhaps a stroll through the grounds.

And, Sara had added, the friendship, as long as they helped Maddie see it for what it was, could benefit both of them.

Quickly reminding herself of her friend and

coworker's words as she unlocked the front door of the bungalow, Lynn called out.

"Maddie? Kara? I'm home, and look who I brought with me!"

"Mama!" The three-year-old's happy squeal came from the back of the three-bedroom cottage. "I'm on the potty!" Her daughter's sweet little babyish voice melted her heart.

"Okay, we'll wait," she called back. "Come on in," she said to Darin, who was standing on the threshold of her house.

"I'm sorry," he said. "I… It's been a long time since I have been in a woman's home."

"I'm not a woman." Lynn laughed. "I'm the nurse who just stitched you up."

"Yes, but I haven't been in your home before, either. Maybe I should wait for Grant."

"My house is no different than any other house." She wouldn't force him, but she hoped he'd come in.

"I just… I think I should wait for Grant."

She supposed they could stand in the doorway for the next five minutes but wished she could help somehow.

"Darin? That is who came home with you?" Maddie's eyes widened as she came walking into the living room just ahead of the little dynamo who pushed past her and flung herself at her mother.

Kara hugged her mother's legs, kissed her leg

through her scrubs and then hurled herself toward Darin, as though she was going to repeat the greeting.

"Hold on there, tiger." Lynn grabbed her toddler by the arm and scooped her up onto her hip. It wouldn't be long before Kara was going to be too big for her to carry around.

"Mr. Bishop has an owie on his leg."

"That's not Mister, it's Dawin." Kara giggled with both hands up to her mouth as Maddie's gaze traveled down the basketball shorts Darin wore for his therapy sessions.

"Your leg is bandaged," Maddie said, her look of wonder turning to one of horror. "What happened?"

"I dropped a weight. Lynn stitched me," he said, his gaze locked on Maddie. "It's okay. I'm fine. Just afraid Grant's going to be mad. Now I have to be careful to not get it wet in the shower."

Standing in her open doorway with Maddie behind her and Kara on her hip, Lynn said, "I told you, he's not mad."

"You should come in and sit down," Maddie said, stepping forward, her focus still on the bandage wrapped around Darin's muscled calf. She grabbed his hand and pulled him inside.

With only a moment's hesitation, Darin stepped over the threshold and walked behind Maddie to the great room with Lynn carrying Kara behind them. As though she were a hostess in her own home, Maddie settled Darin on the sectional couch Lynn and Brandon had picked together to furnish the family room in their two-thousand-square-foot home. Before she'd gotten pregnant and Brandon had met Douglas and finally admitted to himself that he wasn't a happily married man.

As Darin sat down, Maddie moved the ottoman under his injured leg. "Do you want water?" she asked.

"Yes, please."

"Do you want a bottle or a glass?"

"A bottle would be fine."

"Okay, wait a minute and I'll be right back."

Lynn could have gone for the water. Or offered him some juice, which would help raise blood sugar levels after his loss of blood. But Darin hadn't lost enough blood to be a concern. And he hadn't been showing any signs of dizziness.

Maddie's attention to her injured friend choked her up and made her smile at the same time.

"I want wataw," Kara said, playing with the gold ball post in Lynn's earlobe.

"How about apples?" Lynn asked, putting the little girl down. "Darin, would you like some apple slices?"

"No, thank you," the tall man said, sitting completely still and upright on the section of the sofa where Maddie had left him. Kara, who'd run back toward her room, came out again, hurtling toward them as fast as her little legs could go with Sammy in her hand.

"This will help you," she told Darin as, with the stuffed toy still in her hand, she used both hands to help herself climb up on the couch.

"Be careful of Darin's leg," Lynn instructed. She'd have liked to have insisted on her toddler calling the older man by his respectful title, but figured she'd be fighting a losing battle on that one.

And for no real gain.

With Sammy bunched in one hand, Kara started to slip and Darin reached out, pulling the little girl up beside him.

"This is Sammy," Kara said. "You can kiss him." She pushed the stuffed toy up to Darin's face.

On her way to the kitchen, Lynn heard the smacking sound the man's lips made as he acquiesced.

GRANT KNEW LYNN'S yard. Intimately. He really, really wanted to know the woman intimately, too.

She was independent. As much in charge of her life as Grant was. With seemingly as little time to spare. Maybe they could hook up. Just for a little adult pleasure.

He walked up the couple of steps to her front door and knocked.

She was still in her scrubs—black bottoms and a peachy-colored top today. A medical professional who was helping his brother.

Maybe he'd stick to fantasizing about those adult pleasures he'd imagined.

She was smiling, and her gaze collided with his. Maybe it wouldn't be all fantasy....

"Come on in," she said.

He did. And stood there in her hallway, not noticing at all the house he'd been so curious about.

"I was just going for some apples and tea. Can I get you some?"

Voices came from the distance. The words weren't distinguishable, but the laughter that followed them was.

"He doesn't seem to be any worse for wear."

"All he's talked about since I first saw him was you being angry with him. The stitches in his leg, on the other hand, don't seem to be fazing him a bit. I asked if he wanted a cane, tried to take his arm while he was walking, but he was having none of it."

Grant laughed. He couldn't help himself. "I told you, my brother's a determined man. He's also had his share of stitches. Starting long before the diving accident."

"Something tells me you both have."

Her grin immediately reminded him of last night's fantasy....

Voices floated in to them again. He recognized Darin's. The other one was quite distinguishable, too.

"Maddie's here?"

"Yeah."

"Does she live with you?" It made sense, the two of them sharing a place. Since they both were employees. Other than Lila, whose apartment, he'd been told, was in the main building, Lynn and Maddie were the only two who lived at The Lemonade Stand full-time.

"No. She has her own bungalow in the first commons. But she tends to panic if she's left along in the dark for too long, so there's another woman, Gwen, who stays with her at night. Gwen has her own home, and is never here during the day. Her husband works nights. He drops her here on his way to work and picks her up on his way home every day."

So Maddie was never completely unsupervised with her daughter. Other than maybe for lunch sometimes, he amended, remembering that afternoon and the peanut butter and jelly sandwiches Maddie had promised the little girl.

But they hadn't been heading toward the first commons....

Curious, he figured he shouldn't ask questions, but he couldn't help a raised brow. These women, their lives...they were unconventional, and yet they seemed to blend together perfectly.

"Gwen was a resident," Lynn said, more forthcoming than usual as they stood in the hallway. He wasn't sure why they weren't going to collect Darin, but as long as his brother was engaged in a conversation that he seemed to be enjoying, Grant had no problem spending a few minutes alone with Darin's beautiful nurse.

"Her first husband, her abuser, came after her a couple of times once she'd recovered, made a new life for herself and remarried. He's been in jail, but is out again. Gwen was terrified to stay alone. Her husband, someone we all know here, didn't want her to stay alone, and Maddie needed a life helper. It worked out for all of us."

"So Gwen gets paid for her time here? This is her job?"

"The state pays a stipend for Maddie to have a companion. Gwen donates it to the shelter."

"She works seven days a week?"

Lynn shook her head. "Five. Sunday through Thursday. On Fridays and Saturdays Maddie either stays here or at one of the other bungalows. She likes to have slumber parties with the younger girls and they seem to enjoy having her."

Maddie laughed. Too loudly. As she did on occasion. Darin laughed, too, and he could hear Kara's squeal. Maybe the slightly odd woman and her curly-haired imp had been invited for dinner.

Lynn still didn't move toward them. And Grant leaned one hand on the wall behind her, not close enough to touch her, but closing them into a more intimate stance.

What he wanted to do was kiss her.

She hadn't moved out the half circle he'd created around them. He'd left room for her to step back. Plenty of room.

He hadn't forgotten the way she'd shied away the second he'd gotten too personal before, and he wasn't about to blow any chance he had to be close to her before he even found out if he had a chance.

"I need to talk to you," she said with a glance toward the other room.

He stepped back. What guy didn't know those words were the kiss of death?

"Okay." He'd come on too strong.

In his world, his behavior had been circumspect, but he had to remember that he wasn't in his world here. The Lemonade Stand was a special place, almost a sacred place.

"Not now," she said, looking again to the other room. "Can you come to my office on Monday before you start out in the yard?"

"We're going to be here all day. Monday is the day my guys are coming to help lay the fountain."

"I know. But you said it was okay to leave Darin alone with them. I'll be in the office by seven."

He didn't want to wait that long.

But whatever she had to talk to him about, she clearly didn't want his brother present. And Darin would be with him all day Sunday. Every Sunday. And every Saturday night. And Friday night. And any other time a man might ask a woman out on a date.

He could ask Maura to stay with his brother....

The thought occurred to him and was quickly dismissed. Maura checked on Darin during the day the first few days his brother was out of the hospital. He'd scheduled her for two weeks. Darin had been up, dressed and insistent on going with him and spending the day in a chair on the job site after the third day.

Darin wasn't going to be okay with a babysitter.

And Grant couldn't do that to his brother, anyway. Darin was injured. He wasn't a baby.

"I can be there at seven," Grant said.

Lynn smiled and gave him another glance. A warm, personal glance that included his mouth.

He grinned. She was interested.

"Can I get you some tea?" she asked, as though nothing momentous had just passed between them.

Her nipples were protruding against her scrubs. Clearly she didn't wear a padded bra.

And unless she was suddenly cold in a very warm house, she was every bit as affected as he was by their proximity.

Grant's first instinct was to refuse her invitation to tea. Darin did better when they ate on schedule. His medication had to be taken with meals.

His brother laughed again.

"Tea would be great," he said, and would have followed her to the kitchen, but she deterred him.

"Darin's in there," she said as they passed an archway. He could see the sectional. See the back of his brother's head and Maddie perched on some kind of stool in front of him. The toddler, Maddie's daughter, wasn't visible at all.

And Grant remembered his first and foremost priority. "Hey, big bro, I hear you've been showing them that you're tired of playing Little League," he said, grinning as he joined the threesome. And hoped Lynn would be quick with the tea. He was going to have to leave soon and wanted to spend as much time as he could with her.

Darin's laughter was cut short and the look in his eyes was all worried-little-boy as Grant rounded the corner of the sectional.

"I'm sorry, Grant. I didn't follow the instructions."

"I'm not sorry, bro," Grant said, punching his brother on the shoulder and trying not to make too big a deal of his perusal of Darin's newest injury. "You didn't become a star baseball player by only practicing when you were told."

"I didn't know you played baseball," Maddie said in her slow drawl.

"I did." Darin sat up, and Kara climbed down from the couch, snatching a stuffed toy away from Darin's lap.

"Hi, Mister, this is Sammy. You wanna hold him?" The words were legible, if he listened carefully.

"Sure," Grant said, taking the animal and then wondering what to do with it.

"I think you're supposed to kiss it," Darin said, grinning up at him.

So Grant did. And was rewarded with his brother's full-bodied laugh, tinged with a bit of out-of-control little-boy guffaw.

Maddie just sat there, watching Darin.

Kara said, "Mama! Look! Mister is here!"

Grant's gaze went to Maddie, who was still watching Darin, who was smiling at her. So the toddler was aware that her mother was…slow? She realized that Maddie hadn't noticed him standing there? How long ago had Maddie been injured? Before Kara was born? Or more recently?

And could a three-year-old adapt that quickly?

Thoughts flew through his mind.

"I see, Kara."

That's when Grant realized he was the slow one.

Kara wasn't looking toward Maddie. She was looking at the woman who'd just walked into the room carrying Grant's cup of tea. The woman who'd just replied to her.

Lynn was Kara's mother?

Any hope Grant had had of some kind of quiet,

on-the-side liaison with Darin's nurse flew right out the window.

There'd be no after-bedtime sex at his place.

Lynn was as tied down as he was.

CHAPTER ELEVEN

LYNN WAS UP by four in the morning on Monday. Not because she'd had a call, but because she couldn't sleep. She couldn't stop thinking about the fact that she was going to have Grant Bishop all to herself, alone in her office, in a matter of hours.

Just the two of them.

Because they had matters to discuss, it went without saying, but...

The man did things to her libido that even Brandon had never done. Brought fires out in her when she hadn't even realized there had been embers.

She couldn't wake Kara for another hour and a half. Five-thirty was morning. Potty time. And then fifteen minutes of playtime before they washed up and were ready for breakfast at 6:10. Which put them out of the bungalow at six-thirty.

Or on a day when Maddie was coming to stay as opposed to Kara's going to day care, they'd be ready at six-thirty and Lynn wouldn't have to leave until 6:45.

It was 4:05 a.m. So she took a long hot bath. With rose-scented bubbles.

She'd never been so aware of her intimate parts as she was as she lay in the candlelit, quiet room, and let her mind wander. It was a luxury she almost never allowed herself.

She could control her thoughts—had learned the hard way after Brandon's life-altering revelation. She couldn't seem to completely control her body. But what it was doing felt so good, she wasn't sure she wanted to.

When she got out of the tub, she put on blue scrubs—not rose-colored for passion, or purple for spirituality—blue for calm.

She pulled her hair back in its usual ponytail, ignored her makeup drawer and cleaned the bathroom.

She emptied the trash, changed the sheets on her bed and, because she wasn't sure she'd put on deodorant, went back to the bathroom one more time. Where she passed her makeup drawer.

And stopped.

The conversation with Grant was important. She needed to feel confident. A little bit of mascara wouldn't hurt.

HE BROUGHT COFFEE. Black with fixings on the side in case she wanted them. Grant wasn't sure if Lynn drank the stuff, but if she did, she'd realize that he'd brought the good kind. He'd stopped, ordering it in a thermal cup, just before pulling into the back lot of the Stand and sliding his temporary pass key in the security keypad that would allow him inside the residents-only section.

"Who's that for?" Darin had asked as he'd passed his older brother his usual large, dark, black cup of Colombian, kept one for himself and put the third in the cup holder behind him.

"Lynn," Grant said. "I have a meeting with her this morning." He'd already told Darin three times. But reminding him of that fact, if indeed he'd forgotten, would only serve to trigger his brother's depression.

"I remember. It's not even light yet."

"Crazy, huh?" He said words. They didn't really mean anything. They didn't have to.

"She's pretty."

"Lynn?"

"Well, yes, Lynn's pretty, but I was thinking about Maddie. We have therapy together today." Darin spoke slowly, explaining with a serious tone, as though Grant didn't know a thing about his plans.

Darin's gym bag, with his workout shorts and T-shirt, were in the back. He'd worn jeans for the morning's early labor.

"Just remember to keep your extremities out of the way if you're going to push yourself beyond recommendation."

"Yeah, I know. My leg stings. I'll remember."

Glancing sideways, Grant said, "You said it doesn't hurt."

"I didn't want to complain. And it's my fault." The comment was offered in such an offhanded way that Grant heard the old Darin.

And took heart.

Life might seem to be upside down at times, but it always righted itself.

HER DOWNFALL WAS coffee. She'd never fallen prey to chocolate. Or soda or pizza or chips. But coffee...

In any form.

Just like the man who was handing it to her?

"I... Thank you," she said, taking the tall, nondisposable cup he was handing her as he came through the back door from the grounds toward her office.

She'd been waiting. In case he forgot and tried to come through the front.

She took a sip. The cup's plastic lid had a sipping hole. It wasn't big enough for the gulp she needed. So she took it off. Took another gulp. Turned.

And knocked into the man who'd been standing close enough to be touching her.

He jumped back, holding his arm out as he hissed in a breath.

"Oh! I'm sorry...."

"It's okay."

His wrist was dripping with coffee. Steaming hot coffee.

"It's not okay." Taking hold of him from the underside of his arm, she led him quickly inside the examination room closest to them. "I'm so sorry," she said again, grabbing sterile bandages to pat at the burn. "I can't believe I did that."

She wasn't usually a klutz.

"It's not a big deal."

Leading him to a chair, she said, "Sit," swatting his hand away gently when he would have used it to brush at the liquid still dripping from parts of his arm.

She got those last drops, too, and then looked at the damage.

Not as bad as it could have been. But it was going to blister.

"I've got some aloe gel," she said. The Lemonade Stand used natural and holistic remedies whenever possible. Lifting another sterile pad out of the glass jar on the counter beside them, she stretched a little farther to open the cupboard above and get a small, individualized packet of gel.

His nose touched her breast.

Lynn squeezed the packet so tightly some gel oozed out of the closed end. She didn't move immediately.

"I've got extra packets of this," she said quickly when she did move, as though to make up for lost time. As though she could cover up the fact that she'd just stood there letting her breast touch his face for no other reason than because it felt good.

Hot under the skin and on top, as well, Lynn expertly applied the salve to a sun-bronzed, hair-covered, muscled forearm.

And knew, when he sucked in a rush of breath, that his reaction had nothing whatsoever to do with the burn she was treating.

WHAT GUY DIDN'T fantasize about doing a nurse on an examining table? It was normal, right?

Except that, until that moment, he'd never so much as entertained the notion.

Lynn's medical attentions were excellent. His arm barely stung. The rest of him was burning up, though. And he couldn't flirt.

Or pick her up and have his way with her.

He looked up at her beautiful face, saw that she was concentrating on one spot on his arm and glanced away.

How did one woo a woman who'd been possibly mistreated and was obviously mistrustful of men?

Why would he woo any woman when he didn't have anything to offer but a few minutes with his body and a late-night phone conversation or two?

Lynn had a small child. There were already too many complications. Kara put the kibosh on the deal that was already a no-deal before she'd even entered the picture.

"I want to kiss you."

She stepped away. Not just back, but completely across the room. "You'll need to leave that exposed to the air if you can while you're working today. That will help it heal much more quickly and with less chance of infection."

He really didn't give a damn about a spot on his arm. His hands and fingers had been hammered and had rocks dropped on them and been blistered so many times that sometimes he'd look down and see a mark and try to wipe it off only to find it was a blood blister and he had no idea how he'd gotten it.

He didn't give a damn about that, either.

She moved to the sink. Washed her hands. Took a long time to dry them with the paper towel she'd pulled out of the metal dispenser above the sink.

The examining room door was open. He wanted to close it. And knew better.

That early in the morning no one was around. And it wasn't as if they were going to do anything that required privacy.

He wanted the door closed.

"Did you hear me? I said I want to kiss you."

"Yes." Her back was to him and she didn't turn around. "I heard you."

He knew she had. Now what?

"I'm pretty sure sometimes that you want to kiss me, too." Or, at least, want him to kiss her, which was basically the same thing.

She didn't respond. He took that as an affirmative. If he'd been wrong about her, she'd have immediately denied his allegation.

And suddenly he felt better. He wasn't going to kiss her. She wasn't going to let him.

But at least now they both knew they wanted to.

"You said you had something to discuss with me."

Lynn turned, a nurse in control, and a woman, too, when her blue-eyed gaze climbed up to meet his. All the way up. From his groin on… "We have a problem."

You're telling me, lady.

He wanted her to offer to touch him. To have a quick romp up on that table, get it out of their systems and get back to being the practical people they both were.

"Maddie likes Darin."

He blinked. She folded her arms across those full, soft, very feminine breasts. He'd never known a man could be jealous of his own nose.

"She thinks Darin likes her, too."

"I'm sure she's right," he was quick to assure her. And then he remembered that mother-hen way she'd protected the other woman the first day Darin had been in for therapy. "Darin's a nice guy. He likes most people, as long as they're decent and treat people well."

"I'm not worried about Darin taking advantage

of her," she said, meeting his gaze and taking a step forward, arms still crossed.

He'd bet she'd drop those arms if she knew that the position was pushing her breasts up, making them appear even more lush than they were naturally, drawing his attention to them like never before.

"At least, I'm not worried that he'd be anything but decent with her," she said. "The problem is bigger than that. She doesn't just like him, she *likes him* likes him."

"As in, a male/female attraction kind of like?" He asked the question, but couldn't wrap his mind around the ludicrousness of it. "She does know that Darin's not quite right, doesn't she?"

Feeling like a traitor to the man who was right then outside with Luke and Craig working at whatever he could manage to do four weeks postsurgery and with stitches in his leg, he wanted to wash his mouth out with soap.

"I doubt she finds him anything but normal," Lynn said. "Even if she's noticed lapses, she'd likely just roll with them."

Had she just opened the door to Maddie's past? He worked his mind around a way to enter delicately. And then he said, "Did the bastard who put her here hit her in the head?"

Every time he saw the slender, pretty woman,

he wondered about the man who'd hurt her. She seemed so fragile. So sweet and tender.

Not that any woman, no matter how strong, should be mistreated...

His thoughts tripped over themselves again, and Grant felt kind of like what he imagined walking in a mine field would feel like.

"I'm in scrubs in an examination room, but I'm not talking to you as a nurse right now," she said. "I'm not talking to you in any official capacity. Though Sara might seek you out to do that."

Feeling mines populating his mental field a dozen by the second, he watched her lean against a side wall, about four feet away from him. And cross her arms again.

"Maddie has HIE. Hypoxic-ischemic encephalopathy." The worlds rolled off her tongue like a foreign language.

"You said you weren't a nurse right now." He crossed him arms, too.

He'd wanted the door closed. Now he wanted it open.

"She suffered a lack of oxygen to the brain when she was born. She's not mentally distressed, just... slow...in some areas."

"Like Darin."

"For different reasons, but yes, a lot of their symptoms are the same. Maddie can't understand the value of a dollar, for instance. Or read nuances.

Everything is black and white to her. She also has a hard time controlling her emotions. When something is bad, it's all bad. When it's good, it's all good."

"When she likes a man, she really likes him," Grant said, not at all happy with what he was hearing.

"Right."

The solution was obvious. "We'll have Darin moved out of her therapy session. That should take care of it."

"I think he likes her, too. The other day, he wouldn't even come in my house without you. Until he saw Maddie there. She pulled him in and he was like a puppet on her string."

"The short time Darin's been here has already showed me that by keeping his life contained, I've isolated him too much. He needs to get out more."

They'd watch the games in bars from now on.

"The reason they didn't notice Kara running toward your hole in the ground on Saturday was because Darin had just told Maddie that he felt happy when she talked to him."

"Like I said, he needs to get out more."

"I don't disagree with that. But as far as his liking Maddie is concerned, it might be too late to just stop him."

"I love my brother. I think his life has a hell of a lot of value. There are many things he has yet to do, many things he can contribute, but there's no way he's mentally equipped enough to have an actual one-on-one relationship with a woman. He can't always remember what day it is. Or if it's time for breakfast or dinner."

"I'm not disagreeing with you, Grant." Pulling over the other hard-backed plastic chair in the room, Lynn sat opposite him, her elbows on her knees.

Exposing her cleavage, damn it. Though he was absolutely one hundred percent certain she was unaware of that fact.

"Neither Maddie nor Grant can live alone. Neither one is completely self-sufficient. But they both have feelings. Normal ones."

He didn't want to think about his brother getting turned on. It was… Uh-oh.

"Could you sit up please? That…" He motioned toward her V-necked cleavage. "It's distracting."

Clearly appalled, judging by the horrified expression on her face, the rush of color, Lynn sat up. Lifted both of her arms, hands toward her chin, in front of her.

He swore. Like a sailor. But managed to keep it silent.

"I'm…having feelings, too," he said, when the awful expression didn't leave her face.

She blushed again. And he smiled, a sheepish apology. She grinned. Nodded. And he wanted to take her to bed.

CHAPTER TWELVE

GRANT HAD TO focus.

He might be in an exam room with a beautiful woman with whom he shared a mutual attraction, but life wasn't about fantasy.

"I've been caring for my brother exclusively for seventeen years. The idea of him and a woman… It's never come up. It never dawned on me that it would."

"His doctor never talked to you about the fact that Darin's sexual urges were intact?"

"Of course he did." The doctor had been male. Close to sixty. And Grant had still been beside himself with grief. "He mentioned wet dreams as a way his body might have of dealing with the situation."

There was a clock on the wall. Analog. High up. He stared at it.

"And I imagine he talked to you about the fact that Darin might exhibit sexually inappropriate behaviors such as masturbation in front of people."

"Something like that."

"Has it ever been a problem?"

Chin tight, Grant took a deep breath. Swallowed. And looked her straight in the eye. "No."

"Often times TBI—sorry, traumatic brain injury—"

"I know what that one is."

"Often it causes low libido. But it can also have the opposite effect and make someone more inclined to experience sexual arousal."

"I know."

"Which one is Darin?"

She was doing her job. And being a friend, too. They had a situation he had to face. And when he remembered that Maddie was also involved here, and Lynn obviously cared a great deal for the woman, he completely understood her concern.

"Neither. We've been lucky where Darin's sexuality is concerned," he said, making eye contact and holding it. "He's pretty much normal in that area in his ability to experience it, but also in his awareness of social mores."

"TBI patients often forget little things," Lynn said. "Like the need for the use of protection."

"Darin's not going to have sex."

"You don't know that."

"Yes. I do. He… We have…magazines…for him to…"

There were just some secrets a guy didn't tell. She nodded, then looked away. And if she was wondering if he ever borrowed his brother's magazines… "The answer to your question is no."

"No, what?"

"I don't use them."

She blushed again. Nodded again. She seemed to be having a difficult time breathing.

"I think we'll be okay here, you know." He was driven to comfort this woman. To make life better for her.

He had no resources to do so. Not time or money or mental focus, either. He could barely keep up with the business and Darin, let alone take on a woman.

No way could he handle a child.

"Darin and Maddie are never really alone. They see each other in therapy, and maybe to walk across campus once or twice a week. That's it. Maybe this friendship is a good thing." Once he got going, he was on a roll. "The change in Darin these past weeks is stupendous, really. He's up before I am, doing all he can, pushing himself, eager. Hell, he's remembering our schedule better than I am somedays. I can't speak for Maddie, but I know that Darin would never hurt her. He's just not the type."

"Sara believes that Maddie needs to get through this if she's ever going to recover from her past. So while I'm apprehensive and would very much like to see the whole thing disappear, I'm to understand that it's good for her."

And really, other than making certain the two didn't ever have an opportunity to make a baby, what could a friendship hurt? It wasn't like either of them had the ability to take it any further than a walk or a talk.

"I have to ask, since you mention Maddie's recovery, mentioned her past, what happened to bring her here?"

"I can't talk about my patients. But I don't see Maddie professionally. Unless she gets sick. I came to you as someone who cares deeply for her as a friend, as someone who looks out for her and—"

"Lynn." He leaned forward, covering her hand with his. "It's okay. I know you'd never betray your professional ethics. But, as you said, we have a situation here and since I'm directly involved, as my brother's caregiver, I need to know what we're facing. For Maddie's sake as well as Darin's. He might have questions. I need to have answers."

She turned her hand over. A very small movement. He slid his fingers softly between hers.

"Maddie was integrated into a regular school curriculum. From what she's said, and what I've been told, some of the kids teased her, were mean to her, but overall, it was a positive experience for her. Mostly because from grade school on there was one little boy who was her self-appointed bodyguard. From the first time he noticed her hovering at the back of the classroom, he was her instant friend and protector.

"She has a pretty good sense of humor when she's relaxed, and he appreciated her jokes. Laughed at them with honest humor. He was impressed by her good heart, is what her parents said he told them.

"He saw her through junior high and high school. She was actually on the cheer squad because of him. She didn't get all the cheers, but they had her join in for the easy ones. She was on student council with him, too.

"When, after graduation, he approached her parents and told them he wanted to marry her, they were skeptical at first. He was a perfectly normal, intelligent young man with his whole future ahead of him. He'd trained in high school to be an auto mechanic and had a decent job with benefits. He bought a house. Put money in savings. And approached them again. This time he asked Maddie first, though. And, of course, she was elated."

"It must have been hard for her when her parents said no."

"They didn't."

"Maddie was married?"

He'd been expecting caregiver abuse. Or maybe parental.

"Yes."

Dropping Lynn's hand, Grant sat back.

"Apparently, as he matured, and was ready to

move up in the world, go to college and get a degree in business, he grew increasingly frustrated with her inability to keep up with him. Her parents did what they could to free up his time so he could focus on school and he ended up with a whole new set of friends. And was embarrassed by his noticeably slow wife.

"She'd make a stupid choice, and rather than patiently helping her see the right way, he'd hit her. He was smart, though. He kept the abuse to parts of her body that didn't show. And told her that his temper was her fault. He always held her afterward. Told her that he was sorry. He told her that he'd love and protect her forever. Remind her that he'd always been her bodyguard. And he'd tell her that if she told anyone what was going on, they'd take her away from him and she'd be put in a home because her parents were getting too old to care for her. Maddie's parents had no idea what was going on."

He'd asked. He hadn't been prepared for the truth. "How long did it go on?"

"She was married fourteen years. The abuse went on for about twelve of them. When Maddie caught her husband in bed with another woman, she called her parents and told them everything. They called the police, got her out of there and brought her here. He's currently serving a ten-year sentence in the state penitentiary."

"Darin would never hurt her." It wasn't nearly

enough, but all he could come up with. "He'll be a good friend to her."

But Maddie had had one of those before.

"According to Sara, she needs to be able to trust herself to have a man for a friend if she's ever going to have a hope of recovering from the damage her ex-husband did. Sara thinks Maddie's reaching out to Darin like this is a small miracle."

"So, it's good for Maddie, it's good for Darin. And now it's up to all of us to make sure that their friendship remains just that. A friendship."

He was looking her in the eye again. She looked back. And they weren't just talking about Maddie and Darin.

"Agreed," she said, her voice heavy with conviction.

"Good."

And to seal their bargain, to give evidence to the fact that friendship was all they could ever have, to make certain they both understood the insurmountable walls between them, he said, "I didn't know you had a daughter."

"THAT DAY I told you that Darin was at the park, I said he was with Maddie and Kara." She stood. Returned the chair she'd been using to the opposite wall where it belonged.

She straightened her top. Checked that there were

no smudges on the tips of her tan-colored soft-soled hospital shoes.

Grant was so...there...where she'd been so lonely for so long.

"I thought she was Maddie's daughter. Every time I saw Kara she was with Maddie, and it seemed clear that Maddie was her caregiver."

The thought that someone might mistake Maddie for Kara's mother had never occurred to her. Everyone at the Stand knew that Kara was hers. Maybe Darin wasn't the only one whose life had become too insular.

"I'm sorry," she said, hating that she felt defensive, like her having a daughter made her less appealing.

It made her less available.

It was really quite frustrating that not being available didn't seem to shut down her really strong urge to have sex with him.

She wasn't like that.

Didn't have casual sex.

Or sex at work, either.

She'd never had sex with anyone but Brandon.

He grinned, her stomach flip-flopped and she knew she had to get him out of there.

"Kara adds a depth to my life I didn't know was possible," she told him, holding on to reality for all she was worth. Fantasy might be fine for middle-of-the-night baths. But then you drained the tub and went on. "She's the first thing I think about when I wake up in the morning. The last thing I think about before I go to sleep." He might as well know.

And stop looking at her like he wanted to be there when she went to sleep.

"I hear her little voice and something in me settles. Every single time. You ever think about having children?" she asked, feeling incredibly tired all of a sudden.

Grant stood. "Nope. Didn't see how I could ask Darin to accept a woman he didn't know into his nightmare, to be that vulnerable. And I couldn't ask a woman to take him on for the rest of her life, either. Hell, what am I saying?" His gaze was direct. Purposeful. "I'm not going to leave Darin alone the amount of time it would take to have a steady woman in my life. Or to raise a kid. In a sense, I'm Darin's dad."

She understood. In some ways it would have been easier for him if Darin's injury had been severe enough to render him completely senseless. Instead, he was damaged enough to not be whole, but not so damaged as to not know he wasn't whole.

That awareness was the hardest part.

And the best, too, because it meant Grant hadn't completely lost the brother he'd known.

"What about before Darin's accident? Did you have a woman in your life? Or think about having kids someday?" Why was she pushing this?

"I was in college. I had more woman than was right. And no, I hadn't even begun to think about whether or not I wanted children someday. Which turns out to be a good thing since it's not in my cards."

He didn't sound sorry. Or regretful.

He didn't sound as if he would have loved to have children if things had been different.

And she'd wanted at least a couple more.

When she was married.

Which she wasn't going to be again. Ever. She wasn't giving up what control she had over her life.

There were many things Lynn didn't understand, but one thing was absolutely completely clear to her. Never again was she going to put her life, her happiness, in the hands of another person.

CHAPTER THIRTEEN

GRANT MADE SURE Darin was never alone on Monday, even going so far as to accompany him to his morning therapy session, saying he wanted to see Darin's progress and get updates from Angelica on how much they could push things.

He was just as interested in what they weren't going to push. Namely, Maddie and Darin together.

He'd have stayed for the afternoon session, too, except that as she was leaving the morning session, Maddie had told Darin she couldn't see him at lunch or following his afternoon session because Lynn was taking her to the mall.

She wouldn't have been seeing him at lunch, anyway, Grant could have told her. He'd brought enough sandwiches for Darin to eat with him. And if he hadn't, he'd have taken his brother out for a hamburger. And got him back in time to put in his hour and a half in the kitchen afterward.

He took Darin straight home after work. Told his brother to shower, reminding Darin to cover his stitches, and put on some nice pants and a casual shirt. As soon as he heard the water go on in

Darin's bathroom, he had his own shower, pulled on some black jeans and an off-white button-down shirt, rolled up the sleeves, slid into some soft-sided loafers, ran his fingers through his hair and was in the living room waiting for Darin when he appeared ten minutes later, freshly shaved and looking as if he'd just stepped off the pages of a classy magazine.

Grant approved.

"Let's go," he said, picking up his keys.

Darin followed right behind him, his gait more lilted than it was earlier in the day. "Where are we going?"

"Out?"

"Out where?"

Pushing the button to raise their automatic garage door, he opened the door of his white F250 diesel truck, climbed inside and waited for his brother to get in and buckle himself up.

Darin reached the belt across with his right hand and then switched it to his left to buckle it. The belt sprang back into the door frame. Darin tried a second time.

And while Grant's hands itched to grab the belt and slide it into the receptacle, he started the truck instead.

Darin's belt sprang back a second time.

He backed down the drive.

The belt snapped a third time.

"You've always buckled your belt one-handed,"

he commented casually. These random moments of confusion were difficult. For both of them. "With your right hand."

He pulled out onto the street and couldn't go any farther until Darin was safely buckled in.

"I know."

Easing the truck over to the curb, Grant watched as Darin tried a fourth time. His brother's face was lowered to his task, and Grant couldn't get a good read on his expression. But his tongue wasn't sticking out of his mouth the way it sometimes did when Darin was in a regressive state.

On the seventh try, the buckle snapped into place.

Grant put the truck in gear and drove away.

"WHERE ARE WE going, Grant?" Darin was looking out his window, seemingly entranced by the freshly painted Cape Cod–style homes they were passing, all with professionally landscaped, though smaller, yards.

The seventy-five-home neighborhood had been built with landscaping included.

Grant knew. He'd won the bid for the landscaping.

And they both knew the homes well. They were still in their neighborhood.

"Where do you want to go?" Grant sidestepped his brother's question a second time.

He had a plan. Was taking control. Lynn had

given them a problem and he'd deal with it. That was the way of his life.

But Darin wasn't going to know that.

"I want to go to the beach," Darin said. "I want to see the boats come in."

So they went. A couple of miles from their modest neighborhood was a public access area where they could sit and watch the fishing boats come into Santa Raquel's very small, noncommercial pier.

In the distance, an occasional cruise ship traveling up the coast from San Diego or L.A. might appear, riding out the ocean's waves. Some yachts. Or commercial fishing boats that were headed to other ports.

"I want to dive again."

"No, you don't."

"Yes, Grant, I do."

He took a deep breath and pinched the skin on his nose, though he had no idea what that was supposed to do. It didn't relieve any tension.

"What about your arm?"

"It's getting better."

"Then when it does, we'll talk about this again."

"I don't want to talk about it again." Darin's focus didn't leave the ocean. "I want to dive again."

The words "What if your arm doesn't get better?" were on the tip of his tongue. They would probably end the conversation. And there was a chance Darin would never bring diving up again.

But Grant studied Darin and bit the words right off his tongue. He couldn't lock Darin up any further than the injury his brother had sustained attempting to save a life had already done.

"Until my arm is better, I'd have to stay shallow."

Grant didn't know what to say.

And Darin turned to look at him. "I can't go alone, Grant. I'd need you to go with me."

Darin was completely, one-hundred-percent serious.

And so Grant did the only thing he could do. He said, "Okay." And promised to make the plans.

"HEY, LYNNIE."

She'd known it was Brandon before she'd picked up the call, but the sound of his voice, using his pet name for her, still shot sharply through her.

"Hi, what's up?" She didn't feel like his "Lynnie" anymore.

"I got a favor to ask." He sounded hesitant. And her heart reached out to him. Because it always had.

And, she'd come to realize, it always would. She didn't stop loving someone just because he had a biological predilection that couldn't be helped.

"What favor?"

Walking by the door to Kara's bedroom, she peeked in at the exhausted little girl sleeping in her princess bed—a white wooden bed with a canopy on top that Brandon had spent a couple of hours putting together for her the previous summer, when they'd thrown a moving-into-a-big-bed ceremony.

Just the three of them.

As if they were a family again.

"It's a big favor." Brandon wasn't getting right to the point, which didn't bode well.

She and Maddie had worn Kara out at the mall. Lynn had made macaroni and cheese with peas in it for dinner when they got home and Kara had fallen asleep at the table.

"You sound tired. What's going on?" she asked him.

It was only eight-thirty. The evening stretched ahead of her.

Without turning on any lights, she settled on the sectional in the great room, looking out the sliding glass door to the garden beyond.

It needed more landscape lighting.

And she knew someone who did that sort of thing....

"Douglas was in a car accident this morning. Some guy was drunk and ran a red light."

She sat up. "Oh, my gosh, Bran, I'm so sorry!" And then, more slowly, "Is he okay?"

"He's going to be. He's got a couple of broken bones, some stitches and lots of bruising, but if he does well tonight, I'll be able to bring him home in the morning."

"Good, so that means no internal injuries."

"Surprisingly not. He wasn't going that fast and had his seat belt on. Also he was hit broadside on the passenger's side of the car."

"Thank goodness for that. Is he fully conscious? Have you been able to talk to him?"

"Yeah, he just ate a good dinner. I'm staying here with him tonight."

"You're at the hospital?"

"Yeah. He's resting and I needed to call you...."

She pictured the slim man her husband had moved in with after he and Lynn had divorced. This past year, when California's ban on gay marriage had been lifted again, they'd gotten married.

Douglas was sweet. Gentle. Well dressed, quiet spoken. And a successful stockbroker. He'd always been kind to her and respectful of her place in Brandon's life. Not just as the mother of his child, but as his best friend, too.

"What can I do?"

"I want to bring Kara here for the weekend."

Her heart lurched. He had every legal right to do so. By law, Brandon had Kara every other weekend and one night during the week. Except that he'd moved upstate to San Francisco and the midweek arrangement hadn't worked after that.

He'd never missed one of his weekends with Kara. Every other Saturday he flew down, either with Douglas or alone, and spent the day with her.

Because that's how Lynn had wanted it. Brandon here in Santa Raquel, not Kara up in San Francisco.

She wanted to say no to his favor. To scream it at him.

But Brandon was Kara's father. And a great dad.

He was also still a loyal and true friend to her.

"I'll see what I can arrange here to be able to get away and fly with her." Kara had never spent the night at her father's house.

Lynn had never spent the night without her little girl.

"I'll fly down to get her," Brandon said. "I'm not going to put you out, Lynnie. Douglas's mom is going to stay with him Saturday morning and again Sunday afternoon while I get her back to you. She'd stay with him all weekend, if we needed her to, but I don't want to leave him. And he misses Kara. He didn't get to see her last time."

"And it's time that you have her in your home some, too."

"We've had a room ready for her since we bought this place," he reminded her.

"I know."

"I bought the same exact bed she has at home."

"I remember."

"It'll just be for one night."

"I'll be fine, Bran. I'm not a piece of china, you know."

"You're one of the strongest people I've ever

known, Lynnie. You've got way more backbone than I do."

"That's utter nonsense."

"I just hate hurting you and it seems like that's all I do anymore. I miss the days when I was a blessing in your life."

She wasn't going to cry. It was just allergies.

"You're still a blessing in my life," she told him. And meant it. The world would be a darker place if Brandon wasn't out there.

"If I'd known I was gay, I'd never have asked you to marry me," he told her, something he'd said many times before.

"I know."

"I feel so responsible. So guilty and stupid for not recognizing…"

She didn't blame Brandon. Or herself, either. Logically, medically, she understood that he couldn't help being attracted to men. And in her heart of hearts, she still felt shocked and betrayed.

Not because Brandon was gay. But because she'd thought she'd known him so completely… had trusted that she knew him as well as she knew herself…because she'd trusted that he'd always be faithful to her. Always want her.

Because he'd been her husband and he'd left her.

"Tell Douglas I said hello," she said, keeping her voice light in spite of the heaviness inside her. "And that I'm glad he's okay."

"That will mean a lot to him."

"I mean it."

"I know you do."

"Okay, well, call me as soon as you have your flights arranged."

"I will. Good night, Lynnie."

"'Night."

She'd pulled the phone away from her ear, looking for the end call button in the darkness when she heard, "I love you."

She pushed to end the call.

"Are we going home now?" Darin asked once the brothers were back in Grant's truck after sharing a steak dinner at their favorite place on the main strip in town by the beach. "You missed our turn," the forty-four-year-old man-child continued, swiveling in his seat to look at the intersection they'd just passed.

He'd talked about diving during dinner. And burped so loudly that the people a few tables over had turned to look at them.

He'd flirted with their waitress, who'd flirted right back. Grant was pretty sure the girl had no idea there was anything wrong with his older brother. She'd been absent for the belch.

And he'd talked about Luke and Craig letting him help put pieces of plastic tubing together that day.

"We aren't going home," Grant said now. He had

no idea how this next part was going to go, but he was determined that it would.

Every problem had a solution.

"Where are we going?"

"It's a surprise."

"It's not my birthday."

"You like surprises."

"Yep."

Grinning, Darin crossed his arms and looked out the window.

CHAPTER FOURTEEN

HE'D NEVER ACTUALLY been to the place before. But he knew exactly which exit to take off Highway 101 to get where they were going.

Guys knew these things. Or at least he did. He supposed most guys did. At the moment, he wasn't sure. He was having doubts. Because, personally, he didn't want to spend the evening ahead as he'd planned.

He wasn't changing his mind.

Arms tense, he pulled into the crowded parking lot, hoping his brother either didn't recognize the place, didn't know what it was or wasn't paying attention.

"Coastal Flame." Darin read the sign like a first grader in reading class.

And then he started to laugh. Hand over his mouth, he guffawed. "You made a mistake, Grant! Look where you brought us!"

Grant wasn't laughing. He parked in the back, the only empty spaces he could find. He walked around and opened Darin's door. "Come on," he said. "Let's go."

"Go?" Frowning, Darin eyed the huge pink building. "We're going in there?"

"Yep." Grant yanked at his brother's sleeve and then, when Darin still didn't move, undid his seat belt, grabbed his right wrist and pulled.

Darin didn't resist. He got out of the truck. And stood there, letting Grant close his door for him. "Are you sure about this?" he asked.

"Yep."

Standing there, looking like the most successful gentleman at the gentlemen's club, Darin frowned. "I don't think they'll want me in there."

"You're a man and you have cash. They'll want you."

"But…"

"You'll do fine, bro," Grant said. He would have liked to remind his brother of a bachelor party outing, or any other time the two of them had been to a strip joint together, but there hadn't been any other time.

With a hand on Darin's elbow, he escorted his brother toward the front of the busy establishment. It was packed. On a Monday night, no less.

"Do you know what this place is?" Darin leaned over and whispered. Loudly. As soon as they stepped inside.

"Yes." He was heading toward the pay booth.

Darin shook his head, pulled his elbow out of Grant's grasp and made a beeline past the guy who checked IDs of anyone who looked underage, right by the bouncer who looked surprised and straight back out the door they'd just come through.

Not a good start. At a trot, he followed his brother, ignoring the checker's curious stare and the bouncer's frown.

"Darin."

The taller man was heading straight toward the truck with a purposeful stride.

In the parking lot, a couple of gentlemen, dressed in suits, headed toward the door, but turned to watch Grant chasing Darin.

"Darin," he said again, firmly, but quietly, too.

Halfway to the back of the parking lot, Darin stopped. With both feet firmly planted he turned to face Grant.

"I am not going back in there."

"Come on, bro. It'll be good for us." For him.

"Good, how?" The raised eyebrow was classic Darin. A look that would have cowed Grant in the old days. The tone of voice was petulant.

"There are pretty girls in there, Darin. We can look at them all we want. And there's more. I was going to ask one of the girls to dance just for you."

A private lap dance. He knew what they were. How to procure one. They were perfectly legal.

The thought sickened him. But they *were* legal. And could take care of Darin's need to have some intimate contact with a female without being exposed to disease or prostitution.

Or attempting to get it from Maddie.

It was the perfect solution.

"It's a strip club, Grant."

He knew that.

More slowly, Darin headed toward the car. Grant kept pace with him.

"I'm surprised at you." There was no petulance in Darin's tone now. But there was something else there that Grant recognized only too well.

His big brother's disappointment.

TUESDAY AND WEDNESDAY passed peacefully. There were no new residents. No emergency calls, just well checks. She only had two pregnancies to follow at the moment and both of them were progressing normally and nowhere close to delivery. She'd caught up on her charting. Administered allergy shots. Distributed meds to residents who couldn't be trusted to keep them in their bungalows.

And between her, Sara, Lila, Angelica and Grant, they'd managed to allow Darin and Maddie to take morning therapy together, to see each other on campus a time or two, without ever giving them a second alone.

Sara was hopeful the time together would be enough to get Maddie through her adjustment period. And it appeared another storm had passed.

But with each day that passed, the weekend loomed closer.

Or, to be more precise, Saturday night—and Kara's trip to San Francisco.

On her way home from work on Wednesday evening, she saw Grant off in the distance, bent over a mound of dirt and stone in the area where the rock fountain was taking shape. She saw him because she'd specifically gone that way hoping to see him.

She called out.

He looked up.

She waved.

He waved back.

And for one split crazy second she entertained the idea of asking him to spend the night with her Saturday night.

She wanted an adult sleepover. Just the two of them. The kind where the adults didn't sleep.

MADDIE WAS STILL at Lynn's place when Lynn came out from putting Kara to bed after eight on Wednesday evening.

"I thought you had arts and crafts tonight," Lynn said. A volunteer was coming in to teach the women how to make reindeer Christmas ornaments to sell at the secondhand goods and craft boutique The Lemonade Stand owned a block up from the shelter.

Maddie shook her head. Sniffled.

And that was when Lynn realized that Maddie was crying.

"What's wrong, sweetie?" she said, placing a hand on Maddie's hunched-over back as she sat down next to her.

Maddie got agitated. Nervous. Panicky. Scared to death. Worried. And ecstatic, too. She almost never cried.

"He doesn't like me."

"Who doesn't like you?" she asked, but she already knew. Obviously something had happened between her and Darin.

"Daarrriiinnn." The pretty blonde sounded as though her heart had been broken into a million pieces.

But maybe this was good. Broken hearts mended and Maddie could move on past the relationship stage of her recovery.

"Of course he likes you," she said, because what else could she say?

Maddie shook her head and looked at Lynn with big watery eyes that were red and swollen. Maddie must have been crying the entire time Lynn had been bathing Kara, getting her in her jammies and reading to her. "He doesn't like me, Lynn."

"How do you know that?"

"Because I told him I liked him and then he stopped waiting for me."

"You told him you liked him?"

"Yes. Because I do and you tell me I just have to be honest and so I was."

"What did he say?"

"He s-s-said he l-l-liked me, t-t-tooooo." The last word broke off on a wail followed by another bout of tears.

"He did."

"Yes."

"Well, there you go, then. He does like you."

"I think you should tell him about always telling the truth."

"You think Darin lied to you?"

Sniffling, taking the tissue Lynn pulled from a box on the table and handed to her, Maddie blew her nose loudly and said, "Yes, I do, because he said it and then didn't wait for me ever again."

No matter what was best for Maddie, it hurt to see her so upset. Maddie was the sweetest, most giving person she'd ever known—certainly the most pure-hearted. And she'd suffered enough.

Rubbing Maddie's back, she asked, "What do you mean wait for you?"

"After his afternoon therapy he waits outside of Angelica's room and I finish the day care playtime and Kara and I go to Angelica's and Darin walks us home."

Ah.

"You know his brother is working here full-time

this week, right?" she asked, feeling like a traitor to this woman who trusted her implicitly.

"He's making a new Garden of Renewal," Maddie said, enunciating as purposefully as always, as though she had to stop between thinking the words and saying it so that her brain could tell her mouth *how* to say it. "He took away the gazebo. I have to keep Kara away from there until the yellow ribbon is down around it."

"That's right. And you know that Darin works with his brother in his business, right?"

"Darin can't do much right now. He can't bend over or lift things that are heavy. So he does some work that he can do."

"Well, right now, with Grant here all day, Darin has to go right out to the garden to work after his therapy."

Maddie's big eyes opened wide as the woman looked at her. "Are you sure?"

"I'm positive." She also knew that Grant was collecting Darin from therapy so that his older brother wouldn't have any time alone with Maddie. Angelica was texting him five minutes before Darin was through.

She could feel Maddie's shudders beneath her hand. "Okay?" she asked the sweet woman.

With a big sigh, Maddie fell against Lynn, burying her head against her, and Lynn sat back, her arm around Maddie. "Okay," Maddie said.

She hiccupped. "I like him, Lynn."

Lynn ran her fingers slowly through Maddie's hair, like her mom used to do when she was a kid and thinking the world was going to end over some crisis or another. "I know you do."

"He would never hit me."

"No, he wouldn't. But neither would most men."

"Darin smells good."

She hadn't noticed.

"And he doesn't make fun of me."

"He's a nice person. So is Grant."

"I like Darin."

They were in trouble. Darin was showing signs of completely recovering his left-side motor skills but was nowhere near ready to cut back on his therapy.

And Maddie...once she understood something, it was hard for her to understand it in a different way. She'd believed her ex-husband loved her and she still believed it. In spite of all the years of beatings at his hands.

She also believed she liked Darin. In a boy-girl sense. They weren't going to convince her otherwise.

Which meant certain heartbreak for the sweet woman. They'd avoided it that night. But it would come again.

Lynn had no idea what to do about that.

So she did what she could. She stroked Maddie's hair. And when the other woman fell asleep, she sat there, cradling her, wishing she could promise Maddie, and Kara, too, a world where hearts didn't have to hurt.

A world where hearts weren't vulnerable to the vagaries of other people.

GRANT WAITED UNTIL Darin was in his room with his door closed before heading to his own room Wednesday night.

But just barely. He was like a panting dog, rushing to the water bowl. A panting something...

He'd been thinking about Lynn's jaunty little wave to him all evening.

Lynn got calls at all hours. Hopefully ten o'clock wasn't too late.

"Hello?"

"I'm sorry it's so late." He didn't bother to introduce himself. She'd have seen his number on the caller ID. It was the third time they'd talked on the phone since he'd first visited her at the shelter.

The second since she'd made him aware of the Maddie/Darin situation on Monday.

"It's not too late," she said now. "Maddie just left."

"How's that going?" Lynn was hoping to distract Maddie from thinking that she was romantically interested in Darin. Sara was trying to help the other woman recognize the difference between being friends with a man and being his girlfriend.

"It's not."

Not the answer he'd been hoping far.

"How's it going at your end?" she asked.

"He's never mentioned her to me so I haven't said anything."

"Do you think he's noticed that you aren't giving him any time with her?"

"Doesn't seem to have."

"That's good, then."

"I thought so."

He didn't tell her about his botched attempt to take care of any needs his brother might have. Darin hadn't mentioned it again, either. Which was fine with him.

At the moment he was more interested in his own needs. Ones that would never be assuaged by a trip to a club.

He was beginning to fear that they wouldn't be assuaged by time alone with a woman, either. Unless the woman was Lynn Duncan.

He'd get over her. He knew he would. He was thirty-eight, not eighteen. As soon as he and Darin were done at the Stand, his desire for Darin's nurse would fade.

"Okay, then," he said, still thinking about her wave that afternoon.

"Sleep well."

"You, too."

He hung up.

And took another long shower before climbing naked between the sheets.

CHAPTER FIFTEEN

LUKE AND CRAIG were back on Bishop Landscaping paying jobs, with Grant spending his mornings and evenings doing CEO and design work, and the rest of his days out in the Garden of Renewal.

By Thursday, though, he had to take time off from the garden to mow. The Lemonade Stand grounds weren't growing as quickly as they would when the rainy season came and the sun got a bit warmer, but he didn't want them to look anything other than resort perfect.

He was kind of looking forward to a couple of hours riding the industrial-size zero-turn mower someone had donated to the shelter. Bishop Landscaping didn't do a lot of mowing and had no reason to invest the thousands of dollars it would cost for one of those babies.

And he didn't do a whole lot of the menial yard work tasks at any rate.

But as he climbed aboard late Thursday morning, he found himself on guard for a little curly-haired imp around every corner.

Maddie and Darin were in therapy. Kara would

be at the day care. Unless for some reason she wasn't. No one would have thought to tell him. Still, Kara wasn't the only child at the complex, though, as a rule, kids were either in school or at the day care during the time Grant was around.

He didn't see Kara. But as he rounded a corner, he saw Lynn in blue scrubs walking with a woman and two children. The children, about first and second graders, he figured, clung to their mother, one on each side.

Lynn said something. The children laughed.

She looked over at him.

He waved.

And she waved back.

SHORTLY AFTER ELEVEN that morning, his cell beeped a sound he wasn't familiar with. And vibrated, too. Pulling it out of the holster on his belt, he saw that he had a message from his service provider. He'd reached his maximum minutes for the month and was now being charged a per-minute fee.

His cell was also his business phone. There was no way he could pay per minute every time a client called him.

It was a mistake. Had to be. He'd been on the same phone plan for more than six years. And he'd never reached his minute limit.

Sitting on the stopped mower in the middle of one of the six commons that made up the living quarters of The Lemonade Stand, he dialed his service provider.

A couple of minutes later, privy to the information that there'd been no mistake, he started mowing again. Just until lunchtime. Or until he saw Lynn heading back toward her office unaccompanied.

He did a row. Then another. Leaving a neat pattern of cut grass in his wake. And then he stopped. Maybe she'd returned to work through the building. He wouldn't have seen her.

Yanking the key from the ignition of the mower, he left it in the yard and strode off toward Lynn's office. Rounding a corner too quickly, and not looking where he was going, he almost ran straight into her. Would have if she hadn't held out a hand to prevent the collision.

"Lynn! I'm sorry," he apologized, holding on to her arm until he was certain she hadn't lost her balance.

And then he didn't let go.

"I was looking for..."

"I was coming to find..." They spoke in unison.

The air was a balmy sixty-five, but Grant was sweating in his Bishop Landscaping oxford shirt and jeans.

"What were you looking for?" she asked. "Maybe I can help you find it."

"I have no doubt about that," he told her, looking

into those blue eyes and wishing he could just find a home there. "What were you coming to find?"

"You." She was as focused on him as he was on her. Staring right into his eyes. If she saw something more than their color there he didn't care. She could take whatever she wanted.

"I was looking for you."

A couple of women appeared behind them, talking, but their voices stopped as they rounded the corner and Grant and Lynn came into view.

"Ladies," Lynn said, smiling at them. And then she grabbed Grant's hand. "Come on," she said, pulling him into an alcove between two bungalows, down a small pathway and into an empty, unlocked cabin filled with round tables and chairs. A counter lined three of the walls, with cupboards above and below it.

"This is an arts and crafts room," she said. "It's also used for special parties—baby showers or birthday parties."

He didn't think she really cared for him to know what the cabin was for.

And didn't like the fact that he cared about what she cared about.

Wanting sex with her was fine. Wanting *her* was not.

Giving himself a minute to regroup, he walked around the room, looking out the windows at the various views. He'd mowed and weeded the entire area. But he'd thought the cabin was a storage facility. It had always been closed up and he'd never seen anyone near it.

Turning, he saw her watching him, her sexy butt leaning against a counter on the wall opposite him.

"Do you have parents in the area?" The question came out of nowhere, but he realized that he didn't know. And wanted to.

"No, though I grew up here. My younger sister, Katie, is divorced and living in Denver. She has two small kids and really needed my parents nearby. My father is a lawyer and took the bar in Denver and off they went."

"Why didn't your sister move back here?" She'd told him and Darin, four years before, that she'd grown up in Santa Raquel. He'd remembered.

"She can't take the kids out of the state as part of the custody agreement in her divorce."

"Do you have any other siblings?"

"Nope. It's just Katie and me."

And apparently her parents had determined that the younger daughter was more of a priority than the daughter who'd been abused? If she'd been abused. He knew Maddie's story now, but still didn't feel comfortable enough to ask Lynn about herself.

He wasn't sure he'd ask even if she'd seemed open to talking about her past. She was on his mind too much as it was.

"Mom hates not being closer to Kara," Lynn said

as though reading his mind. "We talk at least once a week, and she visits as often as she can."

"Does she stay here?"

"Yes, though she had to submit to a background check before she was cleared to do so."

"What about your dad? Does he ever come with her?"

"Sometimes. And when he does, they stay in a bed-and-breakfast down at the beach."

He nodded. Envying Lynn her parents. But only for the second it took him to shake himself out of it. He focused on her again.

She was more than enough to distract him from just about anything.

"You said you were looking for me," he said, and when she didn't break eye contact, he moved closer to her.

They were alone again. In a very quiet, remote part of the complex.

"I have a favor to ask." Her lips moved. He wanted to lick them.

To know how the tip of that tongue tasted.

"Then ask."

"I'd like some more landscape lighting in the garden at my place," she said. "I don't know if I can afford it, but I figured you'd be able to tell me how much it would cost and—"

"You tell me what you want and it's yours." He moved a couple of steps closer to her.

"I'm not going to take advantage…." Her words trailed off. But she still didn't look away from him. And he wanted to take advantage. In the worst way.

"I've got a shed full of leftovers and samples," he told her. "And anything that isn't there, I can get from my suppliers. They've given me carte blanche for this place."

"I'll pay you for your time to install them."

"I'd rather you just be my friend." Where the words had come from he didn't know. But once they were out there, he couldn't take them back. And couldn't deny their truth, either.

Somewhere, in the midst of his fantasies, he'd begun to want more than sex.

"I told you why I was looking for you, now why were you looking for me?" she asked, neatly sidestepping the land mine he'd just thrown down between them.

Rightly so.

He had no ability to follow through on any personal relationship offer he'd make. Whether it was accepted or not.

"Darin's been calling Maddie," he said, getting himself back on track. "They've talked over a thousand minutes in the past two weeks."

"That's…"

"Over sixteen hours."

"When?"

"Mostly at night. Since I took on the work at the shelter, we've been spending our evenings separately. Darin goes to his room with the TV on or he's on his computer while I'm working. He plays the television kind of loud, or has his music on and it's still going a lot of the time when I head to my room, which is on the other side of the house. We have a split master bedroom floor plan."

And he still should have known his special-needs brother had been talking long into the night. On several occasions.

What kind of caregiver was he that he hadn't known?

"They talk here, too, during the day."

That he couldn't have known.

"Maddie's usually at my place while Kara takes her afternoon nap."

The timing fit.

"I'll talk to her."

He shrugged. "And say what? That she's not allowed to talk on her own phone? You've already said that Sara thinks this 'friendship' of theirs needs to play itself out."

He'd just realized something else. Something he was deeply ashamed of. He was resentful. Darin had a woman he was talking to half the night while Grant lay in his bed and only fantasized about one.

"I don't think there's anything we can do about

it. Darin and I have a family calling plan with separate lines but shared minutes, and I switched it to unlimited minutes, which is cheaper than paying the overage charge. I'm certainly not going to tell my brother he can't talk on the phone. I just thought you should know what's going on. In case you want to tell Sara."

Lynn nodded and glanced at her watch. "It's almost time for lunch," she said.

He wanted to ask her to have the meal with him. Away from the Stand. Away from Maddie and Darin.

And Kara.

Just the two of them. In a place where nothing else could intrude on their time together.

"You and Maddie and Kara have lunch at your house, right?"

"Maddie and Kara do. I share it with them as often as I can."

She didn't stand up. He took a couple of steps closer to the door, which put him closer to her.

She didn't move away.

But her phone rang.

She glanced at the screen. "I'm sorry, I have to take this."

Grant would have left, but didn't want to go without telling her goodbye. Or so he told himself as he heard her say, "That's fine…. No, I'm sure. It's fine.

I'll have her bag packed and ready. But it's important that you keep her on her schedule."

She paused. The other voice was male. Grant stiffened.

"No, I know," Lynn said, her voice changing. Getting softer. Familiar. "I know. I appreciate that."

Jealousy flared inside him. Adding itself to the resentment that had flared earlier.

What the hell was the matter with him? He was normally an even-keeled type of guy. He didn't often have emotional flare-ups of *any* kind, let alone one like this. Emotions that couldn't possibly go anywhere...

He needed to get back to work.

CHAPTER SIXTEEN

"Okay, I will. Bye."

Grant was pacing by the time Lynn ended the call and slid her phone back into the pocket of her scrubs.

He took a deep breath. Warned himself that this situation was none of his business.

"Whose bag are you packing?" Maybe Maddie was going to visit her parents. Maybe she'd stay awhile. Which might create a bit of a babysitting situation for Lynn, but overall would be a very good thing.

Maybe Lynn had arranged it. Maybe that's why she'd taken the call.

"Kara's."

The kid was only three. Way too young to have a bag to pack.

"She's going somewhere? Without you?"

"Yeah." Lynn didn't look too happy about it. And his hackles rose again. For a completely different reason. If Lynn didn't want her daughter to go someplace, then no one had the right to make her go.

"She's going to spend the night with her father," Lynn said slowly. "In San Francisco."

The city was three hours away.

"Her father lives in San Francisco?" He'd assumed the guy was still in Santa Raquel. Or jail.

"He moved there a year ago."

Grant moved closer to her, wanting to take those shadows out of her eyes.

He'd done a little reading over the past couple of weekends. About abused women. A disturbing percentage of them went back to the life they'd left.

Time and distance changed perspective, softened memories and...

"You think it's a good idea to send her off to be alone with him?" he asked, because it was clear that she wasn't happy about the situation.

"I don't want to send her," Lynn said, a wry smile on her lips. "But yes, I think it's a good idea or I wouldn't have agreed to do so."

"You don't have to send her?"

"Not technically."

"Have you talked to Lila about this? Or Sara?"

"No. Why would I do that?"

He didn't want to make her defensive. When he made Darin defensive they got nowhere fast.

"I don't know. Just in case..."

"In case what?"

Lowering his chin to his chest, he looked up at

her and then away. "I don't know. Do you think she'll be safe with him?"

"He's her father, Grant!"

Wow. He'd overstepped on that one. She'd never given him any reason to believe that she wanted him as a confidant. Or even a friend.

"He's never...hurt...her, then?" Why wasn't he letting this go?

"Of course not!" The horror on Lynn's face couldn't be faked. "Brandon loves Kara more than anything on earth. He'd give his life for her."

He should stop. But couldn't. Even if he pissed her off. Because Kara was...three. And...

"If he hurt you, don't you think there's even a remote possibility that—"

"Hurt me? We're divorced—of course I was hurt—but just because he didn't want to be married to me doesn't mean that he'll ever abandon his daughter. He's a great father."

Jealousy screwed up his logic for a second. He sidestepped it. Forced himself to focus.

"I'm not talking about emotional hurt or abandonment."

She stood, hands out on either side of her. "Then what are you talking about?" she asked, her face lifted up to his. Those blue eyes were wide and searching—and unusually open to the heart and soul he was trying to avoid.

In way over his head, Grant swallowed.

He cared about her. Whether she wanted to be his friend or not.

"I… You're here, at the Stand. A resident. He… Brandon… Kara's father… Your ex-husband…" *Get it out, Bishop.* Everyone present knew who the man was. "Did he hit you?"

He couldn't pretend now that his personal interest was just about sex.

"Brandon? You're kidding, right?"

"No." But he was beginning to think he had her all wrong.

"Brandon would no more lift a hand to me than slit his own throat."

"You weren't abused?"

"No! I had no idea you thought that."

"You're here."

"Because I had an aunt who was killed by her abusive husband," Lynn said. "My mother's sister. And because my own sister was abused. That's why my parents are in Denver and don't get home much. Katie's ex managed to get all domestic violence charges dropped. He not only got joint custody of their kids, but he wants her back, as well. My folks live with her in the hopes they can prevent that from happening. And to watch over the kids. Mom can't bear the thought of losing Katie like she lost her sister.

"Anyway, when I saw how my sister, who'd been raised, as I was—to be completely aware of the signs of mental and emotional abuse—fell prey to it, I knew this was a disease even more insidious than the cancers and viruses I saw at the hospital. I started volunteering here. When my marriage broke up, Brandon offered to put me through the yearlong master's program I needed to certify as a midwife practitioner so that I could work full-time as a chief medical officer for a shelter. I was halfway through the program when the full-time position here opened up. I applied and they hired me, with the mandate that I complete my certification. I did and I've been here ever since."

"How long is ever since?"

"Two and a half years."

He counted backward.

"Your husband left you right after Kara was born?"

"More or less. She was five weeks old when I knew my marriage was over."

The shadows in her eyes stabbed at him.

Grant had no idea what to say. Or do, either.

He shoved his hands in his pockets. And said, "I don't think you should send her up there."

What kind of guy walked out on his wife and brand-new baby daughter?

"I'm going to have to let her go sometime," she said. "And Brandon's so good about bringing her home to spend the night in her own bed on the weekends that he's here for his visitations."

"How often does he come down?"

"Every other weekend."

"He comes down from San Francisco every other weekend?"

He did some more math. That meant the guy had been there, with Lynn and Kara, since he and Darin had been coming to the Stand.

"Yeah. Kara adores him."

So. Good. They had it all nicely wrapped up.

They didn't need him.

Which was fine, because he didn't have room in his life for them, either.

GRANT HAD BEEN different when he'd said goodbye and left Lynn to meet Darin for lunch.

Distant.

She hadn't liked it. At all.

On and off all afternoon, whenever she was in between patients, or in her office and supposed to be charting, she ran their cabin conversation over and over in her mind.

She went in to restock supplies in the exam rooms and thought of the morning Grant had been in there with her.

She'd wanted him to get intimate with her.

That morning, when she'd stood with him in the cabin, she'd actually felt weak with wanting him—wanting him to touch her. And she'd known that if he'd tried, she wouldn't have stopped him.

She dropped the plastic jar that she'd picked up to refill with cotton balls. The lid rolled under the exam table.

It wouldn't have been right. Letting him touch her. She'd have regretted it later.

But she'd have let him.

Opening the sterile sack of cotton balls with gloved hands, Lynn shoved a handful into the jar and set it back on the counter.

He had that way of staring at her mouth. As if he wanted to know what she tasted like.

On her hands and knees, Lynn reached under the exam table, retrieved the lid and dropped it in the sterilizer.

For all she knew, Grant Bishop eyed all the women he knew like he eyed her.

She didn't think so, but what did she know? It wasn't as though she had loads of experience.

But she did know one thing. She couldn't just leave things as they were.

Finished stocking her supplies, she closed and locked the clinic doors and went out the back door, heading straight for the Garden of Renewal.

With any luck, Grant would still be there alone.

GRANT WASN'T AT the garden. No one was there. Lynn walked through the three-acre oasis, hardly able to believe what she was seeing. The garden had always been bordered and shaded by strategically placed maple and oak trees—some of which had been growing on the land before it had been developed. The trees created "walls" for a private roomlike feel, setting the garden off from the rest of the property.

Inside had been mostly ground-cover plants and the gazebo with its wooden picnic tables.

Today, while it was still taped off and not completely finished, the Garden of Renewal was exquisite. A haven. As close to heaven as anything Lynn had ever seen.

Feeling as if she was trespassing, she walked along a mulched pathway that threaded through various-size pine boxes, filled with every kind of plant and flower she could imagine. The scents wafted up, intoxicating her. The colors brought tears to her eyes. Wooden benches set apart for privacy not only lined the pathway but were placed off the path, as well, in the trees, surrounded by ground cover. And in the midst of it all was the fountain. Water trailing down over a boulder. Enough to make the sound of a waterfall, but not swift enough to give any sense of urgency or speed.

As she got closer, she could see why the area was still cordoned off. Electrical wires stood up, capped, around the fountain and the large, kidney-shaped pool that fed the fountain.

There were more wires along a small stream that wound from the pool into another area of the garden—one filled with greenery and a couple of additional smaller benches. This section of the garden reminded her of a prayer forest she'd been to once when she was a kid at camp.

As she looked more closely, she noticed other capped wires set surreptitiously around the acreage.

Lynn wanted to pick a bench—any of the ten or so she could see—and just stay awhile.

"I was going to invite you down when I had it all finished."

If she'd been holding anything, she'd have dropped it. Twirling around, Lynn saw Grant at the entrance to the garden, his brown eyes glinting with that…something…that existed between them.

"I came out here looking for you and then just couldn't help myself. Grant, this is beyond anything I'd imagined or expected."

He shrugged. "It's not done yet."

"I'm just so… I had no idea."

He walked toward her and she met him partway. She didn't want a man in her life. But in the garden, in those moments, the only thing she wanted was Grant. The outside world faded into insignificance for that time.

And she had a man again. For sex. But for more than that. She had what Brandon had taken away from her. A companion by her side. Caring about her and their lives first and foremost.

Not a husband. But more than a friend.

He stopped about a foot in front of her. Close enough to touch, but not touching. "Seriously, Grant, you're wasting your talent on yard work."

His business wasn't any of her business. But what he'd created here...

With a grin lifting one side of his mouth, he cocked his head and said, "You do realize that I don't spend my days mowing grass and trimming bushes, don't you?"

God, she loved that grin. "I know you're the boss. That Luke, Craig and, when he's able, Darin do most of the manual labor."

If he moved a little closer, they could flirt with the idea of something between them. Make innuendo that she could take with her into her bathtub later that night.

"Bishop Landscaping doesn't do yard maintenance," he said. "Except as part of completing a project. Or when we go in for remodel or repair."

He was staring at her lips again. She moistened them and asked, "What do you do?"

"I'm a landscape architect."

Oh. Feeling stupid, she took a step back, glancing over at him. "I'm sorry. I thought you had a landscape business, as in you maintained yards for clients."

"We started out that way," he said. "When Luke and I were at college we made extra cash by mowing yards. That venture grew to trimming trees, and then doing general irrigation systems maintenance. We continued to grow that business until I started getting enough design jobs to support us all."

"I feel horrible that we're wasting your time with mowing and trimming."

"It's not a waste of my time. I've kind of enjoyed the return to the manual part of the business. And the brainless part, too," he added, grinning at her again.

He was such a combination of professional and down to earth, of stereotypical guy and caregiver.

"You said you'd come out here to find me." He had that look in his eye again. Slumberous and vitally alive all at once.

As though he found her intoxicating.

And that was just plain crazy.

"I…" She should just let it go.

And remembered how down she'd been all day. She'd come out here for a reason.

But maybe not a good one.

Reaction without thought spelled disaster. Or, at the very least, heartbreak.

She'd had enough of that.

Vacillating wasn't like her.

He moved closer. Close enough that she could smell the freshly cut grass on him. And something musky, too.

"Before, you said you'd like to be my friend."

His eyes narrowed. "That's right."

"I didn't answer you and that was rude. I…came out to apologize."

That was partially true.

"Apology accepted. Is that it?"

He knew. It was as though his gaze bore right into her brain, as though he could read everything there.

"No. I came to tell you that I think us as friends would be good."

The smile that slowly spread on his face made *her* feel drunk. Or maybe it was the smell of all the flowers getting to her.

"I was actually at your place."

"You were? Did you see Maddie?"

"Yeah. She opened the door before I could knock to tell me to be quiet so I didn't wake Kara."

"A cannon going off wouldn't wake her."

"She also told me you weren't home."

"I had an appointment cancel this afternoon. I was going to make an early day of it, but wanted to stop by here first."

Her lips were dry again. She was moist in other places.

"I took another look around your backyard area. I've got an idea and thought, if you were up for it, I could get those lights installed for you on Saturday. I'll be done with the Garden of Renewal tomorrow."

She'd be saying goodbye to Kara for her first overnight visit. For the first time since her daughter's birth she was going to be in a different city than her.

"Saturday would be perfect," she said.

If anything could distract her from the depression of Kara's absence—from the sadness and grief that continued to linger at the demise of her happy family life—Grant Bishop could.

His head dropped, and then he looked up at her. "Eight o'clock okay?" he asked.

"In the morning?" She heard the question and knew that it was asinine. He wasn't going to install landscape lighting at night.

Brandon was due to pick Kara up at ten.

"Yeah, I thought morning would be best."

He smiled. Her blood ran hot.

"Eight is fine. And…with Kara leaving, Maddie won't be there so it would be the best time to have Darin around." She tried to stay focused. To listen to her mind, which she could trust, and not get waylaid by emotions, which weren't trustworthy at all.

"Do you have early appointments?"

She shook her head. And wondered what his kiss would feel like. "Not until the afternoon."

She planned it that way on purpose so she could be at home when Brandon came to collect Kara. And thinking of her ex somehow led to the reminder that she hadn't had sex in three years.

"But…you have to let me pay you," she said, desperate to keep herself on track. "I make okay money, Grant, and I don't have a mortgage. Let me pay your company the going rate."

He grinned again. A slow grin that made her feel as if he'd just taken her clothes off. "Lady, you can't afford me."

"Try me."

He named a price. She didn't blanch. But if she'd tried to speak she would have choked.

"Too much, huh?" His head at a slight angle, he studied her. She didn't want to fail his test.

"No," she finally managed, and her voice sounded fine. Years of practice in the medical field paying off, probably. "I can afford you."

But she couldn't. Not financially. And not emotionally, either.

CHAPTER SEVENTEEN

HE SAW LYNN twice on Friday. Both times she'd been walking within view of the Garden of Renewal. She waved. He waved back. And his thoughts of her were hotter than the lights he was wiring—the finishing touch on the garden.

By the time he collected Darin from his afternoon therapy session, he was ready to remove the caution tape from around the newly remodeled garden.

He told Darin the second he saw him, lifting his left hand to Darin's right for a high five, a ritual at the completion of every job.

"I don't know why you keep coming here to get me, Grant," Darin said, leaving Grant's hand hanging in midair.

"I like to watch the last few minutes of therapy each day so I can see how well you're progressing," he said, aware of the slightly petulant tone of his voice.

He was hurt. He knew he had absolutely no right to be, but he couldn't help the way he felt.

"You've always liked to have me around," he

added as he headed down the hall and out the back door. Darin kept pace with him.

"I do like having you around," his older brother agreed.

"Then what's the problem?"

"Nothing."

It was a truculent "nothing." Not an assured, truthful one. But he let it go. Because he knew what was wrong—if Grant was there, Darin couldn't wait for Maddie—and was hopeful that if they continued to ignore the issue, it would fade away as so many others had in the past.

"Oh, yeah, look." Reaching over with his right hand, Darin pulled Grant to a stop on the sidewalk. He held out his left leg. Pulled up the leg of the sweatpants he'd worn to therapy that day.

In place of the piece of gauze taped to his brother's shin, there was a line of pink puffy skin. "Lynn came and got me and we went to her room and she took out my stitches."

He'd wanted to be there. If for no other reason than to have the excuse to spend the time with Lynn. "She said seven to ten days," Grant said aloud. "It's only been six."

"But I saw her in the hall before my therapy and I told her I was itching there and she said, 'Let me take a look,' and she did and she brought me right over and took out the stitches and walked with me back over to my therapy. Don't worry, I wasn't late, Grant."

"I wasn't worried. And I'm very glad the stiches are out. Now you can shower without having to make sure it's covered."

"That's what Lynn said." They continued on toward the garden.

And Grant thought about Darin's nurse in the shower. *His* shower.

THAT EVENING, AFTER stopping for burgers on the way back home from The Lemonade Stand, Grant asked Darin to help him find the landscape lights he wanted in the supply shed behind their garage.

While they were in the shed, his phone rang, and he talked to Luke about a problem he and Craig had run into that day on a fifty-thousand-dollar job. At the customer's request they were planting two rows of flowering trees along a river rock walkway and they'd run into some slate ground.

He'd tested patches of the ground himself and found the soil nutrient rich. Telling Luke he'd be at the job site at six in the morning, he made a mental note to check the design blueprint before turning in that night. He needed a plan B for the mini-orange-tree grove at the end of the line of trees if he was going to have to reroute the walkway.

Luke filled him in on the other job they'd been

at that morning. And by the time Grant hung up, Darin had a bin open on the workbench.

"These are the ones you wanted, right?" he asked.

He glanced in the bin. "Yep, thanks, bro."

Darin closed the bin with his good hand and pushed it to the corner of the workbench, turning to replace the other plastic bins he'd pulled off the waist-high shelves. Handled one at a time, the bins were light enough for Darin to move on his own without breaking the doctor's no-lifting rule.

They were light enough to move with one hand, but his brother was using both. Slowly. Awkwardly. But successfully.

Darin's left hand didn't do much more than touch the underside of the bin—a two-or three-inch movement that didn't appear to be weight bearing. But it was a start.

Grant grabbed some wire, clips and extra bulbs, put them in a bag and turned to find Darin standing at the workbench between them, frowning at him.

"What?" Grant asked a little more irritably than he probably should have. He had a problem at a job site—a very lucrative job site—he'd had a long week, his brother didn't seem to want him around and he had formed an unhealthy addiction to a woman he couldn't have. Could you blame a guy for being a little frustrated?

"You know that girl, Maddie, the blonde you saw me with, who was looking after Lynn's little girl,

Kara? The one who was so upset the day Kara almost fell in the hole?"

"Yes."

"I like her."

Play it down, man. It's only a big deal if you make it one. Darin's words to him when he was a junior in high school and wasn't chosen to play first string basketball...

"I like her, too."

Darin stood tall, making eye contact. A sign of a lucid moment. "You don't know her as well as I do."

"No, I don't. But from what I've seen she seems very nice."

"I know a lot about her."

Was this the time to mention the phone calls he knew about?

Or maybe it was time to ask Darin if he wanted to make a run for some ice cream.

"She's very trusting and sometimes gets hurt." Darin had both hands on the workbench.

All Grant could think of to say was, "That's nice." And managed to stop himself.

"We like talking to each other." Darin's tone was growing stronger. And the child in him wasn't surfacing, Grant noted.

He knew he was going to have to engage.

"I had a call from the phone company yesterday," he said, equally serious as he met his brother's gaze head-on. "We were over our minute allowance. They did a usage analysis for me."

"I've been talking to Maddie on the phone."

"Late at night, apparently."

Darin wasn't a child to be disciplined, he reminded himself as he heard the almost accusing tone in his voice. "Which is fine," he quickly added.

His tension was his problem. Not Darin's.

"I'll pay you for the phone bill."

Grant nodded, knowing full well that Darin had no idea how much the phone bill cost, or how much money it would take to cover it. He had a bank account because Grant paid him, and he got federal assistance, as well. But Grant was the executor of the account. And kept very clear records of every dime of Darin's money that was spent.

"You already pay your share of the phone bill, bro," he said, wishing he'd opted for ice cream. Or that Darin had started this conversation while he still had things to do in the shed.

"I'm sorry the phone company had to call you."

"I'm not. You have a friend, Darin, that's fine."

It was just going to have to be. Because his brother deserved a life, for God's sake. Standing there listening to a forty-four-year-old man apologize for talking on the phone—and knowing that his handling of the situation had prompted his brother's remorse—made him sick.

Darin watched him for a long time, which wasn't

all that unusual. His brother took a long time to focus sometimes. And then he said, in a perfectly normal tone, "I want to take Maddie on a date."

Grant needed a beer. A whole case of beer. And a deep breath, too. He'd already screwed up the phone company conversation.

Of course Darin couldn't take Maddie on a date. That was a given. How to handle the situation in a way that respected his older brother, he didn't know.

"I need your help, Grant." Darin could have been in college, and Grant fourteen again. That was how Darin sounded. And how Grant felt.

He waited.

"I can't drive. And while I could pay with a debit card, I'm afraid I'd screw it up and spend too much of our money."

Life wasn't meant to be this way. Logic and knowing mixed with helplessness. It just wasn't natural.

But Darin was alive. With him. He hadn't died with Shelley that day. Or in the critical days afterward when they'd had to do the first of many surgeries on his brain.

"Maddie needs me."

It was a completely adult concept. A completely Darin concept.

"How does she need you?" he challenged, on the defensive again, but managing to keep his feelings out of his tone as he posed the question.

"She needs me to be a man who's her friend."

So any man would do? The words, thankfully, didn't make it out of his mouth.

"And she trusts me not to hurt her."

"How do you know that?"

"She told me."

Grant's eyes narrowed as he and his brother stood facing each other across the workbench—man to man—wishing he knew how much man was really left inside his brother.

Sometimes he was convinced that Darin was all there, just challenged in his delivery.

"And that's why you want to go on a date with her? So that you won't hurt her?"

The old Darin would have known that to lead a girl on would hurt worse in the long run. But the act of trying to prevent a woman from hurting was just like the old Darin.

"I want to go on a date with her because I like her and want to go on a date with her, silly," Darin said. He dropped his head and slurped saliva before scooping the box of lights under his arm. Grant followed, bag in hand, turning off the lights to the shed as they left. He stopped to deposit the morning's supplies in the back of the truck.

Were they done, then? Was that it?

Darin stood back, waiting for Grant, and then followed him into the house. Grant had work to do. He waited to see if his brother would go calmly about his routine, take his shower, eat a snack.

Grant dropped his keys on the kitchen counter. Darin emptied his pockets beside them, something Grant had trained him to do early on after the accident. You could tell a lot about a guy and his day by what was in his pockets.

Grant also always made sure Darin had money in his pocket. Money that would most likely get lost if Darin didn't turn it in every night.

Darin moved toward the archway that led from the kitchen to the living room.

"I want to go diving, too, Grant," he said, and then turned slowly to face him again. "But I want to go on a date with Maddie first."

"Darin…"

"Please, Grant. Don't make me beg for this." Darin's brow was furrowed, and he looked as if he might cry.

"Okay, bro. If Maddie wants to go on a date with you, I'll find a way to make it happen."

Darin laughed then, and followed it up with a full-bodied, unrestrained whoop. A little-boy reaction to a big-boy request.

"And I don't even have to cover my stitches," he said, proceeding toward the bathroom.

Grant was left standing in the middle of the room with another problem on his hands. One he had no idea how to handle.

But there was one thing he did know. Maddie seemed to be good for his brother. He couldn't remember the last time Darin had had so many "real" moments in one span. It was as though Maddie's need for him—and his protectiveness of her—was bringing out some latent instincts that hadn't been diminished by the injury to his brain.

CHAPTER EIGHTEEN

KARA'S BAG WAS packed, and the little girl was sound asleep in her princess bed, covers tucked up to her chin, hugging Sammy.

Maddie had long since gone home. On Friday nights she liked to stay up to watch old movies on some cable station with the younger girls. Gwen, the woman who stayed at Maddie's place while her husband worked, was off for the night.

Lynn didn't even hesitate before pouring herself a glass of wine and heading to her bathroom. The rose-scented candle was already there. As was the bottle of rose-scented bubble bath. Turning on her portable music player, she found her CD of Pachelbel's Canon renditions, stripped down and stepped into the still-running water.

She could do all that was expected of her, do all that she expected of herself; she could contribute to society and be happy, too. She just had to make certain that she maintained control of her heart and, thus, her life.

The warm water sluiced around her ankles as she stood naked in the tub and bent to adjust the water temperature. A tepid bath wasn't going to do it tonight.

She needed enough external heat to melt away the lava burning through her veins.

It wasn't like her to be so emotional. But as hard as she tried not to allow herself to wallow, she was angry with Brandon for breaking his promises to her—for asking her to share his life with him and then changing her life so drastically.

She was illogically jealous of Douglas, who was able to attract her ex-husband when she couldn't.

She was worried about letting Kara go off with her father to another city overnight.

And she was so turned on by Grant Bishop that the following morning loomed amid a mass of anticipation and fantasy....

At first she thought the ringing was coming from her music player. By the second ring, she'd jumped out of the tub and grabbed her phone off the bathroom counter.

Being on call 24/7 meant she could never have more than one glass of wine. And could never be far from her cell phone.

"This is Lynn," she said, pushing the answer button without looking at the LED screen.

"Is this a bad time?"

Pleasant shivers suffusing her body as she slid back down into the water, Lynn said, "No, it's fine. What's up?"

Darin called Maddie at night because he liked her. Did Grant's call mean that he liked Lynn, too?

The thought was followed quickly by another. He was calling to cancel their appointment in the morning....

She took a gulp of wine. Set the stem of the glass carefully on the edge of the tub.

"How does a double date sound?"

"I'm not sure what you mean."

"Darin wants to take Maddie on a date."

"You prevaricated, right? Led him down another path."

"I... Not successfully."

"So you're thinking we should let them go, but go with them?"

"I'm saying I have to help him take Maddie on a date and I'm asking you if you would like to accompany me."

Oh. But... The wine was too good going down.

"You want us to be on a date, though."

His hesitation was sexy. And worrisome, too. What if he didn't want to date her but felt he had to? What if he was only asking her for Maddie's sake? What if he'd asked her because he thought doing so was the only way The Lemonade Stand would agree to let Maddie go on the date?

Maddie didn't need their permission to go. She wasn't a prisoner at the Stand.

"I want to emasculate my older brother as little as possible." Grant's belated answer was offered softly.

"You want Darin and Maddie to think we're on a date with them."

"I want it to be a date."

Oh, boy. She needed to not be naked in the bath at the moment. Covering her pubic area with her hand, as though she could stem the flow of feeling down there, and shield that part of her from a man who saw far too much, she said, "When?"

"Tomorrow night. That's why I'm calling tonight. Otherwise, we could have talked about this in the morning."

Right, so he was still coming in the morning. Good.

"My thinking is to get this done as quickly as possible," he said. "I don't want the date to build into something bigger than it is."

Was he talking about them? Or Maddie and Darin?

"And Kara's going to be gone tomorrow night."

Maddie was her usual sitter, but not her only one. Occasionally, when Maddie was otherwise engaged, other residents watched over Kara for her.

"Okay."

"Really? Just like that?"

She sipped again. Pushed water up over her nipples, stimulating them further. "Yeah, I think so, just like that."

It made logical sense. Put the elephant on the table. Take the bull by the horns. Face the issue.

"Great, then. I'll plan something. Unless you'd rather…"

"No, you go ahead." Mistake. Mistake. Mistake. She used to love it when Brandon surprised her with a special night out, when he took care of the details. She'd felt spoiled. Cared for.

And she'd been left bereft when the details he'd taken care of had no longer included her.

She been brokenhearted, too, but hearts mended. It was the way the life one was building could be completely deleted without warning, when one allowed one's life to be tightly woven with the wants and needs of another, that had nearly killed her.

It was that joining of hearts and lives that she would never again allow.

But she could date. Have sex. Be friends.

Grant asked about her culinary likes and dislikes. She told him Maddie's, too. He asked if she liked the beach. She told him she and Maddie both liked the beach.

He wanted to know her taste in music. She told him about Pachelbel, happening to mention that she was listening to him right then. And added, "Maddie likes country music."

"You're listening to Pachelbel?"

Scooping more water over her breasts, she reached for her wineglass and said, "Mmm-hmm."

"Is that water I hear?"

She'd tried to keep her activities quiet. Until that last time. She'd forgotten.

Taking a sip of wine, she allowed a drop to spill onto her breast. Watched it trickle into the water and set her glass back on the porcelain edge. "I don't know, probably," she said.

"You listen to Pachelbel while you do dishes?"

"I'm not doing dishes."

His pause was quite lengthy. She dipped her hand in the water and wiped the wine off her nipple.

And dipped her hand in the water again, not even trying to be quiet about it.

"You're in the bathtub."

"Mmm-hmm."

"You leave me no choice but to picture you there."

"I'm under bubbles. All you'd see is white."

"Completely?"

Slipping down farther into the water, she concentrated on keeping her phone dry. "Yes."

"Too bad."

Yeah, well, a girl had to do what it took to save herself from mental and emotional breakdown.

"I meant what I said." His voice had dropped down to a very quiet but powerful tenor. "Tomorrow night is a real date."

But he'd only asked because of Darin and Maddie.

"Okay," she said, and left the phone beside the

tub after they hung up, pretending he was still there as she let the hot water touch her body and fantasized about what he looked like naked.

GRANT HEARD DARIN moving about just before he crawled into bed Friday night and, pulling on a pair of boxers, walked in to find his brother at the computer, playing a game of solitaire.

It was an exercise his occupational therapist had recommended years ago. One that Darin struggled to complete with any accuracy.

"I haven't seen you play that in a while." Was this what Darin did at night? Kept trying to succeed where he'd failed? Grant had thought his brother had given up on ever getting solitaire right.

"I was wrong to quit," Darin said now. "Quitters never get anywhere." He sounded like himself at fourteen, going out for the high school baseball team.

And again Grant was struck by the sudden changes in Darin. If having a girlfriend was going to have this kind of effect on Darin, then Grant had to do what he could to encourage the situation.

At the same time, he had to maintain enough control that no one got hurt. Because while Maddie and Darin could experience adult emotions, they were unable to discern between what was doable and not, what was good for them and not. They were both unable to see pitfalls that a normal adult would get from the start.

"I've got some good news," Grant said, watching as Darin moved an ace up to the plateau to place it on a two of the same suit, rather than moving it up to the home four and adding the two on top of it.

At least he was putting the right denominations on the right suit.

"What good news?" Darin asked, trying to put a king up where the aces were supposed to stack.

"If Maddie says yes to a date, we can go."

His brother turned around so swiftly he knocked his mouse to the floor. His mouth hanging wide-open, he stared at Grant.

And Grant wondered, for one horrible, shameful second, how any woman would want to go out with a grown man who didn't always swallow his spit.

Then he thought of Maddie. Who also drooled on occasion when she was talking or eating.

And he remembered sitting at his mother's grave site after all the cars had pulled away, remembered Darin coming to find him and sitting with him there. Just sitting. Until Grant had been able to get up and leave his mother so irrevocably behind.

"Grant?"

He blinked.

"I said she said yes."

He tuned Darin out sometimes. Especially when

his brother was jabbering like a little kid. But he wouldn't have missed a phone call.

"How do you know?"

"I already asked her."

"When?"

"Today. When you were loading up the truck after I didn't get to see her after therapy. We don't know when we'll get to walk together again since you want to watch my therapy and she's busy at the day care and Lynn needs her, so I said we should go on a date because then we could spend the whole time together on purpose."

Grant grinned. His brother had taken control of the situation. "Well, call her back and tell her it's tomorrow night," he said. He felt like whooping right along with his brother.

Instead, he left the room, shutting the door firmly behind him when Darin picked up his phone.

"Hi, Mister, whatcha doin'?"

Grant looked up from the narrow trench where he'd been busy burying an electrical line and was greeted by a pudgy little face topped by reddish-brown curls. Kara's big blue eyes glinted with curiosity.

"Putting lights in your yard so you can see out here, even at night."

In jeans, a T-shirt and tennis shoes, Kara was obviously dressed for her flight later that morning.

"Mama said you was stalling. She said I bettaw not get in the way."

"It would seem that you don't listen all that well, young lady." The soft feminine voice, accompanied by a chuckle, came from behind Grant. "And I said he was *in*stalling the lights." Running her fingers through the little girl's curls, Lynn met his gaze. "Darin said to tell you that he finished putting the bulbs in all the lights."

It was the first time she'd looked him in the eye all morning. They'd hadn't shared more than a brief hello since he and Darin had arrived almost two hours before.

After having Darin help him by holding chalk lines and tape measures, he'd left his brother out front where there was a stoop for him to sit on as he worked at putting the plastic pieces of the light fixtures together.

Darin was about to drive him crazy that morning with talk about his date. In his excitement he'd reverted to repeating himself over and over again, and then laughing when he realized what he was doing.

"I gave him some lemonade and came out to ask if you wanted some."

She licked her lips and he swore she was doing it on purpose to drive him crazy.

Her eyes didn't mention lemonade at all.

And he started to get hard.

In jeans and a white blouse she looked young

and fresh…and he could see through her blouse. Her bra had lace on it.

He was going out with that bra, or one like it, in just a matter of hours.

"I'm going to Daddy's house," Kara said. Lynn's smile faded. And Grant saw a flash of some deep emotion in her gaze before she looked away, saying, "That's him now, sweetie. Why don't you run and tell Daddy hello?"

Grant wasn't going to look across the grassy expanse to the sidewalk leading back to Lynn's bungalow. He wasn't going to intrude on this morning's private goings-on.

With one last glance at Grant, Lynn turned and followed her daughter. He watched her go in spite of himself.

When Kara and Lynn reached Lynn's ex-husband they were too far away for him to hear what was said but he didn't miss the way Kara threw herself at the man. And the way he picked up his daughter, giving her a hug and a kiss, and then leaned forward to give her mother a kiss, too.

The bastard was wearing golf shorts, a polo shirt and deck shoes. His hair was stylishly short and he had a gold watch on his wrist.

He was smiling like a man who loved his family.

The family he'd walked out on.

Resentment flared within him. He'd never have that chance. Never know what it was like to greet his wife and child. To have the right to touch and kiss a woman any time of the day or night. He'd never wanted it before, either.

CHAPTER NINETEEN

THEY WERE HALFWAY through dinner at a little Italian place she'd never been to before when Lynn realized she hadn't thought of Kara and Brandon and Douglas once in the past hour. She probably wouldn't have thought of them at all if Maddie hadn't suddenly blurted out her daughter's name.

"Oh, it's eight o'clock, Lynn. Kara has to be in bed right now and she didn't call to say good-night."

Darin frowned, looking at Lynn. "She's right. Maybe you should call to make sure she's all right."

"I'm sure she's fine," Grant said. "She's probably just staying up a little later tonight."

Maddie was shaking her head before he finished. "Kara's bedtime is eight o' clock every night. Huh, Lynn?" The pretty blonde had worn a bright colored maxi dress with sandals and looked very cute. Some of the girls at The Lemonade Stand had done her makeup for her.

"That's right, Maddie, it is," Lynn said, disconcerted and concerned, too. Surely Brandon hadn't forgotten that he'd said he'd call to have Kara say good-night.

But she'd forgotten the time.

Pulling out her phone, she checked to see if she'd missed a call.

"Call him." Grant, dressed in black casual pants and an off-white oxford shirt, put his arm along the back of her chair as he spoke.

Lynn had already speed-dialed Brandon and was listening for the ring.

It wasn't wrong for her to have lost track of time. Kara was Brandon's responsibility that night, and he was as capable as Lynn of caring for their daughter.

But her lack of awareness still made her uncomfortable.

"Hi, Lynnie—sorry!" Brandon sounded out of breath as he picked up on the fourth ring.

"Bran? Is everything okay?" Darin and Maddie, sitting across from her at the linen-covered table, had stopped eating and were watching her, as if they could hear what Brandon was saying.

Grant took a sip of wine. It was white and dry—a perfect complement to their pasta. He'd ordered a bottle.

"Everything's fine," Brandon said. "I got her in the bath by 7:45, just like your chart said, but it's a double-wide tub and she was laughing and swimming so I let her stay in an extra ten minutes. She's in her jammies now and we were getting ready to call you but I left my phone out in the family room and had to run to get it."

Bless him for being so sweet. He was trying so hard to please her. And she was too unbending.

Aware of the eyes trained on her, she said, "Can I talk to her?" After she'd heard all about the bumpy plane ride and Daddy's bathtub and Douglas's cast, she told her precious little girl that she loved her and to sleep well. As she hung up the phone, she felt like crying.

"Is she okay, Lynn?" Maddie asked.

"Why were they late?" Darin wanted to know.

She put the phone back in her purse and felt Grant's fingers lightly brush her shoulder. She sat there, frozen for a second. It was the barest of touches, but it was enough to bring song back into her night.

He brought his hand down from her chair, and she was disappointed. Until she felt it brush her thigh through the ankle-length black-and-white cotton skirt she was wearing

The cotton was plentiful, pulled together at the elastic waist to give the skirt fullness. But the fabric was light. And she could feel the warmth of his hand through it.

She looked over at him and he returned her gaze.

"Why are you two staring at each other like that?" Maddie asked.

"I think they like each other," Darin replied.

Lynn coughed. Took a sip of wine. And relayed Kara's phone conversation word for word.

She didn't mention Brandon at all.

He wasn't her family anymore.

THE FLOWING SKIRT might have, technically, hidden her body from his view, but it only served to ignite his imagination, to tease him, to draw his mind to what lay beneath. Her tight white T-shirt, on the contrary, showed him smooth, luscious, feminine curves that brought his eyes back to them again and again. Made him want to skim his hands over them. And more.

But with Darin and Maddie within sight of them, Grant had to settle for strolling barefoot beside Lynn, hands in his pockets. Every now and then the water would touch their toes, as the waves ebbed and flowed.

It wasn't all that warm out, maybe sixty, on that first Saturday night in March, but he was hotter than summer.

Lynn and Maddie had brought zip-up hoodies and were both wearing them now—the jackets, not the hoods. Definitely not the hoods. Lynn had left her hair down, and it curled softly around her shoulders to the middle of her back.

He ached to run his fingers through it.

She'd left the jacket unzipped, too.

The shore was mostly beach, with a cliffside or two thrown in, and they lost sight of Darin and

Maddie for a second as the front two went around a jutting cliff's edge.

He considered pulling Lynn into the alcove the cliff provided, to see if she was as eager to get naked with him as he was to get naked with her.

But he hadn't even held her hand yet.

"You and your ex seem to be good friends," he said, raising his voice to be heard over the roar of the surf.

If anything would cool his ardor it would be thoughts of that kiss he'd seen the other man give Lynn earlier that day.

"We are," Lynn said, her hand brushing close to his.

She might be Brandon Duncan's ex-wife, but she was *his* date. "Brandon has been my best friend since junior high," she continued, her voice softening in a way he hadn't heard before.

"You dated in high school, then?"

"I never dated anyone but him," she admitted. "Not until after the divorce. I went on a couple of dates that first year. Dinner or a movie—never both, though, because I didn't want to be away from Kara that long."

"What about when Brandon had her? You said he's never missed a visit."

"That first year I used pretty much all of that free time to study. And after that, we were living at the

Stand and, as you've seen, there's never a lack of something that needs doing there."

He took away one thing from what she'd said. He was her first real date since her divorce.

Not that they were really on a date. They were chaperones.

With privileges?

He'd told her this was going to be a real date. And had lain awake in bed the night before wondering what she'd thought he'd meant by that.

Wondering how far he was going to get.

And knowing that he couldn't go very far at all. Lynn was definitely not the type of woman who would be good with a little mutual fun on the side. She'd want commitment along with the sex.

"I take it that means Brandon is the only man you've ever slept with?"

"Yes."

Wow. He wasn't sure he'd ever been with a woman who'd only had one lover. "I could overhear some of what he said on the phone tonight." He hadn't meant to say anything. But the night, the moon over the water, the waves, his handicapped brother up ahead holding the hand of the pretty blonde walking beside him—they were all conspiring against him. "He called you Lynnie."

"That's his name for me."

"But he still uses it." And the fact rankled. Which made no sense.

"He's my friend."

"He told you he loved you before he hung up."

"He always does."

"You said, 'You, too.'" And he'd wondered, if she hadn't been sitting at the table with the three of them, if she'd have said, "'*Love* you, too.'"

"Yeah." Lynn stepped ahead of him to get around another jutting cliff. And then an expanse of deserted white beach stretched out before them again. Santa Raquel wasn't a huge town and most of the beaches were private. During the summer there might be a few people out and about at night, but for the most part, the coastline was deserted after dark.

"You still love him."

"Of course."

Grant's skin cooled measurably.

"You don't love someone for more than half your life and then just stop." She sounded resigned. Not all that happy about the fact.

Grant was confused. He shoved his hands deeper into his pockets and took small steps beside her, inhaling the fishy sea smells, tasting the salt on his lips. "And he still loves you."

"Yeah."

Was he the only one missing something here? "So, if you don't mind me asking, why did the two of you divorce?"

Her gaze was focused ahead of them on Maddie

and Darin. The other two were standing at the shore, kicking sand into the ocean with their toes and laughing.

"He… When I was pregnant with Kara, he met someone. And the week that I had her, he…was… unfaithful…to me."

Life was messed up. How could anyone…the very week his wife was giving birth…and to *Lynn?* The woman was the perfect combination of sexy and wholesome. Perfect wife material. Why in hell would a man ever have a need to stray from that?

Darin and Maddie, still holding hands, moved on.

Grant took Lynn's hand. She didn't immediately grasp hold of his, but she didn't pull away, either.

He knew now that her hesitance wasn't due to having been abused. He knew, too, that she wanted him. Her signs were too obvious.

A guy knew when a woman was sending vibes in his direction.

But what this guy did not do was take what belonged to another man. In any fashion.

"So you divorced him," he guessed, needing to know quite clearly where she stood with her ex. If they were entertaining a time-out, with a caveat that they might get back together, he needed to know.

He'd still be willing to have sex with her—if she wanted to have sex with him—but he'd need that right out on the table.

"No." Lynn shook her head. "He filed for divorce. I'd have stayed with him."

She didn't sound any happier about that than the rest of it.

"We had a life together, a lifetime planned. We'd been working toward it since we were in high school...."

He couldn't even imagine that one. In high school he'd had a lot of things on his mind, but not one of them included any kind of life plan. Or family plan, either, for that matter.

It was what he'd ended up with, though. Not that he was unhappy about that. He loved his brother. They had a good life together.

Darin and Maddie stopped again and bent down to look at something. Maddie shrieked and jumped back, fell on her butt in the wet sand. Laughing uproariously, Darin reached down to help her up. When she was standing again, he kept an arm around Maddie's waist.

And they moved on. Off in their own world.

Neither of them had glanced back toward Grant and Lynn.

"I don't get it," Grant said, moving a little closer to Lynn, threading his fingers more snugly with hers. "Is he a philanderer? He loves you but doesn't want to be married to you because he wants to have flings on the side?"

"I don't... It's hard to explain...."

What was hard was understanding why a woman like Lynn—smart, successful, gorgeous as hell—would allow a man to treat her that way. Let him divorce her but still do everything she could to keep their "family" intact.

Including allow Kara to fly to San Francisco with the man when she didn't have to let the little girl leave the city.

"Try me," he said. The waves rushed to the shore. And he couldn't let this go. He was on a date.

And wanted, at the very least, a kiss good-night.

He had to know what her situation was.

At least, that was what he told himself. And since much of what was going on with him where she was concerned didn't make a hell of a lot of sense, he just went with what he told himself.

"Brandon doesn't have flings. He's only ever had one lover, other than me."

"How do you know? A bachelor, living alone…"

She stubbed her toe in the sand, lurched and tightened her grip on his hand as she righted herself. "He doesn't live alone."

That was too much. The man lived with his mistress, but still kept Lynn on the hook? Then something else hit him….

"Kara's with her father's lover this weekend?"

Lynn's chin dropped. And he regretted his outburst. He'd been living alone with Darin too long. Lost his ability to have some tact.

"I'm sorry. That was completely insensitive."

She licked her lips. Sucked them in. The moonlight glistened on her face, and he caught shadows of emotions he couldn't read.

His hand holding hers was the only right thing at the moment. Darin and Maddie had made some time on them. They were visible in the distance, but he could no longer hear them at all.

Maybe they should think about turning back.

He had miles to go before he'd be ready.

"I'm sorry," Lynn finally said. Her voice sounded normal. Pretty much. But it wasn't open. Not the same as it had been when she'd talked about her and Brandon being best friends in high school.

"Yes, Kara is with her father and his spouse. But it's not quite what you think. Douglas respects me and my place in Brandon's life. It's a bit unusual, but…it works for us. Mostly."

Darin and Maddie had stopped walking. They were sitting in the sand by the water, but not close enough to get drenched, pulling handfuls of wet sand between them. Grant watched for a second. Remembering.

Darin was the most incredible builder of sand castles. As a little kid he'd begged Darin to take him to the beach and build castles. More times than not, his big brother had done so. Together they'd add wings and build moats and then Grant would start to look for branches that would be trees. He'd use pieces of colored candy wrappers he scavenged on the beach with tiny pieces of drift bark stuck into them to resemble flowers. He'd build shell fountains....

If Darin was going to build a castle for Maddie they'd be a while.

He pulled Lynn behind the jagged side of a cliff that jutted out onto the beach.

He tilted her head up. Looked her straight in the eye. And had to swallow. There was so much there for him to read.

He wasn't sure he could take it all in.

The hurt. The doubt. And the desire to be wanted.

The third part he could handle. But it wouldn't be right if he didn't deal with the other two first.

"Your ex-husband is gay."

"Yes." Her chin started to lower, and with one finger, Grant held her face up to the moonlight.

"Did you know when you married him?" They'd been best friends since high school. They'd made a plan.

Because Brandon had needed help to overcome a lifestyle he didn't want? Because he wanted a traditional family and Lynn was willing to give it to him?

"No!" At least his question had brought some fire back to her eyes. "I had no idea! Brandon and I... We... Our sex life was quite healthy."

"Before you were married?"

"Yes. We were the stereotypical prom-night-things-got-out-of-control couple. Except that…it was…nice. And we knew we were going to be getting married as soon as we were out of college and so…it wasn't a onetime thing. By any means."

It was "nice"? If he'd had a woman say that about him afterward…

Lynn deserved to know what lovemaking was meant to be. With a man who could give her more than *nice*.

Whoa, Bucko.

"So you found out after Kara was born?"

The sand formed a hard mound under the arches of his feet. Tugging gently on Lynn's hand, he sat down, pulling her with him. Her skirt flowed out around her, over his shin. With very little effort he could slide his hand up underneath it.

"She was five weeks old," Lynn was saying. "I knew there was something different about him. I thought he was jealous of Kara. Of how she was completely monopolizing my time and attention. I was breast-feeding and only had eight weeks at home with her before I was going to have to go back to work and…as much as I knew medically about taking care of children, I had a ton to learn about being a mother."

"I'd think it would be unusual if a woman wasn't completely taken up by a new baby's arrival. Especially a first baby."

"Brandon was caught up with her, too," Lynn said. "Which was probably why I let her take over so much. I thought we were doing it together. You know, she was another adventure on our path of life. The most incredible, most important adventure."

One he was never going to have. With her. Or anyone.

"And then he told you he was gay."

"Yeah. He'd never been particularly close with any of the guys in school—he always hung out with me and my friends, but that just seemed natural to us. I asked him once when he'd first had the idea he might be, and he said that he'd wondered a time or two, but put the thoughts down to having settled into a monogamous marriage that meant having sex with only one person for the rest of his life. He didn't think it meant anything.

"Until he found out I was pregnant with Kara. Somehow having a daughter, a family, made him look at life entirely differently. He wasn't as happy as I was—as he'd expected to be. He said he'd expected to feel like his life was perfect when we finally got pregnant, and he didn't.

"Until he met Douglas. And everything fell horrifyingly into place."

"He said that? 'Horrifyingly'?"

"Yeah. If you knew Brandon you'd understand. He really does love me. And he knew what the truth was going to do to me. But he couldn't lie about who he was. Not to me."

"That's when you went back to college, got your masters degree and nurse midwife certification and started a new life."

"Brandon supported me so I could go back to school full-time and also be at home with Kara for most of the first year. I took what courses I could online. He knew being with Kara and getting my CNM certification were my life's dreams."

"Apart from you and him growing old together."

"Right."

"So he gave you what he could." He'd rather have hated the guy.

"Yep. And he still does. He tries so hard to anticipate my needs and be there to fulfill them whenever he can."

Just not her sexual needs.

Which could be where he came in.

And in a strange sort of way, he guessed, it worked.

CHAPTER TWENTY

"WE SHOULD GET back to Maddie and Darin." Lynn jumped up and walked over to peer around the cliff.

"They're sitting right where we left them, right?"

"Yeah. Wow, you should see this castle they're building."

"I've seen more of them than I can count," Grant told her, leaning back on his hands in the sand, his long legs out in front of him.

Drawing her attention to his fly.

She'd just talked about sex with a man who wasn't Brandon. In her capacity as a nurse, she had no problem discussing any and all bodily functions. But she didn't talk about hers, not with anyone. She had a handle on her emotions and on her physical feelings. And that was how she wanted it.

Until she looked at Grant and wanted *him*.

He was watching her. Checking out her breasts. Her skirt. She was wearing a pair of lace panties beneath the thin cotton. The air crept up her skirt, caressing her bare skin.

She grew moist.

"Come here."

Grant had hunger written all over him, along with the confidence of a man whose hungers had been assuaged many times in many ways.

She sat back down next to him.

"I told you this was a real date," he said, staring at her lips.

"I know."

Did he think sex was the norm for a first date? Did he think she'd agreed to a roll in the sand with him?

The thought made her nipples harden. But that was only for her to know. For her to deal with.

Sliding his hand beneath her hair to cup her neck, Grant held her still with no force at all as he leaned toward her.

His eyes were open, watching her, pulling her toward him. Holding her gaze focused on him. He opened his mouth, but didn't say anything. She stared at those lips. Wanting to know how they felt.

And she was going to know.

His face was an inch from hers. She could have pulled away but she waited. Frustrated that he was taking so long.

And then he kissed her.

His lips touched hers. Held hers. Moved on hers. They opened and hers did, too, moving with his, staying with his, as their bodies came closer. His tongue touched her lower lip. A swift stroke. And then again. One more time.

He slid inside her mouth. Gently. Exploring more than conquering. As though he was interested in every single little thing there was to know about her.

And that was when she knew that every little thing about him mattered to her.

Lynn pulled back.

He couldn't matter. Not that much.

She wasn't going to have her happiness, her future, any part of her life, intertwined so intimately with another person's again. She wasn't going risk someone else having a change of feeling, or a latent self-discovery, that stripped her life away from her.

"That was…way better than nice." His voice was gravelly in a bedroom sort of way. Being on the receiving end of it was almost more than she could bear.

It took her a moment to realize he'd used the word she used to describe sex with Brandon.

And realized he was completely, absolutely right. With one kiss he'd completely shattered her idea of what sex should be like.

Her hands were shaking. He took hold of one, turned it over and, with his other hand, he caressed her palm.

"I have a proposition for you, nurse." His voice. The way he said her title. The look in his eye. The scent of him. He was flooding her with sensation. Overriding everything she knew to be true.

"What's that?"

He was going to ask her to let him under her skirt. And, God help her, she almost pulled it up and spread her legs for him right then and there.

Darin and Maddie were going to be working on their castle for a long time. Kara was so far away she couldn't get to her if she wanted to.

And she had needs. Heaven help her, she had needs....

"A partnership, of sorts."

Her heart started to beat faster, if it were possible for it to beat any faster than it already was, and she waited for him to continue.

"I have no room and no time in my life for a committed relationship," he said. He had her attention.

"Running my own business is a huge responsibility," he was saying, as though completely undisturbed by their kiss. But she knew what the bulge underneath his fly meant.

It meant she could be patient and listen to him.

"But a lot of people own businesses," he continued. "However, you add Darin into the mix, and some days it's damn near impossible for me to keep track of everything I've got to do, let alone get it all done."

"I understand." Didn't he get that she was glad he wasn't promising her the sun and the moon?

"And from what I've seen and understood of your life, your needs are pretty much all covered. You've got your ex, who is your best friend. You've got all the companionship you could possibly have time for with all the women at the Stand. You've got your daughter, and a secure family unit…."

He made it sound as if her life was perfect.

"As far as I can see, the only critical thing missing for either one of us is sex."

She coughed. It was one thing to think it. And another thing to say it out loud. In the dark. On the beach. With the moon above and the ocean lapping just a few yards away, the waves reaching toward them with a force that was larger than life.

"Do you disagree?" His fingers had slowed on her hand and his head was turned toward her. Their knees were touching, only the thin fabric of her skirt and the heavier cotton of his pants separating their naked skin.

"No." She couldn't lie about it.

"Then my proposal is that we remain as friends, but with benefits. When time and occasion permits, we have sex."

Was the time and occasion right then?

"I… It's…unusual." But it resonated with her. Her life was unusual. And he was offering her everything she needed without asking for anything more.

"Agreed."

"Okay."

"Okay?" His hand dropped, and hers landed… on the bulge in his pants.

The move wasn't deliberate. On her part or his.

She knew it, and her belief was confirmed by his sharp intake of breath.

The bulge beneath her hand moved. Grew. She didn't squeeze, exactly, but she explored a bit with her fingers while her palm lay still on top of him.

"I expected to have to work harder to convince you," he said, his words sounding slightly choked.

"You knew I'd agree."

"I'd hoped you would. And was prepared to resort to begging."

He wanted her that much?

The proof was beneath her hand.

"I have one condition," she said. "And it's non-negotiable." No matter how badly her body needed his to end this insane climb toward ecstasy, she would walk away with her legs firmly together if he couldn't comply.

He wasn't just hard, he was rock solid. She moved her hand a bit, needing to feel more of him.

"What's your condition?"

If she didn't know better, she'd think he was strangling.

The smile that had been lingering on the corners of her lips faded away completely. He had to know she wasn't kidding.

"As long as we have this…partnership—which is defined as being in place until one or the other of us communicates an end to the other—we are sexually exclusive."

"Monogamous," he said, his lower lip jutting out as he nodded.

"You agree?"

"I took it for granted," he said. "You've only had one lover, Lynn. I know that what I'm asking, what we're doing here, is serious."

"But not for life. It's only serious for the sex."

"Agreed."

She squeezed. Hard enough to make his hips rise up off the ground. "Then I'd say you have a deal."

"The best deal I've ever made," he said, his voice lowering as he leaned in to kiss her again.

His lips touched hers. And his hand slid under her skirt to her knee.

"Lynn? Lynn? Lyyynnnn!" Maddie's voice rent the air. First with excitement, and then with very quickly escalating panic.

"Maddie?" She jumped up, calling out. "Maddie? We're right here!"

Thank God she was still fully dressed. She rushed around the corner, afraid of finding Darin prone on the ground.

Or gone.

Instead, she found the two of them racing around the beach, looking frantically in every direction.

"Hey!" Grant's voice boomed. "Over here, bro!"

Darin's head shot up and, grabbing Maddie's hand, he hurried her over toward Lynn and Grant, who were running in their direction.

"Where were you?" Darin asked as Maddie, still clinging to one of Darin's hands, threw her other arm around Lynn and started to cry.

"I thought we were lost," Maddie said. "I thought we were building our castle and forgot about you and got lost."

She thought she'd been left.

"Hey," Lynn said, both hands on Maddie's shoulders as she faced the other woman. "We aren't ever going to leave you, not anywhere, you got that?"

Maddie nodded.

Lynn persisted. "You know that, right? Alan was very, very bad to take you out to that cabin and leave you there, Maddie. Good people would never do that to you. Remember?"

Maddie nodded again. "I remember," she said, sounding as if she had more marbles in her mouth than usual. Then she grinned. "I was just being a dope, wasn't I?"

She looked back at Darin.

"No, you weren't," Darin said. "It was dark and we couldn't see them and neither of us can drive." He turned to Grant. "I asked you to let me talk to Maddie alone because it was a date and you did and I'm glad," he said. "Thank you. Now do you want to see our castle?"

"Of course," Grant said. He was a step back from the three of them.

"Yeah, we came to find you so we could show you our castle." Maddie grinned up at Lynn.

Knowing that this was what real life was all about, Lynn took Grant's hand and went to marvel at a castle in the sand.

CHAPTER TWENTY-ONE

HE DIDN'T HAVE sex. But he was going to.

As soon as Darin had retired to his room on Saturday night, Grant picked up the phone.

"I was wondering if you'd call." Lynn's sexy drawl greeted him after one ring.

"It's such a waste." With his phone to his ear he walked through his room into the adjoining bathroom.

"What is?"

Shrugging out of his shirt, he tossed it into the clothes hamper. Which was overflowing.

"You there, without Kara for the night, and me here."

"Maddie stayed here tonight. By the time we got back, all the lights were out in the girls' bungalow where she has weekend sleepovers. Remember I told you that Gwen has Friday and Saturday nights off and Maddie either stays here or with a group of young girls who like to do makeup?"

"Right. I forgot." He lobbed his pants over to cover his shirt. "Is she sitting right there?"

"No. She's in her room."

Stepping out of his underwear, Grant tossed them, too, turned off the light and, penis hard and heavy, walked back to the bedroom, pulled back his covers and lay on top of the sheet in the dark.

"We need to figure out when we're going to finish what we started."

There was a long pause. "Where are you?"

"Home."

The moon cast shadows on his ceiling, creating shapes. One looked like the silhouette of a woman's breast. And that one…a thigh. Or maybe a butt… "I figured you were home. I heard Maddie talking and suspected she was on the phone with Darin. Are you in bed?"

"Yes. Are you?"

"Yes." Her tone dropped.

"What do you wear to bed?"

"A nightgown."

"With panties underneath?"

"No."

His penis was ready to explode.

"What are you doing tomorrow?"

"Kara's due back by noon. And Sundays are grocery, laundry and cleaning days."

"Darin and I do laundry on Sundays, too."

"He can do laundry, then?"

"He can't sort the clothes but he's obsessive about listening for the dryer to stop and changing loads—I put a chart on the washer that tells him what temperature to set for what color. And the soap dispenser is marked for how much soap to put in. I just always make sure I sort the loads first. And I made some wooden signs that I put on the loads after I sort them that tell him the color."

"Is he color blind?"

"No, but if something's plaid, or striped, and has white and blue, for instance, he freaks out over which color to call the load."

He wasn't going to have sex tonight. And talking was better than lying in the dark with nothing to distract him from his hard-on.

"He's also a whiz at folding and hanging. He's good at pretty much anything that's done the same way every time. Which is fine because I like a neat closet."

"I hang my clothes all facing the same way."

"Short sleeve with short sleeve?"

"Yes."

"I hang my T-shirts."

Her chuckle set his groin in motion again.

"When are we going to get together?"

"I'm not sure. It'll have to be a time when you don't have Darin and I don't have Kara."

"Or when Kara's asleep. People who have kids still have sex."

"Right."

Was she having second thoughts? He almost asked but didn't want to chance the answer.

Running his hand through his hair, he wondered if that was a coffin he saw up there on the ceiling. Were the shadows changing? He couldn't find the breast.

"So when does that leave us?"

And wasn't this precisely why he wasn't in a relationship? There simply was no time or occasion with the obligations he had.

"I was thinking…maybe…depending on your schedule…a week from Wednesday? I checked my book and, unless I get an emergency, I don't have an appointment between three and four, which is when Kara has predance class at day care and Darin's in therapy. I can block out the time now so that nothing gets scheduled."

She'd already checked her book. Didn't sound like second thoughts to him.

"At your place?"

There was the breast again. How could he have missed it up there?

"Yeah. We can say you were working on my landscape lighting."

It was already installed.

"In your bedroom?"

"No one is going to know you were in my bedroom."

Good. They were on the same page. "So we're agreed that no one will know about the change in our…situation."

He had to be discreet. For Darin's sake. His brother didn't deal well with change.

"Of course."

He was making an appointment to have sex.

Feeling tired all of a sudden, Grant pulled the covers up over his waist. His life wasn't typical, wasn't for everyone, but it was his.

And he had it under control.

LYNN WAS HOME with Kara Sunday evening, enjoying some rare alone time with the precocious three-year-old, when her phone rang.

Lila was with a woman at the clinic. A new arrival with obvious injuries. She had no idea how serious they were and the woman refused to let her call an ambulance, certain that her husband would get to the hospital and finish off what he'd started.

Lynn would have liked to think the woman's fears were grounded in drama and overreaction, but she knew better. According to Bureau of Justice statistics, a woman died of spousal abuse in the United States every six hours.

Maria Cleveland was not going to be one of them. While her injuries had been serious enough to require a trip to the emergency room, Lynn had accompanied her and stayed with her. And she and Maria had signed paperwork to allow Maria to be released into her private care.

It was almost two in the morning by the time

Maria was settled in a bed in the bungalow closest to Lynn's, with one of the residents sitting up with her, waking her every hour, so Lynn could head back home.

A light was on next to the sofa, and she could hear the television.

"Hi, everything okay?" Amy, a sixty-year-old grandmother who had been at the Stand for a little over two months, greeted her. The worried frown on her face had been perpetually there when she'd first come to them. But it didn't show itself as often these days.

"She's going to be fine," Lynn gave the rote answer. The only one she *could* give until Maria signed occupancy papers that would allow those within the walls of the shelter to share in her care. She might or might not opt to share her personal story with other residents. That was one of the choices she'd be making when she was able to make decisions about her immediate future. Right now, she just needed to rest and allow her body to heal.

Amy nodded, shoving some yarn and needles into a big cloth bag. "I'll be getting on home, then," she said. "Kara had the apples you had assigned for her snack at seven-thirty, her bath at 7:45, went down at eight, fell asleep during the first story and hasn't made a peep since then. I've checked on her every half hour."

Other than the half hour checks that weren't necessary because there was a monitor in Kara's room with receivers in the family room and both of the other bedrooms, Amy's recounting of events was exactly as had been designated by the schedule on the refrigerator.

"Thanks, Amy," she said. "I've already alerted security that you need a ride back to your bungalow. Tammy's waiting outside for you."

Tammy Swenson was one of the Stand's full-time, police-trained security personnel. There were four full-time officers on staff and another three, two of whom were male, worked part-time to relieve them. They mostly watched over the main house and the public buildings outside the locked campus, but at night, there was always one patrolling the private grounds.

She slid a twenty down into Amy's knitting bag. Amy had been a housewife her entire life. One who'd been beaten, on and off, for forty years because she'd had no means to leave the man who claimed to love her but forgot about those feelings any time he drank.

At sixty, with all of her kids out on their own, she couldn't take it anymore. But so far, the bastard had managed to tie up all their assets in court. And since Amy had no training, and was near retirement age, she wasn't having a lot of luck finding any kind of work to tide her over.

And residents who did volunteer work were

not allowed to get paid. Which meant that Lynn couldn't pay her for watching Kara.

"You already paid me for the dress I knitted your little one," Amy said.

"No, your work was exquisite and worth far more than you charged me."

Amy shook her head.

"Tammy's waiting," Lynn reminded the older woman, and saw her out the door.

She pulled her cell phone from the pocket of her scrubs, peeked in on Kara and headed to the bathroom to take a shower.

Grant had called. She'd had her phone on vibrate all evening, but she always checked her calls in case there was an emergency with Kara. He'd left a voice mail.

She listened to it as she undressed.

He'd asked her to call. No matter how late she got in.

His voice didn't have that sexy undertone she'd grown to crave. But if it had been an emergency surely he'd have said so.

Pulling on her robe, she texted him first. And wasn't even in the shower yet when her phone signaled a return text. Followed by a second vibration indicating his incoming call.

"You're up late," she said, picking up the call.

"I've been asleep for three hours. I just heard your text." His voice sounded groggy. And…the sexy tone was back. She heard it all the way to her toes.

"You said to call no matter how late."

"I wanted to speak with you before tomorrow." He sounded sleepy, but not the least bit put out to be talking on the phone in the middle of the night.

"It's already tomorrow."

"Are you just getting in?"

"Yeah. We had an emergency tonight."

Seeing herself in the mirror—the tired eyes, no makeup, hair pulled back—she turned away from it.

"I called you just after Kara's bedtime."

"I left here at six-thirty."

"Wow."

"Yeah." She kept her voice low, just in case, although Kara slept through almost everything, and slid down to the floor, her back to the wall.

"Is everything okay?"

"I think it will be, physically, at least. In the meantime, I have a patient in the bungalow next door."

"How old is she?"

"Thirty-four."

"Was it her husband?"

"Yeah."

"How long were they married?"

"A couple of years."

"She got out early."

"Yeah, but it was still almost too late." Some abusers were stronger than others.

"Were there any kids?"

"Two from a previous marriage. She was widowed. The kids are with their paternal grandparents until tomorrow after school."

"Will they stay there, then?"

"Possibly. So they can remain in school. Or they could come here if she decides to leave her husband and become a resident. It will be partially up to the woman. She wasn't in any state tonight to make those kinds of decisions."

"I took it for granted she'd already decided to leave him."

Lynn knew she had to get to bed, get in a few hours of sleep before she had to be back to check on Maria and continue with her day. But talking to Grant right then, rather than lying in the dark alone, seemed more peaceful than sleep.

"She ran away from him out of fear. That's an in-the-moment thing. It might last, it might not."

"Can't the police step in?"

"Only if she decides to press charges."

"They can prosecute if they have enough evidence, right? With or without her? You said you took her to the hospital. Aren't they under an obligation to report the abuse?"

She could hear the frustration in his voice. And wondered when she'd begun to accept the facts of domestic violence rather than being shocked by them.

"The police were called tonight. But unless Maria is willing to go to court and testify, they won't have a case against the guy so probably won't waste the money to file charges on a case they can't win. You'd be surprised how many women change their stories, say they were just upset or mad or jealous and lied about how they got hurt."

"They actually return to their abusers."

She thought everyone had known that. "Yes."

"And you think tonight's woman might be one of them?"

"I hope not." She couldn't let it get to her one way or the other. If she didn't keep professional boundaries she wouldn't be good for anyone.

"I called to ask a favor," he said now, "but after the night you've had I don't think—"

"It's fine, Grant. Tonight wasn't all that unusual, I'm sorry to say. I'll grab some extra sleep tomorrow, rearrange some well checks if I have to. And there's always someone to keep an eye on Kara. What do you need?"

"I was hoping Darin and I could have dinner at your place tomorrow night."

They were both approved to eat at the cafeteria. As paying guests, of course, just like any other staff member or visitor.

"Here at my house?"

"I know, I shouldn't have asked...."

"No! It's fine." Grant wanted to sit at her table and have dinner with her. Like a family...

She shook her head, rubbing her neck. She was tired. What sounded good tonight couldn't be relied on in the cold light of day.

"Darin has talked about Maddie all day—specifically about when he could have his next date."

"I had a feeling one wasn't going to be enough."

"I think now, more than ever, it's not a good idea to leave them alone together. They might have the minds of kids, but they've got the bodies of adults. And while, ordinarily, with Darin, I wouldn't give it a second thought, he's really taken with Maddie."

"This is the first time it's ever happened?"

"Hell, yes, it's the first time! I'm in deep water here."

He obviously didn't like the feeling any better than she did.

"So you want me to invite Maddie for dinner, too."

"I was under the assumption that she usually ate with you and Kara."

"She stays sometimes, depending on how late I am getting home. I always plan meals to include her just in case."

"We could go out again, but with Kara and our schedules, I just thought, since Darin and I are going to be there at dinnertime, anyway..."

"It's fine, Grant." She had hamburger in the freezer, could thaw that, and switch Wednesday's spaghetti for Monday's tuna casserole. And even if she didn't, she'd make do. The thought of seeing Grant again so soon was too tempting.

Only because she was so tired. And they hadn't actually had sex yet.

"Darin will be glad to hear that. He insisted that I take him to the store for everything he'll need to make lasagna. I told him Kara might not like it, so he picked up macaroni and cheese, too."

"Darin's making dinner?"

"You didn't think I was going to invite us over and expect you to cook, too, did you?"

"I wouldn't have minded," she told him. "I like to cook." She had loved making dinner for Brandon and sitting down with him after a long day to discuss everything that had happened since they'd last seen each other.

"So when you issue the invitation, you can cook," he said. As though already assuming there would be another time.

"You've got a deal."

"And maybe, if we're lucky, Kara can occupy Darin and Maddie long enough for me to at least get in a kiss or two…."

Her reaction to him was swift and immediate. Lynn crossed her legs.

"You make me feel a hell of a lot better-looking than the picture I see when I look in a mirror."

It was a two-in-the-morning thing to say.

"Then you need to figure out what's wrong with your mirror." His reply was quick and sure. "'Cause I gotta tell you, lady, there's nothing wrong with the way you look. Except maybe that you look too good to resist."

Her entire body suffused with pleasure—from the heart outward. Grant's voice was growing on her. His lack of subterfuge. His dedication to his brother, and the sensitive artistic nature that drove the creation of the Garden of Renewal.

Lynn rubbed her eyes and thought about the pillow awaiting her. After a quick shower.

She had responsibilities. A life that she loved. One she'd worked hard to achieve and had under complete control. That was her priority.

Any extracurricular pleasures, no matter how delicious, had to stay down on her list where they belonged.

CHAPTER TWENTY-TWO

Darin made his lasagna, which Kara loved, and he watched and cheered while Maddie and Kara played a video game afterward. Grant ended up on the opposite end of the table from Lynn—Maddie's doing; she'd set the table so that she was by Darin and next to Kara—and while it felt strange, it was also kind of nice looking up from his brother's pasta to see Lynn's face at the end of the table across from him. He had no idea how she felt about any of it. He'd tried to get Lynn into a corner in the laundry room, but each time he almost had her to himself, either Maddie or Kara would notice her missing.

It was clear to him, more than ever, that the lives of those two revolved around her. And hers around them, too. Just as his life revolved around Darin. Which was exactly as it should be.

Still, when he didn't get so much as a good-night kiss on Monday, he was more determined than ever to do so as soon as possible.

He looked for her on Tuesday afternoon when he got to the shelter after a full day of work on a new bid that Bishop Landscaping had just won—a brand-new upscale housing project that consisted of a total of fifteen yards and six acres of common area in a gated neighborhood.

After wasting as much time as he could possibly afford without seeing any sign of her, stopping short of dropping by her office or her home, he set to work pulling recalcitrant weeds from the planted flower beds in front of each of the bungalows on the property. He'd sprayed for weeds, but, as always, there were those hardy few that inevitably reared their ugly heads.

As he walked around the property, pulling the determined green pests, he entertained himself with thoughts of the following Wednesday, just eight days away, when he'd be spending his afternoon work hour getting a workout in Lynn's bed.

Several of the flower beds had no weeds at all. One had six. He bent over to yank them out.

And felt something touch his butt—and slide upward. "I hoped I'd see you out here."

Standing and turning so fast that dirt from the weeds in his hands bounced off the front of Lynn's scrub shirt, he said, "I looked all over for you."

She glanced at his fly. Then up to his lips—and, finally, his eyes. He was waiting when she arrived there. And didn't even try to hide the fire he was feeling.

"Was last night as excruciating for you as it was for me?" he asked softly.

They were out in public. And while the grounds at The Lemonade Stand were never crowded, there were always women out making their way to some-place.

"I thought dinner was kind of nice," she said, looking at his lips. She knew exactly what she was doing to him. He could see it in her eyes. Hear it in her voice. She couldn't have been more obvious if she'd crooked a finger at him.

"Dinner was nice," he told her. Two could play this game. "Every time I looked up there you were…at the other end of the table."

"We could do it again."

"Exactly what I was thinking. Only this time I want to sit next to you so I can put my hand in my lap under the table and have it end up in yours."

"How about tomorrow night? I know Maddie's already asked Darin to watch a movie." She named the romantic comedy that had bored him to tears the first time he'd seen it. "And if you want to fa-cilitate that, it would be best if they were together at my place instead of hers. I wouldn't want to put the responsibility for them on Gwen's shoulders."

"Tomorrow night is fine if you don't mind me bringing my laptop. I have work to do." And no pa-tience to sit and watch the romantic comedy she'd just named.

Now if he could be doing creative things to

Lynn's body while the movie played in the background, that would be a different story....

SOMEHOW, ON WEDNESDAY night after dinner and before starting the movie, Maddie and Darin roped Grant and Lynn into a repeat performance for Friday night. Gwen wasn't going to be there. And Maddie would be spending the night at Lynn's, anyway.

It seemed to make sense, until they put on the movie and Grant realized he was enjoying his work more than he had in years. For no reason other than the fact that he was able to see Lynn every time he looked up from the computer. Just knowing she was there was exciting—even with no sex involved.

Lynn Duncan was the first thing he thought of when he woke up in the morning these days. And he fell asleep with her image in his mind every night.

It was a no-win situation.

He was going to have to do something about it. Maddie and Darin couldn't continue on this way, either. It was unnatural, everyone convening at Lynn's house as though they all lived there.

He was going to have to find a way to deflect his brother's attention from his new girlfriend and on to something else.

Like diving.

Before he and Darin arrived at Lynn's for dinner Friday night, he made plans to take Darin down to the water on Saturday. It would be cold. But they both had wet suits leftover from earlier days.

He thought about telling Darin the news before dinner so his brother would have something besides his dinner companion to think about, but Maddie found him and Darin out on the property at quitting time to walk with them over to Lynn's.

She had Kara with her.

"Hi, Mister." The little girl put her hand into Grant's as they started to walk.

"Hi, Kara. How are you?" The tiny hand in his felt strange. So small…and yet seemingly monumental, too. Did her hand in his mean he was responsible for her well-being as long as she kept it there?

Like her father had been on Saturday when he'd walked away with Kara, her hand entwined in his, her little legs half jogging to keep up with him?

Brandon seemed like a great father. Maybe a perfect one.

And now that little hand was in his.

"I didn't dance today."

"Were you supposed to dance today?"

"No." She skipped along next to him.

He wondered if she could tell his hand was sweating. If she'd let him go with a squeal of "gwoss."

"What did you do today?"

He was failing a test. He was sure of it.

And he didn't want to care.

"Colored a picture for Mama," she said, sounding as happy as ever. She seemed to be waiting for a response from him. Didn't little kids jabber all the time? Nonstop?

"Where is it?" It seemed to be the next logical question.

She stopped, but still held his hand, so while Darin and Maddie went on ahead of them, Grant had to stop, too.

"Don't you know about pictures, Mister?" If she continued to look up at him like that with those little eyebrows drawn and the painfully serious look in her big blue eyes, he'd be wanting to change his name to "Mistah."

"I don't think so, Kara," he said, deeming that he ought to treat her question with equal solemnity. "Do you suppose you could help me learn about them?"

"Sure!" She started skipping again, swinging his hand in hers. "Come on," she said, pulling at him. "Dawin and Maddie are almost home."

And so he walked faster.

Still unsure what he had to learn about pictures.

But completely sure he'd never know what it felt like to be a dad.

LYNN DIDN'T MAKE it home for dinner. She was on her way there, determined to talk to Grant about her concerns regarding the false impression they were giving Maddie and Darin—the impression that Lynn and Grant would make it possible for them to continue spending so much time together.

Grant and Lynn had lives. She hadn't had time alone with her daughter in over a week.

Grant's business files and all of the supplies he needed to work efficiently were in his home office, not on her kitchen table or in his laptop case.

Darin liked sports.

Lynn didn't like the television on every evening.

Things were getting out of control.

Her phone rang when she was halfway across the yard to her house. Maria Cleveland, the thirty-four-year-old she'd accompanied to the emergency room Sunday night, had pulled some stitches and was bleeding profusely. She was at the clinic.

When Lynn had to call Grant, to let him know to start dinner without her, she felt utterly disappointed. She'd been looking forward to seeing him all day.

She had a whole list of things she wanted to talk to him about, in addition to discussing Maddie and Darin's relationship. Like the fact that the Stand's founder had paid the shelter a visit and told her that he'd won a medical grant to give her a raise. It wasn't a huge increase, but it would give her a little extra to put away for Kara's college fund.

And she had questions about his new project. Had he decided to put at least one fruit tree on every lot like he'd been thinking? And could she see the finished drawing of the water feature he'd been working on Wednesday night?

She needed to know if he still had that slumberous, hungry look in his eye when he saw her.

She'd needed to share the burden of worry that was growing steadily in her with regard to Maddie and Darin.

Where they were concerned, she didn't have any answers.

And she needed some.

"How's MARIA?" MADDIE asked when Lynn made it home shortly after ten that evening. Maddie met her at the door, holding it open while Lynn set her bag on the bench in the entryway and stepped out of her shoes.

"She's okay," Lynn said. Maria had signed papers earlier in the week, agreeing to share her life with the other residents at the Stand. Lynn couldn't disclose specific medical information because of HIPAA laws, but she could fill Maddie in on the most recent development. "Her husband called, telling her that if she didn't do what he wanted her children would pay. Maria left the Stand and was going to get her kids and pulled her stitches trying to hail a cab."

"She shouldn't have done that."

"You're right. She shouldn't have."

"She should have called Tammy and Lila," Maddie said, referring to the night-time security guard and the Stand's managing director.

"Yes, she should have. Because it's important to follow the rules," Lynn said, traipsing through to the kitchen in purple cotton scrubs and stocking feet.

"Sometimes it's hard to follow the rules." Maddie followed her, watching while Lynn looked in the refrigerator.

"Grant grilled the chicken and I made the salad, but Darin helped cut vegetables," Maddie said, sitting at the kitchen table. "There's some left in the container with the blue lid."

Lynn had already seen it. Grabbing the container, she snatched the ranch dressing and a fork and carried all of it to the table. Maddie pulled a napkin from the holder and put it in front of Lynn and then stood. "I'll get you a glass of tea while you go check on Kara."

Maddie knew what she drank. And that she wouldn't sit down to eat without first checking on her daughter. No matter how late it was or how hungry she was.

What she didn't know was that Lynn had almost forgotten. Because she'd been too busy feeling envious while she listened to Maddie talk about the dinner that she had missed.

"DID YOU KISS her good-night?" Maddie asked as Lynn returned to the table a few minutes later.

"I did."

"Good, because I promised her that you would and I don't lie."

"I know you don't, Maddie. You're the best and I don't know what I'd do without you."

Maddie was family. Closer to her than her own sister had ever been, though she loved Katie dearly.

"I love you, Lynn."

"I love you, too." She loved how Maddie just said whatever was on her mind or in her heart.

"And I love Kara, too—of course you know that…."

Looking up from her salad at the peculiar tone in the other woman's voice, Lynn caught Maddie biting her lower lip.

"Maddie?"

"Yeah?" The slender woman continued to chew her lip, and didn't meet her gaze.

"What's up?"

"I'm afraid you'll be mad at me, but I thought it was okay, but now I don't know if I think it's okay and I'm afraid you'll be mad at me."

"For what?"

Maddie chewed. And Lynn pushed the bowl of leftover salad away. Had Maddie done something they couldn't undo?

"Nothing happened to Kara, did it?" she asked.

She'd seen her daughter. Her color had been good and her room neat, with everything in place exactly as it should have been.

Her knees bouncing up and down, Maddie said, "No, nothing happened to Kara."

"Does this have to do with Darin?"

"No."

Lynn's tension eased as she studied her unhappy friend, whose chin had lowered to her chest.

As long as Maddie and Darin hadn't done anything crazy, like have sex, then she could patiently play twenty questions.

"What time did he leave?" If she could get a time stamp on the incident, it might help her to determine the magnitude of the catastrophe.

Maddie had been inconsolable, crying herself to sleep one night, after she'd broken one of Lynn's drinking glasses.

Because it matched a set and now there wasn't a full set.

The woman had only ever used the plastic glasses in the cupboard ever since.

"It was 8:18." Maddie's voice was barely audible.

Eight-eighteen. Precisely. Because Maddie was precise. All black and white and no shades of gray.

"So Kara got to bed late?" It didn't please her, but it wasn't the end of the world.

"No."

She was exhausted. And out of questions.

"Tell me, Maddie. You know how I get more upset when you won't talk to me than I do about whatever happened."

Maddie nodded.

And Lynn understood that whatever Maddie knew, her sense of self-preservation when it came to confessing her supposed mistakes was ingrained. It was a residual instinct due to all the punishment she'd taken over the years.

"I'll just sit here and wait," Lynn said. "Take your time."

The only way to undo the damage caused by Maddie's past was to replace the negative memory responses with positive ones.

"I let Grant read Kara her bedtime story!" Maddie blurted the words so loudly that if Kara hadn't been a heavy sleeper, she'd certainly have awakened.

Grant had been in Kara's room? And she wasn't there to share the moment?

Lynn couldn't breathe. She should've been there to be part of the experience. To see him tell her daughter good-night. He'd taken the time to read to Kara? A bedtime story?

It meant something.

Her stomach cramped, but her heart raced.

"Kara kept asking me all during her bath could Mister read her bedtime story, and he heard her and he said he would. When I said that only you or I read her bedtime stories unless Amy's here, he just told me you wouldn't mind."

"He's right, Maddie. I don't mind."

The other woman's chin came up. Frowning, she met Lynn's gaze. "But you said I always had to follow the list. Always. And that if anything happened and I couldn't follow the list I had to call right away. You or Tammy or Lila. And when I had my cell phone in my hand and I was calling you, Grant told me I didn't have to bother you at work because you were on an emergency, but I already knew that. Then Darin said I should do what Grant said, so I did." Chew. Chew. Chew.

Lynn reached out and took Maddie's hand. "Maddie, I do want you to follow the list. Always. That is the right thing to do." If they strayed from that, she couldn't let Maddie watch Kara anymore. Because Maddie would panic if she didn't have exact orders to follow.

"So I did the wrong thing." The hand beneath hers was trembling and Maddie's eyes filled with tears. "I'm sorry, Lynn. You won't want me to watch Kara anymore."

"You were in an unfamiliar situation, and you didn't know if you or Grant was in charge," Lynn said, knowing from Sara that it was more important that she help Maddie understand rather than merely comfort her.

"I'm sorry."

"I know. And your apology is accepted."

Maddie looked over at her. "You aren't mad at me?"

"Of course not. You should be mad at me for putting you in that situation," Lynn said.

It was the truth. Maddie relied on her. She'd agreed to watch over the other woman.

And by allowing Grant and Darin to come over for dinner even when she couldn't be there, she'd failed Maddie.

"I'm sorry, Maddie. I promise it won't happen again."

"I'm sad about this," Maddie said. "I'm sad that I can't be like you and decide what's best."

"You are you, Maddie, and just right as you are. We are all meant to be different," she reminded her friend. "Think how silly the world would be if we were all walking around exactly alike!"

Maddie nodded. Her chewing stopped.

"So, can we both be done feeling sorry and just not talk about this anymore?" Lynn asked.

It was late. They had to get to bed.

"Yes!" Maddie's voice was too loud again, but she was wearing a big grin. All was well with the world for that night.

Almost. As Lynn left to shower and get some sleep, she wished she could ask Maddie about story time. She wanted to know every detail. Did Grant sit on the side of the bed? Read fast or slow? Did he do the characters' voices? Show Kara the pictures?

Had her baby girl stayed awake for the whole book tonight?

Or fallen asleep with Grant Bishop's soothing voice in her ears?

She wanted to know, but couldn't ask. She and Maddie had just agreed not to talk about the incident anymore.

It didn't matter, anyway. Other than the sex she and Grant were going to have, she was going to have to keep the Bishop men out of her home.

Before there really was a catastrophe with Darin and Maddie. The woman hadn't strayed from what she knew to be right until Darin had said it was okay.

Maddie had followed Darin's dictates rather than her list.

And that could mean disaster.

CHAPTER TWENTY-THREE

GRANT TOOK A bottle of beer to bed with him. It was his second-best chance to actually get some sleep, since the thing that would help the most—sex—wasn't going to happen for another five days.

He was counting.

And he knew that the past week could not be repeated.

Toasting the thought, he sat up in bed, in the dark, the sheet over his bottom half.

He was going to get up in the morning. Take his brother for the first of many diving excursions. And then go to a Bishop Landscaping job for the rest of the weekend. He'd keep Darin so busy he didn't have time to think about Maddie, let alone talk to her.

There had to be a way to maintain Darin's new zest for life without everything getting completely out of control.

He drank from the bottle.

Grant was up for the challenge. He could handle his brother, tend to him, all by himself.

Except for the therapy, of course. Darin had regained about a quarter of the use of his left hand and arm. They had a way to go before he could pull the plug on The Lemonade Stand completely.

Another second, another sip.

As for the landscaping, he'd committed to keeping up the place indefinitely. And he would. He'd just have to rein himself in on any extra projects, or hire a part-time kid to help him out.

He sipped. Yeah, that was a plan.

He'd hire a kid that the management of The Lemonade Stand approved of.

The thought was good enough to seal with another sip from his bottle.

Or not. Onetime sex with Lynn wasn't going to work. He already knew that.

The knock on his door almost made him miss his mouth as he lifted the bottle to it. Darin didn't wait for a response. Grant's door opened and his brother was silhouetted from the light down the hall.

"You're in the dark." His brother, still dressed in the jeans and black pullover he'd put on after therapy, stood looking at him from the doorway.

"I know. It's nighttime. I'm going to sleep."

"No, you're not. You're sitting up."

Grant was tired. Exhausted, really. And wasn't sure if he was facing man or boy as his brother stood there.

"I'm on my way to sleep."

"You can't sleep with a bottle in your hand."

He wasn't putting it down yet. Not even to prove a point.

"I have to talk to you," Darin said, not moving from his stance by the door.

"Can't it wait until morning?"

"No."

The unequivocal answer got his attention. "Okay, what's up?"

"I would like you to turn on the light."

With an inward grumble, he reached up to the bedside lamp and did as his brother requested, blinking against the brightness the low voltage bulb shot into the room.

He'd preferred the darkness, and the thoughts of having sex with Lynn while he poured beer down his throat.

But life wasn't about what he wanted. It was about maintaining control of what was.

"What's up?" he asked Darin, hearing another date request coming on. One he was planning to sidestep until after diving the next morning. At which time, if the fates smiled at him, the date request would be pushed to the back of Darin's mind. And then slide, unnoticed, into the ether that had taken over the better part of his brother's brain.

Walking farther into the room, Darin stopped at the bedside, standing over Grant. His expression was serious, alert, and Grant had to swallow. Hard. Had to fight a memory of Darin coming into his room to tell him that the court had placed him in Darin's custody. To let him know how much he was loved and wanted. And to ask Grant to treat his wife with the same respect with which he treated him.

He had. Always. A day didn't go by that he still didn't miss his sister-in-law.

"I want to get married."

The bottle of beer slid down his hand to rest in his lap, his hand atop the mouthpiece. He picked it up again. Put it to his mouth. Emptied it.

"Drinking is not the answer, Grant."

More words from the past—and he didn't have an answer. He'd give Darin the world if he could. Give him anything and everything he asked.

But he couldn't let his brother be a husband.

"It's a little early to be thinking about marriage," he said, his tired mind scrambling and coming up empty. "You've only known her a few weeks."

"We're together every day but one, which is Sunday, and that's enough time to know I want to marry her. Mom said she knew the night she met Dad that she was going to marry him."

Reaching for his robe at the end of the bed, Grant slid from beneath the sheet and covered himself, then grabbed a pair of basketball shorts hanging on a hook on his bathroom door.

When he turned around, Darin was seated on the edge of Grant's unmade bed, toying with a loose thread on his pant leg.

Grant had no plan. He wasn't prepared for this. There was no literature written—not that he'd found at any rate and he'd been through pretty much everything out there—on how to tell your big brother that he was too damaged to have a wife.

"Can we talk about this in the morning, bro?"

When Darin looked up, Grant's heart sank. His eyes were filled with tears and determination. Passion and fear. "No, Grant, I want to talk about this now."

Something else hit him. "Have you already asked her?"

"No. I'm not stupid, Grant. I know I can't just propose. Maddie and I can't live alone."

Grant took a seat next to his brother. "But you've talked to her about it, haven't you?" He'd softened his voice, feeling his brother's pain more than his own frustration in that moment.

"We've talked about being together every day, making dinner and eating together like we do at Lynn's. And about sleeping in the same bed and talking that way instead of in different beds and being on the phone."

He and Lynn had skipped the talking-in-bed part of the plan and gone straight to talking about sex.

But this wasn't about him and Lynn.

"She needs me, Grant."

Or was it that Darin needed to be needed? And if so, there was nothing wrong with that.

"And you can be there for her, as a friend," Grant said gently. "We don't lie to each other, right?"

"Right."

"So as much as I want to tell you we'll find a way to work this out, I can't do that."

"Can, too." Darin's chin stiffened, jutting out as he said, "You aren't trying."

"I'm not trying because I can't get past the fact that I cannot possibly take care of Maddie, not like I take care of you."

"I'll take care of her."

"What if she has female issues that she doesn't understand or needs help with?" He was pulling at straws and he knew it, but he had to help Darin see, to nip this in the bud now before it flowered into a hellish mess.

"I know all about them. I was married before, remember?"

"She can't stay alone all day. And she definitely can't come with us on job sites."

He had all he could handle with one handicapped family member. He couldn't take on two. No matter how much he loved his brother.

Could he?

Was he actually considering this asinine idea?

No. He was not.

"We could take her to The Lemonade Stand in the morning and pick her up on our way home at night. I can give her half of my closet. My clothes don't fill it up, anyway. And she can borrow my computer and watch my television and use my soap."

"Who would budget your money?"

Darin looked over at him, frowning. "You, of course."

"Maddie lives by lists. Who'd make out her lists?"

"Nuh-uh, Grant. Maddie doesn't live by lists. Lynn does. Maddie just has to follow the list to watch Kara. At Maddie's house there aren't any lists."

Darin had been to Maddie's house? After all their careful supervision?

"When were you in her house?"

"I don't know." Darin shrugged. "One time."

"Can you remember anything about the time?"

It was a question he regularly asked his brother because Darin had no sense of time beyond being able to count days on a calendar.

"No."

"Did you have your stitches then?"

"I don't know. I don't think I looked at my leg."

"What about your arm? Do you remember if you did anything with your left arm?"

Darin wrinkled his nose. His brow furrowed. And then his eyes opened wide. "Yes, I remember right now that I tried to hold the door open for her as we were leaving but my arm wouldn't move and the door hit her and I was afraid she was going to cry, but she laughed instead. And later she told me that she hoped that therapy worked because it made her sad that I couldn't use my arm. That's when I first really wanted her to be my friend. When she looked at me like that and said that."

All of which put Darin in Maddie's home the first week they'd been at the Stand.

Before anyone was specifically keeping an eye on them.

"Have you been back since?"

"No."

"You don't… You guys don't…"

"Don't what, Grant?"

"Have you kissed Maddie?"

"A man doesn't kiss and tell, Grant."

"I'm your brother. It's okay to tell me."

Darin studied him, as though weighing his options. "Yes, I did kiss her. And she tasted good and we both liked it. A lot. And we want to get married. And I farted, too, and she laughed. And then she farted and I laughed. I want to live with her forever. It would make me very happy, Grant."

"You do realize this is a huge decision, right?"

"Yes. And you don't think I can make it, do you?" Darin's gaze was clear for a moment. And then it clouded over.

"What I think is that it's too big a decision for me to make tonight," he told his brother.

"But you aren't saying no."

"I'm not saying yes, either."

"But you aren't saying no."

He had to go to bed. Darin needed to go to bed, too. They were going diving in the morning.

"No, I'm not saying no."

Darin jumped off the bed so fast he almost fell and had to catch himself on the nightstand, knocking over the empty beer bottle. "Gee, thanks, Grant. Okay, good night," he said. And strode from the room.

Presumably to call his intended.

Reminding himself that intentions didn't mean anything without action, Grant picked up the empty beer bottle, set it back on the nightstand and went to bed.

OH, GOD, GRANT, where are you?

Walking outside on the grounds, and then on to the public sections of The Lemonade Stand, Lynn looked everywhere for Grant's truck Saturday morning. He was always there by eight on weekends. To get in a full day's work so he could be free to work on his paying design projects during the week. Grant was a workaholic. Dependable. A do-what-you-say-you're-going-to-do type of guy.

And she couldn't find his truck anywhere.

Let alone find him.

Darin's therapy was due to start in half an hour. Neither brother would let him skip it.

She just had to remain calm.

Kara was tied up for the morning in a specially designed developmental-play class that a child life specialist was giving to the toddlers in the private day care. There could be thirty or more living at the Stand at any given time. At the moment, there were only six.

Twice as many babies. And more than twenty five-and-overs living at The Lemonade Stand.

Still no Grant.

Five minutes before Darin's therapy was due to begin, their truck finally pulled into the back parking lot closest to the secure entrance to the complex, and Darin got out, slamming his door and, without saying goodbye to his brother or seeming to notice Lynn, stomped off in the direction of the therapy room.

"What's up with him?" she asked Grant. Just seeing him and looking into those brown eyes settled her nerves.

"He said he wanted to start diving again. I took him diving."

"And it didn't go well? Because of his arm?"

"It went very well, in spite of his arm."

He locked the truck, the epitome of hot in his tight jeans and black Bishop Landscaping polo shirt.

"He seemed upset."

He didn't ask why she was there.

Or seem to notice that she'd put on makeup with

her favorite pair of black scrubs. She'd thought about leaving her hair down, too, but it just wasn't practical.

"I just signed him up for a diving class he used to teach."

"Does he know the teacher?"

"No. It's a kid who was probably in grade school the last time Darin did any real diving. He's mad because the class meets four nights a week. Right after therapy."

Her confusion cleared.

And so did some more of her tension.

"I'm guessing he talked to you, then."

Maddie had hit her with the news first thing that morning.

"Oh, he talked to me all right." Clipping his keys onto his belt loop, Grant started toward the locked garage where the landscaping equipment was stored. She walked beside him.

And wanted him to want her. Even then.

"I told Maddie that they couldn't possibly marry," she said, having to walk fast to keep up. "I told her that you'd have to sign paperwork giving Darin permission to marry and that you'd never do that."

His silence was not encouraging. On any level.

They passed through open common ground and turned a corner before they reached the garage. Pulling his keys from his belt loop, Grant unlocked the door and strode inside. Lynn waited for him outside, wondering what she'd done to piss him off.

His hand shot out, grabbed her wrist, and she was inside the garage and in his arms before she'd had time for another thought.

Grant's lips seemed to devour hers. His tongue moved with hers as though they belonged together, as though they were *meant* to be together.

She clung to him. She hated the need that prompted her, but she gripped him hard anyway. Maybe even hurting him in her need to hang on.

Breathing wasn't easy, but it didn't seem necessary, either.

When she finally had a chance to gasp some air, her nose and lungs filled with the scent of gasoline, grass particles and machinery.

She kissed him again, her arms locked around his neck, wanting to hold him to her permanently.

The word permeated her fogged brain, and Lynn's hands fell away.

She backed up. "Wow. Um, I guess…"

"Yeah," he said, wiping his mouth with the back of his hand. "I guess."

His eyes finished the sentence. And her entire body tingled.

Whatever doubts she'd harbored about their plan to have sex diminished. Wednesday was coming. And when it did, they'd be naked. He was going to be inside her.

How in the hell was she going to wait that long? And how was it ever going to be enough?

She watched him gather supplies. And she needed so much more than sex. Though the distraction was incredibly welcome.

"I, uh, guess you told Darin he couldn't marry Maddie."

"Nope."

She straightened, folding her arms, and remembered Darin's request for a date. Grant hadn't been able to tell his big brother no then, either. "You didn't tell him yes, did you?"

Turning, one foot on the zero-gravity mower, he looked at her. "I tried to point out that he was not in any shape to marry. He had an answer for everything."

"What answer could he possibly have for the fact that they can't even live alone?"

"Me."

"You?"

"He expects me to do for the both of them exactly what I do for him. I'm already doing it. So it stands to reason that I could just expand my duties a bit and—"

"You can't do that." He was practically killing himself as it was. Hell, he was a thirty-eight-year-old man who had to schedule an hour of sex more than a week in advance.

Grant's silence didn't tell it to her straight.

"Are you considering it?"

"I told him I would."

"Are you?"

"At this point, I've done everything I can to avoid thinking about it."

She didn't blame him. How did you give your whole life to raising your older brother, invest every part of yourself into maintaining and preserving his well-being, encouraging him to push himself and try everything he wanted to try to get the most out of life, and then tell him he couldn't have what he wanted most because he was handicapped.

She moved closer. He took her hand, resting it on his upraised thigh. All she wanted to do was pull him into her arms and promise him that they'd get through this together. That he wasn't alone and it would be okay.

"I was hoping I'd distract him," Grant said, his voice low, dejected. "The diving lessons... I thought I was doing a good thing."

"Clearly, he didn't."

"All he cared about was that they were going to interfere with his only chance to spend time with Maddie. I thought he'd lost the ability to be single focused. Maybe it's just that after he lost Shelley, he didn't care enough anymore. And now, with Maddie..."

"Maybe we should rethink his therapy. I can make some phone calls. Try to get him moved. At least temporarily. And I could take away his cell phone, I guess."

They stared at each other. Lynn was such a mixture of conflicting thoughts and emotions that she didn't even recognize herself.

"Are we being fair to them?" she asked.

"I feel like a selfish ass," he blurted at almost the same time.

"I think we have to discourage any thoughts of marriage but allow the friendship for now."

"He's living life again." Grant's voice sounded different to her. Not controlled.

He sounded lost. "For the first time since the accident, I'm seeing parts of him I thought were gone forever."

"Maddie's good for him."

"It seems that way."

Squeezing his hand, Lynn said, "We'll keep a close watch on them, Grant. I'll be right here beside you all the way. Doing my part."

He nodded.

"We should do what we can not to make it too easy," she continued. "Like, come up with excuses instead of allowing them to have dinner together so often."

He didn't agree immediately.

But the idea was sound. Good. Even though she wasn't excited about it.

"Maybe…once a week?" he suggested.

"Okay." Once a week she'd have Grant at her dinner table. One hour out of one hundred and sixty-eight. She could handle that.

He touched her nipple through her shirt. And then slid his hand up underneath her scrub top and touched it for real. As though he had every right to do so. He was looking her straight in the eye. Claiming his right to touch her intimately.

She closed her eyes and felt her knees go weak.

And with one more quick kiss because she couldn't help herself, she got the hell out of there.

CHAPTER TWENTY-FOUR

THEY SCHEDULED THEIR once-a-week dinners for Friday nights. Lynn wanted a set time for her calendar—apparently it *was* Lynn who lived by lists—and, truth be told, so did he. His schedule was too tight to allow for all this spur-of-the-moment stuff.

He'd be much more relaxed if he could at least get his time back under control.

And have sex, of course. As soon as Wednesday arrived, he'd have a whole new world on his hands.

With the promise of Friday dinners, and Grant's agreement to consider the possibility of a wedding, Darin had agreed to the diving lessons. With Angelica's full support. The water activity was good exercise for Darin's arm.

His brother wasn't as coordinated in the water as he'd once been, but after just a couple of lessons, some of the skills were coming back to him.

All in all, Grant's life was pretty damn good. If he ignored the constant pain he carried around in his loins. Or the cricks he kept getting in his neck from constantly swiveling around whenever he was working at The Lemonade Stand. Looking for Lynn.

Always looking for the long-haired beauty who had a look in her eye no other woman had.

A tone to her voice that no one else had.

And as soon as he had a chance to sink his body into hers, to get relief, then life would be perfect.

He stood for an extra long time in the shower on Wednesday morning. Shaved under the hot water so that he got the smoothest skin he could possibly manage. Took time to blow-dry his hair. And grabbed the newest pair of black briefs he could find before pulling on jeans and a Bishop Landscaping shirt. There was only so much he could do. Wednesday was a workday—though he was CEO all the way today. He wasn't about to sweat.

And once he got to Lynn's house he wasn't planning on keeping the clothes on, anyway.

"Grant! What's taking so long?" Darin called out from the front room.

Technically, they didn't have to leave for another twenty minutes. But on a normal day he'd have been on the road already.

"Coming," he called, opening his nightstand drawer to grab some condoms out of the box and shove them into his wallet before sliding it into the back pocket of his jeans. He snapped on his watch on the way down the hall.

"Phew, you stink!" Darin wrinkled up his nose. "What did you do?"

"It's just my normal aftershave." He'd given it a few extra squirts so that it lasted throughout the day.

"No, it's not. It stinks."

"Have you got your diving gear?" Darin was wearing his sweats and carrying his duffel bag. After Grant had sex, he had to take Darin swimming.

"Yes, and a change of clothes for working in the cafeteria, too." As per usual, Darin would be spending the day at The Lemonade Stand while Grant met with clients and oversaw job sites.

Off they went. He'd be a different man when he returned that night. More peaceful. Satisfied. Not quite as hungry, and, if he had his way, with a steady Wednesday afternoon sex date on his calendar for as long as the foreseeable future.

LYNN WAS AT home eating lunch with Maddie and Kara, listening to chatter she wasn't hearing as she checked her mental list. As soon as Maddie left to take Kara to day care, Lynn would throw her sheets in the washer.

It wasn't laundry day, so she'd just do the one set. While they were in the wash she could dash to her office to finish the morning's charting and see one prenatal patient for a quick monthly check.

And grab some condoms from the free supply at the clinic.

Once she got back, she could throw the sheets in the dryer with an extra dryer sheet and take a hot bath.

The bath had to be rose-scented. She couldn't forget to shave her legs and pits. She was going to wear black leggings, leftover from her days as another man's wife, and a thigh-length short-sleeved sweater dress, and hadn't decided yet on whether or not to answer the door barefoot....

"Lynn?" Maddie was looking at her.

"Yeah?"

Kara banged her empty cup on the table. "I just asked you if I could get Kara another cup of milk."

"Oh. Yes. I'm sorry," she said, thankful for once that she spent so much of her time with folks who couldn't overanalyze her actions. She was gearing up to make some small talk, to make sure her loved ones didn't feel slighted by her lack of attention, when there was a knock on the door.

"Lynn?" Elaine, one of the daytime security guards, poked her head in the door. "Come quickly," she said. "We've been trying to call you, but you didn't pick up."

Jumping up from the table, Lynn reached into the pocket of her scrubs for her phone. It wasn't there. A first. She'd left it someplace.

Because her mind wasn't on her responsibilities.

"It's Missy," Elaine was saying as she grabbed Lynn's emergency bag from beside the door and headed out. "She's gone into labor."

Missy, the young woman who'd been spotting a few weeks before. At thirty weeks they could safely deliver. But because of the earlier spotting, the risk of complications was a little higher.

"Maddie…"

"I know, Lynn. I'll watch Kara and take her to class and feed her dinner and give her her bath and I'll call Lila to find someone to spend the night with Kara if you're not back by bedtime."

"Thank you," she said, and with a quick kiss on her daughter's messy cheek, she hurried after Elaine, taking Kara's "See you soon I love you" out the door with her.

GRANT WAS STANDING in the middle of an acre of dirt behind a half-million-dollar home, helping the new owner envision the naturally landscaped swimming pool and outdoor living area that were represented by the detailed drawings in the portfolio he'd just presented to them.

The expensively coiffed, redheaded wife wanted to know about adding the built-in kiva fireplace cook station he'd recommended the first time he'd met with them.

"Absolutely," he told her cheerfully, mentally calculating how long it would take to revise the quote, and where, in the next forty-eight hours, he could find that time.

His phone vibrated....

"Excuse me," he said, only long enough to glance at the LED screen. Darin came first. Always.

It wasn't Darin. And Grant itched to take the call. Lynn. Probably confirming their date that afternoon. He could hear her voice. And imagine the innuendo with which she'd coat her words...

But he had work to do.

So he spent the next half hour fighting off images of Lynn's long hair splayed across her naked breasts as he closed one of the more lucrative single-home deals of his career.

SHE'D CALLED TO cancel.

To say Grant was disappointed would be an understatement. But he understood, too. A baby's imminent birth was a far more pressing concern than Grant's overstimulated sex drive.

As was the new resident who'd needed a physical upon arrival the following Wednesday afternoon. And Lynn's meeting with an attorney to give her deposition regarding the state of a woman's physical condition the Wednesday after that.

Pretty much the only good thing, where Grant's sex drive was concerned, was that he and Lynn were talking on the phone late into the night a lot. Commiserating about their painful states and feeding each other promises of what would be when they finally did get into the same bed at the same time.

It helped, too, that anytime he had something on his mind, she was there to bounce ideas back and forth with. Whether it was something Darin had said, a design he was working on or something going on with his employees, Lynn wanted to know about it.

Darin's diving lessons went well enough that he and Grant had put on tanks and gone down alone a couple of times. And their Friday-night dinners were equally satisfying, if one didn't count the fact that Lynn had missed two out of three of them.

What was it with springtime and men getting violent? Or dinnertime and women reaching out for help?

Lynn had time off. Just not enough of it when Grant happened to be around to spend it with her.

The third Saturday in March, after Lynn had missed Friday night's dinner, he'd suggested another double date, just so he could get her alone long enough to feel her up. The few moments they'd been managing to steal in the landscaping garage just weren't cutting it.

Brandon was bringing Kara back at bedtime, and had agreed to put his daughter to bed and read to her, and Amy, Lynn's overnight babysitter, had agreed to take over from there so Kara's father could catch his flight back to San Francisco.

The date went well. He couldn't remember when he'd ever laughed so much or seen Darin laugh so much. But it was raining, too, which precluded the time alone on the beach he'd hoped to have.

If he didn't know better he'd think the fates were conspiring to keep his penis hard and his nerves frayed.

And so, the following Monday, the last Monday in March, he made a point of getting to The Lemonade Stand in the early afternoon. He was going to call Lynn and see if they could find a few minutes that afternoon to be alone. They didn't even have to touch. He just needed to see that special look in her eyes. The one that said she needed him to have his wicked way with her.

He'd hoped to be there in time to have lunch with his brother, too, but didn't make it until it was time for Darin to start therapy. Because he hadn't been sure he'd be able to get away, he hadn't told anyone his plans and figured he'd head over to Lynn's place to see if anyone was home.

He'd barely parked and locked the truck when his cell phone vibrated against his hip bone.

Hoping it was Luke or Craig needing him, something easy he could handle in seconds, he glanced at the screen, recognizing the number as an exchange from The Lemonade Stand, but not one he knew.

"Grant? This is Angelica, Darin's physical therapist," the person on the end of the line said in a voice that was either confused or distressed. Or both.

His heart started to pound. "Has something happened to Darin?" Thank God he'd come early. Thank God he was there.

Immediately switching the direction he was walking from Lynn's bungalow toward the main building, Grant heard the therapist say, "I don't know, that's why I'm calling you. He didn't show up for his session. I thought you'd know where he was and just forgot to let me know he wouldn't be here."

Maddie.

The thought was instantaneous. And sure.

"I called Carmelita at the cafeteria, in case he'd been held over there. She said he was there during his shift and that she saw him sitting at a table alone and eating afterward."

Darin had last been seen forty-five minutes ago. That was more than enough time for two people to have sex.

"Has anyone tried to get hold of Maddie?"

"Yes, sir. She walks with him to therapy sometimes so I called her first. Her parents stopped in for a visit today after lunch and took her out shopping to get some things for her room."

Maddie was with her parents.

And Darin was missing.

Growing cold, then hot, Grant continued to stride toward the main building, picking up his pace a bit. He glanced around at the same time, eyes peeled for the black sweatsuit with white stripes that his brother had been wearing when they'd left the house that day.

"How did things go this morning?" he asked, turning a circle in the grass as he tried to take in the entire area at once.

Maybe Darin had gotten discouraged. Was hiding out in the trees, cutting therapy like an unhappy kid would cut class.

"We had a great session. He got his arm three-quarters of the way up in the air with no assistance at all."

Any other day that would have been worth a toast. A night of them. At the moment he hardly cared.

"I'll call him," Grant said, ringing off abruptly to immediately push Darin's speed dial number. His brother always picked up. It was a rule.

The seconds it took to connect were interminable. He half ran toward the Garden of Renewal. It seemed like a place a kid would choose to hide out if he didn't want to be found.

Darin's phone went straight to voice mail.

Grant dialed Lila. Within a minute, she was sending security out to scour the property. All bungalows would be checked. As would the public buildings that were part of The Lemonade Stand complex. They'd check security cameras, as well. One good thing about having his brother at a women's shelter was that they were prepared for emergencies.

By the time Grant hung up he was running. And didn't quit running until he reached the Garden of Renewal.

"Have you seen a man around here?" He interrupted what had obviously been a very serious conversation between two women he didn't recognize. "He's tall. Probably had on a sweatsuit?"

"Are you looking for Darin?" one of the women, a redhead, asked.

"Yes. You know him?"

"We all do," the woman said. "He works at the cafeteria at lunchtime. He's really sweet. And kind."

"He's my brother."

"We know," the plump blonde answered this time.

"You do the landscaping. Darin told us." The redhead again.

He didn't have time for chitchat. "Have you seen him?"

"Yeah," the blonde said. She turned and Grant saw the faded bruising on the left side of the woman's face, continuing back to her ear. A bright pink jagged scar ran from her ear down her neck and into the neckline of her shirt. "At lunch."

Grant tried to focus on her eyes. They seemed to dare him to blanch.

"He showed us that he could use his left hand to serve the potatoes," the redhead said quickly. "He was proud of himself." Her smile was in such direct contrast to the rest of the emotion suffocating the moment.

"And you haven't seen him since?" he asked. Telling himself to calm down. The world wasn't filled with evil.

Darin was fine.

"No." The redhead shook her head. The blonde did the same.

He hurried through the garden, anyway. Looking under benches Darin couldn't possibly fit under, behind trees and in the natural underbrush that he'd been careful not to disturb during his renovation. He even took a peek into the waterfall pond he'd constructed. It wasn't deep, but it was long enough to hide a man who was submerged.

Darin wasn't there.

"Did you check the park?" the redhead asked as he approached their bench on his way out of the garden.

"No, but I will, thanks," he said.

"He likes the park," she added while the blonde woman silently watched the exchange, her expression pained. Grant had a feeling she wouldn't have known if Darin had crawled across her feet.

He obviously hadn't covered his reaction to her injuries well enough.

He felt bad about that.

But he had to find Darin.

Clicking on his phone, he did the only thing left he could think to do at the moment.

He called Lynn.

LYNN HAD JUST finished with a patient when Grant's call came in. She heard the panic in his voice as soon as he started speaking.

"Where are you?" Locking her office door behind her, Lynn held her phone to her ear and, checking each of the exam room doors to make certain she'd locked them, headed out the back door.

"At the park."

Grant sounded as frantic as she'd ever heard. More harried than he'd been four years before when Darin had come from surgery and they hadn't known if his brother was going to survive his brain surgery.

"I'm on my way."

"I have no idea where he'd go," Grant said. "If we were home, or on a job, I'd go to my truck. He hangs out in the backseat sometimes. I found him asleep on the floor in the back once."

Looking around her as she half ran across the complex, she let Grant ramble, trying to think of anyplace Darin might have gone.

"Is there anyone at the park?" It was still early enough in the afternoon that all of the kids would be at school.

And the private day care had its own little fenced-in playground.

"No. There was a woman here with two small children, but she said she hadn't seen Darin. They left."

She could see him, standing there in his jeans and black Bishop Landscaping shirt, looking strong and virile and lost.

"I'm here," she said. Turning, he saw her, returned his phone to its holster as he approached and grabbed her hand as soon as he was close enough to touch her.

"Thanks for coming." The words were plebian compared to the panicked look in his eyes.

"We'll find him." As soon as she'd taken Grant's call, she'd sent the one resident in her waiting room, a well-check appointment, over to Lila. She'd need to have someone reschedule the rest of her afternoon.

"It's just not like him. Darin doesn't ever leave familiar territory. He got lost once and wet himself. He's never forgotten...."

"Then he's someplace familiar," she said, hoping she was right. "We just have to figure out where that is."

He was still holding her hand, and she gave his

fingers a squeeze. "Let's go check my place. He seems to be thinking of that as home. Maybe something upset him or spooked him. He wouldn't have been able to run to you or your truck since you weren't here. I was in back-to-back appointments all morning. And Maddie's out with her folks. She walked Kara back to day care after lunch and her folks were picking her up from there."

"Angelica already called Maddie and confirmed that she's with her parents. She didn't know where Darin was."

Another alarm went off. "Did she let Maddie know he was missing?"

"I'm not sure."

"She'll be frantic if she knows. And her folks aren't great about helping her through her panic. They tend to panic about her panic."

Which was one of the reasons why Maddie wasn't living with them. Pulling her phone out of her pocket she called the slender blonde.

"Maddie? This is Lynn." Still holding Grant's hand in hers, she hurried with him across the sidewalk that meandered through the grounds and across the grass toward her bungalow.

"Hi, Lynn, I'm with my parents shopping right now."

"I know. That's why I'm calling. I wanted to make sure you remembered that you wanted to get some more of that special soap you like."

Cherry-scented hand soap. Lynn had extra that she intended to give Maddie, but she'd needed a reason to call.

"Yes, Lynn, I remembered. And I thought you were calling about Darin. I didn't walk him to therapy today because I'm with my parents right now."

"Okay, sweetie. We just forgot to tell Angelica about your visit with your parents. You're fine."

"I don't want to get into trouble."

"You aren't in trouble." The woman was obviously not worried about Darin, either. Which meant that she hadn't put Angelica's phone call together with the idea that Darin might be missing.

"Did Darin tell you if he had anything to do after therapy today?"

"He was going to miss me. And help his brother, Grant, with yard work because he can do it all now because he can bend over and lift things."

Darin had been released for full activity a couple of weeks ago.

"That's right. Good. I thought maybe I'd see if he wants to make his spaghetti again for dinner on Friday night."

"Okay, Lynn, I like his spaghetti, and Kara does, too. I have to go now. I'm shopping. And please tell Darin I'm sorry I didn't walk him to therapy. And…tell him I miss him, too," she added in almost a whisper.

"I will," Lynn assured her.

They'd reached her house.

"I take it she doesn't know where he is."

"She doesn't know he's missing." Which wasn't all that reassuring. As much as Grant and Maddie talked, if he'd intended to stray from his normal itinerary, surely he would have told her.

And Maddie would have told Lynn. Or at least confessed that she knew something she couldn't tell her.

DARIN WASN'T AT Lynn's house. Or anywhere on the secure premises of The Lemonade Stand. All residents had been put on alert—a one-shot text to their cell phones covered most of them. A message over the speakers installed in all of the bungalows and at the main house covered the rest.

The atmosphere at the complex wasn't one of panic. Everyone at The Lemonade Stand was taking the situation seriously but no one was panicking. It was far more likely that Darin had just wandered off—and a grown man of his size, even mentally handicapped as he was, should be able to keep himself alive until he was found.

Grant was panicked, though.

"This just isn't like him," he said, running fingers through hair that was already standing on end. He felt like a fool.

And a failure, too.

There had to be something he could do.

The police had been notified. And were on their way to The Lemonade Stand to take his statement.

"He's going to be fine, Grant," Lynn said. "He's been out and about enough lately to know to ask for help. Or maybe even recognize someplace close by. He rides on these roads with you every single day."

They were in Lila's office waiting for the police.

Lila was seeing to a resident in crisis. An abused, recovering drug user whose children were going to be removed from her care later that day. Just until she could get clean and find a way to care for them.

As far as anyone could tell, Darin had only been missing about an hour and a half. No one had seen him.

Lila's landline rang, and Grant tensed as Lynn picked up immediately.

He could hear a male voice, but couldn't make out a single word.

She looked at him and shook her head. Then said, "You're sure?" Her tone was biting.

He heard the male voice again. The frown encompassing Lynn's entire expression eased as she gave him a quick smile and a shake of her head. Her lips mouthed the words *Not Darin.*

"Uh-huh."

More male voice. More "Uh-huh."

She was looking at him. His tension eased a bit, but not enough.

"Okay, thank you."

She hung up, a frown marring her brow.

"What?"

"Nothing to do with Darin," she said. Then she picked up the phone again and dialed.

"Lila?"

She was on the phone, but staring at him intently, and Grant read that she was going to let him be privy to classified information without actually telling him what was going on.

"I just had a call from the police. No, nothing to do with Darin Bishop— We're still waiting for an officer to come take our statement on him. Another officer, one on regular patrol, noticed someone hanging around the area. Apparently he's been watching him for a couple of days, but the guy didn't do anything particularly suspicious. He went for a burger across the street. Sat on a bench..."

Grant didn't need to hear the guy sat on a bench. What in the hell was going on?

And where was his brother?

"But today he seemed to be eyeing the door to the public day care a little too closely. Not enough to arrest him, but the officer has been making extra rounds to keep an eye on him. He saw the guy go into our boutique. And then later he was hanging around our public entrance. The officer approached him for loitering and told him he'd have to move along, and the guy got belligerent so he arrested him."

Grant was watching her, on alert. He'd stayed away from the residents as he'd promised, but he'd learned some things during his weeks at The Lemonade Stand. These woman...they were fragile. They had men in their lives who'd hurt them. Men who, by and large, seemed to think women were property—their property....

"Turns out it was Dan Cleveland, Maria's husband," Lynn was telling Lila on the phone.

Maria Cleveland. Grant knew that Maria was the woman who had moved in next door to Lynn. One of their first late-night conversations had been about Maria, though he hadn't known her name then. Lynn had texted Grant at two in the morning after spending the evening in the emergency room with Maria. And had been called out another time to tend to her because she'd ripped out her stiches trying to hail a cab to get to her kids.

"I don't know, I called you first," Lynn was saying into the phone, apparently in response to something Lila had asked.

"Okay."

Lynn hung up. "Lila's sending someone over to make certain Maria's in the group counseling session she was scheduled to attend this afternoon."

"He was really going to try to get to her if he could."

"Of course. This is no drama mart we run here,

Grant. Do you know how many women die every day in the United States from spousal abuse?"

He did know. She knew he knew. She was the one who'd told him.

"It's a good thing the police in this town are so observant."

"The city allots monies for extra patrols around our block. All of the officers on this beat know what to watch for."

"Then surely they'd have noticed if a confused-looking man was wandering around out there."

She came around the desk. Took his hand again. "We'll find him, Grant."

She didn't look him straight in the eye when she said it. But he was glad she'd cared enough to say the words anyway.

THE POLICE CAME. Took Grant's statement. They talked to Angelica and Carmelita, too. And many of the residents who were gathered together in a recreation hall in the main building.

Maria Cleveland was absent. She was in a private counseling session with Sara, being encouraged to press charges against her husband for spousal abuse so the police could keep him locked up and away from her.

A few of the residents had seen Darin that morn-ing. None of them remembered anything different about him. Or knew anything about where he could be.

But in the past ten days, he'd been seen all around the grounds helping Grant with the landscaping. He could mow now. And trim. And had been doing a lot of both. The ladies were used to having him around. They might not have noticed anything amiss.

Darin had been gone two hours, and Lynn could tell that Grant was starting to let his panic get the better of him. She was surprised he'd remained calm as long as he had. For seventeen years his life had revolved around Darin.

"It's almost time to go get Kara," she said. "Let's pick her up early and take another walk around the grounds."

Maybe her precocious offspring would distract Grant a little bit. Either way, Lynn was going to collect her. There'd been too much danger that day. Lynn needed Kara close.

She took his hand as they walked through subdued hallways toward the private day care where Kara had been taking dance class that afternoon. "Did we look in here?" Grant asked, stopping by a janitor door. "Maybe he got locked in someplace by accident...." He didn't let go of her hand.

With her free hand, Lynn pulled open the door. There wasn't room in the supply closet for a man of Darin's size to stand, let alone hide.

Security had already checked the landscaping garage. And they'd been back a second time.

"I don't understand this," Grant said. "If Darin wasn't missing, I'd be thrilled to hear that he'd actually gone someplace on his own. He clings to the familiar. Always."

"Other than that one time he wet himself, he's never just wandered off but found his way back?"

"Not once. In seventeen years, not once."

They'd reached the day care. Grant squeezed her hand and let it go, standing off to the side as she opened the door and stepped into the small foyer.

"You can come in," she told him, holding open the door.

Leaving him in the front entryway, she went through another door, down a small hallway and peeked into the dance class, praying that it was ending. Kara wouldn't be happy about being pulled out early.

The class was still underway.

But she couldn't see Kara at first. So she moved over to get a different view from the big window into the room. And still, even when she peered in the mirror straight ahead of her to get a view of the back of the room, she couldn't find Kara.

With all that had been going on that day, Lynn's nerves were frayed. She was staff. A nurse. She could interrupt any function on campus. So she did. Pulling open the door, she stepped inside, an apology to the teacher on her lips as she sought her toddler out from the other seven or eight kids, male and female, absently registering that they'd brought kids over from the public day care to take part in the class.

But not really caring at the moment.

"Where's Kara?" she blurted out over the children's music blaring from a boom box on the floor by the instructor.

"Kara?" The twentysomething woman asked. She'd been abused by her mother's boyfriend, if Lynn remembered correctly. Sexually. Thankfully there'd been no internal damage.

"My daughter. She was signed up to take this class."

"I thought she was with Maddie," the girl said. "I saw her in the hallway…walking behind Maddie. They told me Maddie has jurisdiction over her and I thought she'd decided not to put Kara in class…."

The girl was babbling. Seemingly unaware of the other kids in her care—most of whom were standing there staring, as if someone was getting in trouble and they didn't want it to be them.

"Maddie isn't here this afternoon," Lynn bit out. Everyone knew, *everyone,* that where the kids were concerned, no one assumed anything. "She'd have had to sign her out and clear it with you face-to-face if Kara wasn't going to be in class. She knows the rules."

And clearly this young woman didn't.

Lynn would have to deal with that later. Right now, she had to find Kara.

Pulling her phone out of her pocket, she tore out of the room—and straight into Grant Bishop's arms.

CHAPTER TWENTY-FIVE

WHEN LYNN'S BODY slammed into his, Grant knew, instantly, that something was terribly wrong.

She turned before he could pull her fully into his arms, and righted herself. She was on her phone before she said a word to him.

"Lila, I need a lockdown. Immediately. Kara's missing."

She hung up and called the police. A tense fifteen minutes later, a couple of detectives met them in Lila's office.

They wanted pictures. Descriptions of clothing and shoes and distinguishing marks. While the female officer was on the phone, checking for any reports of unattended children in the area, the male officer, Detective Smith, talked to Lynn.

She answered his questions as stoically as she had earlier when the police had requested the same information for Darin.

"There has to be some connection here," Grant said as he paced the office. He needed everyone on the same page. "Kara and Darin know each other. They eat dinner together regularly. Darin thinks he wants to marry Kara's caregiver—who happens to be away from the complex at the moment. They have to be together."

Lynn stared at him openmouthed. "You think Darin and Maddie have Kara?"

"I think that Darin wouldn't set foot in your home that first time he was there—because he won't go anyplace he hasn't been before unless I take him—but the minute he saw Maddie there, he went in."

He could see the confirmation of his memory in Lynn's gaze.

"He would never wander off on his own. But for Maddie…"

"You think her parents are in on it?" Lynn asked.

"Where is this Maddie person?" Detective Smith asked.

"With her parents," Lynn told him. "Shopping."

She pulled out her phone. Dialed.

"I'll take that," Smith said, reaching for the phone. Lynn elbowed his hand away.

"Maddie's…special. She'll clam up if you…"

Grant understood. Smith was male. Maddie was scared to death of men.

Except Darin.

"Maddie." Lynn turned her back to speak on the phone as the door opened and more officers entered the room along with Lila and some of the security personnel from The Lemonade Stand.

"We're on lockdown," Lila told Detective Smith,

after asking who was in charge. "All staff and residents have been ordered to check their offices and bungalows and report to the rec hall stat."

"We'll want to speak with each one of them," Smith said. "No one is to enter or leave this campus until we release them."

"I understand, Detective. Thank you for your prompt response."

Grant would have added his thanks if anyone had noticed him standing there.

One thing was clear: once a child was involved, the search and rescue policies escalated.

He nodded to himself, quietly going out of his mind. Would his brother really stoop to kidnapping to be with Maddie? Would Maddie put Kara at risk that way?

He just didn't think so. Couldn't find a way to make the pieces fit. Darin and Maddie both knew right from wrong. They might not realize how much of a panic they would create if Kara went missing, but they'd still know that it was wrong to take her in the first place.

The female detective called Kara's father. The police had insisted on making that call so that they could get a true read on him. The conversation was short. From the tone Grant heard coming from the other end of the line, Brandon was shocked and distraught. Not the sound of a guilty man.

"He's on his way to the airport," the detective said as she ended that call.

"Maddie just about had a meltdown when we strayed from Lynn's list of instructions just to let me read Kara a bedtime story when she asked. There's no way that woman would take Kara without following protocol." He was speaking to the room at large. Everyone, except Lynn, who was on the phone in the corner, stopped talking to look at him.

"And if she tried, my brother would tell her that they had to ask permission first. I know they think they're in love and that they give each other courage to do things they might not normally do, but the one thing we can count on with both of them is that they don't break rules."

He didn't mean to hold the floor. But after seventeen years of living and breathing Darin, he knew his brother.

"If we waste time assuming they're fine and together, we're letting the danger they're in escalate."

He did agree with one point: Darin and Kara were most likely together. The thought didn't relieve him at all.

Darin wouldn't have just wandered off with Kara. Which meant that something had happened...

Lynn dropped her cell phone back into her pocket and walked up to stand beside Grant. She leaned into him and said, "I spoke with Maddie *and* her parents. I spoke to her mother and father individually so they didn't repeat to each other what was going on in front of Maddie. They are definitely together. At the strip mall on Mountain View. They're bringing her back immediately. They aren't telling Maddie that either Darin or Kara are missing. Her mother, Martha, did say that Kara was upset when Maddie left her at class. She wanted to go shopping, too. Maddie started to get upset at leaving her that way, so her parents each put an arm around her and rushed her out."

She looked at Grant. "Maddie's dance teacher said that she saw Kara walking behind Maddie and thought they were together."

"Kara never walks behind Maddie," Lila blurted out before Grant could.

"Maddie either holds her hand, or lets Kara run in front of her where she can see her," he added. Though now that he thought about it... "Ever since Kara almost fell into a service hole I had opened, Maddie has clung to the little girl's hand anytime they're outside."

An image of Darin walking beside Maddie on the sidewalk outside, his head held high, took his voice away.

He recalled his older brother's laugh when Maddie had belched loudly at the dinner table the other night.

Grant swallowed back tears.

They'd find him. And he'd keep him under lock

and key after they did. No more relaxing, leaving Darin to walk by himself anywhere. No more…

"Wait." Lynn's weight against him grew a little heavier. Standing with her, shoulder to shoulder, hip to hip, he gladly withstood whatever she had to give him. "They weren't outside yet," she was saying, her gaze darting around from one of the serious expressions in the room to another. "Kara was walking behind Maddie inside the day care. The dance teacher is new. She thought Kara was going with Maddie. She didn't seem to know that every child has to be physically signed out before any of the children are released."

"She knew," Lila said. "I'll take care of that. But could this mean that Kara did walk out of the day care behind Maddie?" she said aloud what Grant was thinking.

"It sounds like it," Smith said. "We need to know how Maddie and her parents exited the premises."

Lynn already knew. And told them.

Did this mean that Darin wasn't with Kara? That the little girl was out in the world somewhere, wandering the streets by herself?

"Maybe she followed them and when they took off in their car without her, she couldn't get back inside the locked facility."

"She could still be out there…" Lynn said, and the detectives dispatched a flurry of officers to comb the area.

Lila followed them to the door. "I'm going to go talk to the women and children gathering in the rec hall. We don't want panic to ensue."

The managing director left, her expression calm but solemn. Grant wondered how these women did what they did day after day. Week after week.

The constant dangers and emotional and physical traumas would drive him over the edge.

Hell, he couldn't even keep him and Darin together.

SHE WAS GOING to fly out of her skin and burst into a million pieces that would never be able to be put back together.

Lynn knew the thought was crazy. And she couldn't stop it. Leaning against Grant, she listened while the detectives dispersed to perform their various duties, all revolving around finding Kara. It had been less than half an hour since she'd discovered her missing.

She was grateful for the tremendous response. Still…

Her phone rang. Grabbing it from her pocket with shaking fingers, she had to push three times to engage the answer button.

"Lynnie? Oh, my God, Lynnie. I just had to talk to you. Please tell me what's going on."

She laced her fingers through Grant's and talked to her ex-husband, keeping an eye and ear on the detectives in the room, as well. Brandon was booked on a flight to Santa Raquel but wouldn't be arriving for another three hours.

He was distressed, pacing the airport, he said, but determined that they would find Kara and she would be fine.

Lynn agreed. And after she hung up, she laid her head on Grant's shoulder. It was either that or fall apart, and a mother lying supine on the floor was not going to help her toddler at all.

"We should be out there," she told him softly as those in charge made decisions and gave orders around them.

"They want us here for now."

She knew that. She just didn't agree with the decision to keep her and Grant in Lila's office, the current search headquarters, so that they could be available to anyone involved in the search at any time.

To identify a body? She tried not to think so. And was scared to death for the sweet man who'd been injured trying to save his wife's life, as well as for her precious little curly-haired angel.

"I pray they're together," she said.

"If they are, Darin will keep her safe." Grant spoke softly, and this time, he looked her in the eye.

She knew that if Darin was with Kara he would do all he could to help her. There were just too many ifs.

BEFORE MADDIE EVEN made it back, the phone rang
again. Smith's phone.

"It's Detective Martinez," he said to the room at
large, as if the name meant something.

Grant had no idea who Martinez was but hoped
he was part of the search team. And was calling
with good news.

The helplessness, as he stood there with Lynn,
moving from one part of the room to another, shaking his head right along with her every time Smith
suggested they sit down, was diminishing what bit
of control he had thus far managed to maintain.

Smith had told them it could be a long night.

The man had no idea.

Smith still had his disconnected cell phone in his
hand as he approached Lynn and Grant. Her scrubs
were purple today. The color of lilacs.

It was an inane thought that kept his feet on the
ground.

"Martinez is in our forensics lab. She's going over
the security tapes."

His heart was pounding. Lynn's chin held high.

"She identified Kara on them, wearing the denim
overalls and red shirt you described. She sees her
running out after Maddie. Sees her stop when Maddie's parents drive away. And she sees Dan Cleveland approach her...."

Oh, God, no. Lynn's sharp intake of breath, her
only reaction as she continued to give the detec-

tive her hard, focused stare, resonated all the way through him. Cold seeped into the room.

"He grabbed her, pulling her out of the camera's range."

"You talked to him, right?" Lynn asked. "Ask him where she is."

Grant did some calculations. "He couldn't have had her long," he said. Based on the time stamp reported on the tape and when the man was arrested.

"He was still in the area when he was arrested," Lynn said.

Smith nodded. "They're talking to him now. We'll get a call as soon as they know anything. I just wanted you two to know where we're at."

"Is there any sign of Darin on the tapes?" Lynn asked the question.

"We don't know yet. Not to that point there wasn't. Martinez stopped viewing them as soon as she saw Kara."

"But they're resuming looking at the footage now, right?" Grant asked.

"They've got a team on them at this point. If your brother is there, we'll know soon."

He needed to get out of the room. Get outside. Breathe air. And comb the streets for the one person he couldn't live without.

Except that he couldn't leave Lynn standing there all alone. She was leaning on him. And he couldn't let her fall.

MARIA CLEVELAND'S HUSBAND buckled as soon as he was told he was caught on tape trying to snatch Kara.

"He did try," Detective Smith told Lynn and Grant quietly fifteen minutes later. Maddie and her parents had arrived and were in another corner of the room with Sara and a couple of other police officers.

Sara had given a whispered message to Lynn as she'd come in. Maria had agreed to press charges. And was filing for divorce.

"He said he figured if he couldn't get to his wife's kids to use them for leverage, someone else's kid would do just as well. He figured the women who were keeping his wife hostage from him would release her to get one of their own kids back."

Lynn's stomach cramped. She didn't have time to be sick but was afraid she might be anyway.

"You said he tried." Grant's voice was firm beside her. Strong where she felt weak. "Not that he succeeded."

"That's right. He said there was no way he was going down for kidnapping when he didn't do it. He said he saw Kara come out, tried to grab her, but some big guy came out of another door from the locked area, hit him once, hard, grabbed the kid and ran."

"Darin?" Grant asked. "What other man would have been in the locked area?" She could feel his renewed tension as he stiffened. They were sitting on a leather couch, having finally given in to Smith's persuasions to do so, holding hands.

"Yes," the detective said. "As soon as we knew that your brother exited via another gate, we had the team switch cameras and they saw him. It was just as Cleveland said. He seemingly comes out of nowhere, hits Cleveland, snatches Kara all with one hand and runs off camera."

"Darin saved her life!" Lynn jumped up. "They're together and he saved her life!"

Grant was beside her and she grabbed his hand again in both of hers. "They're together, Grant."

"And we have no idea where they are," he reminded her. "Kara's three and Darin's got limited abilities," he reminded her.

"I know." She did, too. And she could see that Grant was heavy with the weight of responsibility for his handicapped brother. If Darin failed Kara, Grant would never forgive himself.

Which was crazy. No matter what happened, Darin had saved Kara's life. It was on tape.

Her little girl was going to be all right.

CHAPTER TWENTY-SIX

ONCE GRANT KNEW for certain that Darin was outside The Lemonade Stand complex, he couldn't wait any longer.

The fact that he had Kara Duncan in his care, a child caring for a child, nothing was going to stop him from going out to find them.

He wasn't all that surprised when Lynn backed up his idea, saying that she was going to accompany him.

Smith didn't like the idea.

"We're free citizens," Grant stated in no uncertain terms. "If Darin sees cops looking around, calling his name, he's just as likely to hide as to come out," he said, thinking clearly for the first time in more than two hours.

The fog had lifted. He had to help his brother.

"Lynn and I know all of the places he's been in the area," he continued. "And if Darin hears us call, he'll respond, even if he's hiding."

"He lacks problem-solving skills," Lynn said, as though she was Darin's nurse, not a friend. "And has emotional lapses, as well. We stand a much better chance of finding them before dark if we're out there looking for them."

They'd waited for official word. It was time to act.

THEY CHECKED BOTH restaurants they'd been to on their dates, including bathrooms and alcoves. They'd shown Darin's and Kara's pictures around and were told officers had already been there looking for the pair.

Grant found corners and crevices, potential hiding places, everywhere.

"You really think he'd cram himself and Kara into a corner and just wait?" she asked him.

"I know he would if he felt threatened," Grant said as they climbed back into his truck. A vehicle Darin would recognize if he saw it and be willing to approach. "He got scared one time when I told him to stand outside the grocery store while I wheeled the cart back inside the door. When I came out he was standing between a pillar and a trash receptacle. Once, on a job, I had him wait outside while I delivered a bill to a woman and when I turned around he was under a stairwell."

He sounded ashamed. Like it was his fault that Darin had felt unsafe enough to hide. Lynn's heart went out to him so completely in that moment when all aspects of normal daily life were stripped away.

If she focused on Darin and Grant, she could

still breathe. Could push forward and find Darin and Kara.

As Lynn kept her gaze peeled out the window, Grant drove slowly, ignoring the honks he was getting. If he heard them he didn't seem to notice. He stopped a couple more times. Jumped out of the truck to look behind a bin and under a stoop.

Lynn's phone rang while he was bent over, peering beneath cement on a quiet street a mile or so from the Stand.

It was Maddie's number.

"They told me I could call you, Lynn," the woman said, her slow speech even more garbled than usual. The poor woman's lip was probably bleeding from chewing on it from nerves. And would need salve for the next several days.

"Of course you can call me," she said with a heavy ache in her heart. Why couldn't this be a normal day? With Maddie and Kara at home waiting for her?

Why couldn't life ever just be what you thought?

"I told them I had to call you because I think I know where Darin and Kara are," the woman continued as though Lynn hadn't spoken. "I know because I did a bad thing and you're going to be mad at me, but I have to tell you now because you have to find Darin and Kara and..."

She sniffed, and Lynn, impatient and frantic, said, "Maddie, just tell me where they are."

The other woman started to cry. "I…I…"

She took a deep breath. And glanced at Grant as he climbed back into the truck. *Maddie.* She mouthed the word. And tried to tell him with her eyes that she was about to fly out the window. To ask him to hold her in place and breathe life into her lungs so she could get through this.

She needed the peace that he brought her.

"It's okay, sweetie. I'm not mad, I swear to you, Maddie. And you know I never lie to you, right? That's our deal."

"But you yelled…."

"I didn't yell, sweetie. I'm worried about Kara and Darin and we need to find them in a hurry. That's all. I'm in a hurry."

She knew how to help Maddie express herself. It was up to her to stay calm. Her panic would incite Maddie's.

"Please, sweetie, we're family, right? We've talked about that. And right now Darin and Kara need you to be strong for them. To not worry about someone getting mad at you. For Darin and Kara. You understand?"

She hoped Sara was on the other end of the line with Maddie, listening in. Doing what she could to keep the woman's panic at bay so she could think clearly.

"Now, tell me where they are."

"At the beach." Maddie's voice was firm. A tone unfamiliar to Lynn. Something she'd ponder later.

"At the beach?"

"Building a sand castle," Maddie said, and Lynn's hopes dashed to the ground again.

"That's what you and Darin did," she said now. "Not what Darin and Kara are doing."

"No, Lynn, Darin and I went to a different place on the beach without you and Grant, and I know that's where they are and I told the lady police officer when she told me that I could save them, but they don't know exactly where and you do so you could go get them."

"I know where they are? But it's not the same place you and Darin built your sand castle?"

She put the phone on speaker and whispered to Grant, "Head toward the beach."

He had the truck in traffic immediately, his face lined with tension.

"Yes, Lynn. Darin and I… A couple of weeks ago Grant dropped Darin off early in the morning a long time before his therapy and he was going to pick weeds, but he didn't. He came to my house and we snuck out the back door that Darin snuck out today. He knew where to find it because of going through it with his brother, Grant."

"You two have left campus before?"

A heavy sigh on the line had her taking another

deep breath. "Yes, and I knew that you would be mad. We're in big trouble."

"You aren't in trouble," Lynn assured the woman. "You are being a big help, Maddie. Now tell me the rest."

Maddie could only do things in Maddie's time. Regardless of how pressured the rest of them felt. Or how serious the emergency.

Maddie's mind only worked so fast.

"Darin has been watching the roads every day when Grant drives him and he said he knew how to get us to the beach so we could build another sand castle like we did on our first date. And so we did."

Her pulse thrumming, Lynn exchanged a glance with Darin.

"You two made it to the beach and back."

"Yes, Lynn, and I'm sorry. I didn't follow the rules and now I might have to leave here and…" Her voice broke.

"You won't have to leave, Maddie," Lynn assured the other woman. She'd take Maddie into her own home and hire a nursemaid if the need arose, but Maddie wasn't going to lose her home or her family.

She also knew Lila well enough to know that she would not require Maddie to resign her position, although there would be some kind of accountability for having broken the rules.

Grant made a quick turn and another, sending

her sideways in her seat as he took a back route to
the beach.

"Well, if I do have to move I'll still save Darin
and Kara," Maddie said now, her voice thick with
tears. "Darin said anytime either of us gets in trouble, we should have a safe place to go and he said
the place we built the sand castle wasn't safe because it's out in the open. He says *our* safe place
would be where we can build sand castles and not
be out in the open, and I think he went there."

"And I know where that is?"

"Uh-huh."

She tried to be patient, but blurted, "Where is it,
Maddie?" managing to keep her tone soft, at least.

"Do you remember when we went on our date
and went to the beach and Darin and I built that
sand castle and then we got scared because we
couldn't find you to show it to you?"

Grant turned again. And was pulling into the
public lot he'd parked in that night.

She looked all around her, hopeful. And saw
nothing except an expanse of beach and massive
waves that were strong enough to wash a three-
year-old out to sea in the space of a blink.

"Yes, I remember," she said, afraid they'd just
wasted more precious time on a goose chase.

"Well, Darin and I said our special place is where
you and Grant came from when we found you. Be-

cause that was our safe time. You found us because it wasn't out in the open."

"The little cove?" she asked, remembering the cliff face jutting out onto the beach. The cove where Grant had first kissed her.

"Yes, Lynn, that's where they are. I just know it."

They were out of the truck, striding across the sand. Lynn cursed the thick substance that squished when she walked and slowed them down.

"Have you talked to Darin, Maddie?" she asked.

"No, Lynn. He doesn't answer his phone."

Promising Maddie that she would call her back soon and reassuring her that she was very proud of her for telling the truth, Lynn rang off with an "I love you" that came straight from her heart.

Maddie was challenged. And sometimes challenging, but Lynn loved her dearly.

And she understood the pained expression on Grant's face as they sprayed sand behind them with the swiftness of their gait.

Just as she loved Maddie and Kara, Grant loved his brother.

Would they find them?

And if they did, would they be alive? Uninjured?

She took his hand as they drew near to the cove. He held on.

And as they rounded the corner, they started to run.

Up ahead, protected by a giant cliff face, sat a

tall man and a very small girl, side by side in the sand, their expressions serious as they built the most magnificent sand castle Lynn had ever seen.

"I'M SORRY, GRANT. I left."

Taking one hand off the wheel of the truck, Grant gave his brother's shoulder a squeeze. "You don't owe anyone an apology, Darin," he said, swallowing back the emotion he'd been hard-pressed to contain during the long, grueling hours they'd just passed. First, finding out that his brother was missing, then Kara; the helplessness of not being able to do anything; the frantic search.

And finally, spotting Darin and Kara on the beach, calling out to Darin and hearing his brother's voice say, quite calmly, "See, little Kara, I told you that if we built a very big castle, they would come to see it and take us home. I told you the bad man couldn't get us here."

"You saved a little girl's life today, bro," he said with a sideways glance at his brother.

He couldn't stop looking at him.

And was thinking about hunting down the baby monitor he'd placed in Darin's room for the first couple of years after his brother's accident. It was out in the shed. In a bin on the top shelf with other old electronics.

It might possibly be the only way Grant was going to get any rest that night.

Unless he crashed on the couch. Darin would have to get past him to get to the front door.

"I just showed her how to build a sand castle, Grant," Darin said now. "You and Lynn saved us."

"You saved her from a man who was going to kidnap her."

"I hit a bad man, but it wasn't hard to do. It hurt my hand, though."

Life in Darin's world was so simple. And more complicated than he felt equipped to handle some days.

But his brother was with him. Safe. He'd saved Kara's life.

Grant had nothing more to ask.

LYNN WAS IN her room, purportedly to sleep. The lights were out. And she lay, fully clothed, on top of her covers.

She'd reached Brandon before he'd boarded his plane and now that he knew Kara was safe, unharmed and unaware of the horror she'd narrowly escaped, he'd decided he would wait and fly down as usual over the weekend.

As far as Kara knew, she'd spent the day with Darin playing in the sand. She'd been unaware of the "bad man" Darin had talked about, thinking only that he'd snatched her up because she'd been left behind by Maddie's car.

It had all transpired so quickly, Kara hadn't known what was happening.

But she'd rattled on and on about her and Darin's castle. To her father on the phone. At the dinner table, through her bath and bedtime story. And was probably asleep dreaming about castles and princesses at that very moment.

Lynn knew about the bad man. And the near-miss. And she couldn't let her guard down enough to get undressed, let alone sleep.

She could have lost Kara that day. Risked losing the little girl every single day.

Just as she'd lost Brandon. Her experience with him had taught her that loving someone made you a hostage to fate—to their choices, their fates.

She'd kept herself free from any kind of romantic commitment so she didn't have to face again the burned ashes of an empty life.

But in reality, any kind of love held her hostage. And she couldn't stop her heart from caring.

Tension emanated from her pores and she couldn't make it stop.

As evidenced by the way she jumped at the knock on her open bedroom door.

"Lynn?"

The voice was Maddie's. She'd insisted that the other woman spend the night with them. Because Kara hadn't liked it that Maddie had driven off without her. Because Maddie had saved Kara's life and was in perpetual panic mode at the thought of being in trouble for breaking the rules with Darin.

And because Lynn had needed her family together.

"Yes?" She sat up. Turned on the light.

She wondered if Grant was asleep. Or sitting up like she was, listening for any sounds from Darin's room, wondering how to prevent a repeat of the day, of the fear of losing the one most dear to you.

She wondered if he missed her anywhere near as much as she was missing him, her partner in fear that night.

"You're wearing your jeans and red shirt just like at dinner." Maddie, her slender little body dressed in the pink-and-white pajama bottoms and top she kept in a drawer in the spare bedroom in Lynn's house, came slowly into the room, a frown on her pretty face.

"I know."

"You were in the dark."

"Yes."

Sometimes it was nice not to have to answer unspoken questions. Because Maddie had simply been observing a shift from the norm, not asking a question.

"I didn't wake you."

"No."

The other woman nodded, picking at a thread on Lynn's comforter.

"Would you like to have a talk?" Lynn asked softly, her heart going out to Maddie. No one on earth tried harder, or wanted to do right, more than Maddie did.

The other woman wouldn't look at her. Her lower lip sucked into her mouth, her teeth biting into it.

"Come on," Lynn said, patting the end of the bed. "Have a seat and let's chat a bit. It was a different kind of day, and I'd like the company, too," she said.

Nodding, Maddie climbed up to sit cross-legged on the end of the mattress, pulling at the hem of her pajamas instead of Lynn's bedding.

"You were amazing today, Maddie," she said. Lila had called a gathering in the rec hall that night. She'd had Maddie and Kara sit up front with her. She'd invited Maddie's parents, as well, but they'd been tired and eager to get back home.

She'd told everyone how Maddie had helped them find Kara and Darin. And then talked about the fact that there were rules at the Stand for a reason, emphasizing how mandatory it was that they all follow the rules as a contingency to their residency with them.

She didn't name names. But Lynn knew that Kaitlynn, the new dance teacher, had received her warning. If the young woman had simply made a mistake, she'd learned from it. If she'd been disrespectfully careless, she wouldn't be with them long.

"I'm going to be in trouble," Maddie said. She

chewed on her lip and picked at her clothes, but she wasn't wild-eyed any longer.

"I'm pretty sure you already learned your lesson about breaking rules," Lynn said, knowing that Lila was not going to bring up Maddie's infraction. Maddie wasn't a prisoner at the Stand. She could leave if she wanted to.

But Lynn needed the other woman to know that the rules were there to protect her—and everyone else. She needed to know that Maddie's breaking of the rules was a onetime thing.

Or she couldn't entrust her daughter to her anymore.

She couldn't risk another debacle like the one they'd had that day.

"It wasn't your rule-breaking that was the problem today," she said slowly. "It was Kaitlynn's. She didn't keep Kara safe. She let her go after you. Do you understand?"

Eyes wide and serious, Maddie nodded. "Yes, Lynn. Kaitlynn could've got Kara hurt really bad. I started to cry when I dropped her off, but I didn't know she ran out behind me," the other woman continued. "If I knew she ran out behind me, I would've taken her hand and walked her back to her class."

"I know."

Folding her bottom lip over her top, Maddie continued to pick at her hem.

"So, we're agreed?" Lynn asked. "No more breaking of the rules. Even for Darin."

"I won't break the rules again," Maddie said. "I won't sneak away. If Darin wants me to go someplace with him, I'll tell him yes but I have to let you or Lila know first."

She didn't want Maddie leaving with Darin. But she had a much better chance of preventing them from going out alone as long as she knew ahead of time that they planned to leave. So Lynn nodded.

"Are you tired now?" she asked, thinking about calling Grant.

She'd hoped he'd call her.

"I'm not tired, Lynn, because I have to have an appointment with you."

She frowned. This was a new one. "An appointment with me?"

"Yes, Lynn."

Maddie didn't seem panicked. But she did seem…different. Because she'd been brave today and grown stronger from the experience?

Because Darin had kissed her on the lips when they'd arrived back at The Lemonade Stand from the beach that afternoon?

"Why do you need an appointment with me?"

"Because I missed my period."

Jaw dropping, Lynn told herself to be calm. This was Maddie. Her heart pounded, anyway.

"You missed your period," she repeated in lieu of the words she'd have liked to find.

"Yes, Lynn." With a very strange peacefulness, Maddie looked straight at her.

"You were due a week ago," she said, knowing Maddie's cycle because women's cycles were her business, because Maddie spent so much time at her house—and because their cycles were pretty much the same.

"Yes."

She tried to think back. To remember if Maddie had had her usual few hours of cramps. If there'd been extra trash in the bathroom can, or things used from under the counter.

And couldn't recall.

"You probably had it and can't remember," she said now. But Maddie was usually pretty good about her period. It was regular. And so something she counted on.

"I didn't have it, Lynn." Maddie would panic at the thought of having Grant read Kara a bedtime story, but she didn't seem to be the least bit frightened of something that would strike terror in a lot of women.

"Okay," Lynn said slowly, watching her houseguest. "Well, there are lots of reasons for a woman to miss her period. It's nothing to worry about. You'll probably get it this coming week."

Maddie shook her head. "No," she said emphatically. "I need an appointment with you, Lynn, because I missed my period and I'm going to have a baby."

Oh, God. Not tonight. She was beat. To a pulp. Completely spent and in need.

Of Grant.

"You aren't going to have a baby, Maddie. You know it takes a man and intercourse to make a baby."

"I know that, Lynn. Darin is a man and we had intercourse."

Lynn's hands dropped to the bed. She stared at the mentally handicapped woman.

And knew that life had just taken an irrevocable turn.

CHAPTER TWENTY-SEVEN

THE TEXT CAME shortly after eleven on Monday night.

You up?

Yeah, he was up. In more ways than one. With Darin safely home, but the day's emotions still running amok, he'd been sitting in the dark thinking about the woman who'd been by his side through the second worst day of his life.

The first being the day Darin had injured himself trying to save his wife's life.

He'd been thinking about the fact that their regularly scheduled sex date was less than forty-eight hours away. And determining that the odds were in their favor of actually consummating their agreement this week.

Just the thought had him hard.

Yeah. His thumbs typed the message back to her.

He was sitting in the dark in nothing but a pair of silk basketball shorts, prepared for a long night. He looked forward to Lynn's next message.

His phone rang. Her moniker popped up on his screen.

"Hello," he said, his voice low, a grin spreading across his face.

"Can you talk?"

The strangled tone in her voice made him sit up straight. "Of course," he told her. "What's up?" He'd help her handle it, whatever it was.

"Maddie and Darin had sex."

"What?" Grant was on his feet before he realized it, and had to rein in his volume, as well. "There's no way. No chance…"

And just as Lynn started to talk again, he remembered Maddie's voice on the phone that afternoon, telling them how she and Darin had snuck away from the The Lemonade Stand to spend an early morning on the beach.

"There's more."

What more could there possibly be? They'd been through the entire gamut of life's crises already that day. "What?" he asked, still stuck on the fact that his brother had had sex.

And was probably going to be wanting it again.

So much for his "just friends" speech. His ridiculous idea that he'd be able to distract Darin from Maddie.

With diving.

"I think Maddie's pregnant."

Her voice dropped on the last word. But it rang in his ear with the strength of a gunshot.

"You think she is or you know she is?" The numbness filtering through him was welcome. He'd take more of it.

He just wasn't going to think.

"I went to the clinic for a home pregnancy test and ran it on her. It's positive. It's only been a week, and it could be a false positive, but it's an early-detection kit. We keep them in stock because we need to know as soon as possible if an abused woman is pregnant by her abuser when she arrives at the shelter."

She was talking too fast. Faster than he could think.

Because he wasn't going to think. Ever again.

With the exception of the one hope she'd given him. He'd concentrate on that.

"What are the chances of a false positive?"

"Slight. More often it would be a false negative because a woman's body produces hormones at different speeds. Maddie already has elevated levels of the hormone a woman's body produces when she's pregnant."

"It's got to be wrong."

"I agree. But I doubt it."

She sounded stiff. As if she had a scarf tied too tightly around her neck. But try as he might, he heard none of the panic that was raging through him as he listened to Lynn.

"She said that making a baby was Darin's idea."

Of course. Blame it on the guy. That thought was quickly thrown out for the nonsense it was.

This was Darin and Maddie they were talking about.

"She said that when you wouldn't agree to their marriage, Darin told her if they got pregnant, we'd have to let them marry."

His brother had the problem solved!

The momentary glee he felt quickly crashed with a string of mental swear words.

"They can't have a baby."

"Maddie is considered medically sound enough to make that decision for herself. We can't force her to abort the child. And she is adamant that she's going to have it."

"I'll make Darin change her mind."

He heard how ridiculous he sounded. And knew, down where it counted, that there was no way on earth he'd choose to have his brother's child aborted.

"What are their chances of having a mentally sound child?"

"Darin's handicap was caused by a diving accident and Maddie's was caused by a lack of oxygen at birth. There's nothing genetically wrong with either one of them."

His tension hit an all-time high. "There's no way

they can live on their own and raise a child." Frustration getting the better of him, he ran his fingers through his hair. Paced his darkened living room and swore as he stubbed his toe.

"Sorry," he said into the phone when he realized she'd heard his expletive.

"I said the same thing when I saw the test results."

"In front of Maddie?"

"She wasn't there. I told her the test results won't be ready until the morning and sent her to bed."

"You don't ever lie to her."

"I am the bearer of the results and I won't be ready with them until the morning," she said, sounding tired more than anything.

"What are we going to do?"

"I have no idea."

He had an idea. A ludicrous one. But he had to think about it—long and hard—before he voiced it aloud.

He needed some encouragement from her, too.

"Okay, well, I suggest we try to get some sleep and talk about this tomorrow."

"I've already rescheduled my morning appointments," she told him. "I'm planning to take Kara to day care as usual. Maddie's there in the morning, as well. As soon as they're safely settled, I'll come back here."

"I can call Luke to cover for me and meet you there after I drop Darin off at therapy."

"Okay."

That was it. An agreement.

And lives that had just changed forever. He was facing an enormous challenge and waiting to meet with Lynn before attempting to solve it. Before making any decisions.

He wasn't going it alone anymore.

Whether the change crept up slowly while he was busy ignoring the signs, or whether it was just borne that day, brought on by the near-crisis they'd avoided, Grant didn't know. What he did know was that he needed Lynn.

Hanging up with her, he stood in the living room that, in all these years since Darin's accident, had always brought him peace but now only seemed to fill him with emptiness.

He stood there and saw his life. He was a thirty-eight-year-old man with…responsibilities.

A man who'd been so determined not to be struck down again, not to have life pull the rug out from under him again, that he'd quit living.

A man without a wife. Without children of his own, or any hope of having children of his own.

A man who'd fallen for a woman who'd just come through a harrowing day with calm and aplomb.

She hadn't fallen apart when Kara went missing,

and didn't fall apart after the little girl had been found, either. She'd hugged Kara, held on to her for the rest of the time Grant was with them, but she'd been incredibly calm.

As if she had no real needs at all.

She wanted him physically. But other than that?

Darin certainly had needs. Maddie had them. And Kara and Brandon. But seemingly not Lynn.

No, she was in complete control. Always.

Was it because of what she'd been through with Brandon? Because, like him, she couldn't cope with the idea of having her life change so completely again?

Or because that's just how she was? How she had always been?

The funny thing was that up until that day, he'd thought himself to be just like her. In complete control. And yet here he stood, in silk shorts and nothing else, with a life that was completely out of control.

He cared about Darin. And Maddie and Kara, too. So much so that he hadn't wanted to leave them that night. He'd wanted to keep every one of them, Lynn included, under his roof where he could protect them.

He looked out into the night, into the darkness that mirrored emptiness back at him, and saw a picture of his life to date.

A wasteland.

LYNN SPENT A sleepless night. She accomplished very little. A couple of loads of laundry. Some ironing.

She watched late-night television.

And made decaffeinated coffee she didn't drink.

By morning, she was exhausted beyond her ability to cope. But she fed Maddie and Kara. Walked with them to the day care, telling Maddie that she'd have her results for her at lunchtime.

The other woman didn't seem the least bit concerned.

She'd submitted to the test because Lynn had insisted that that was what would happen if she came to the clinic to see her. But she hadn't needed the results to know what her body was telling her.

She was pregnant.

And not the least bit upset about that fact.

Because Maddie couldn't problem solve. Which meant that sometimes she couldn't see the real problems in her life. She had no idea how much she'd just complicated her life.

Back at the bungalow, Lynn figured she had an hour to rest before Grant arrived. By her best estimation, they'd have another hour, give or take a few minutes, to find a solution to their problems.

And then she'd be facing lunch. And Maddie.

She went to bed and stared at the ceiling. After wasting five minutes of sleep time she moved out to the couch—hoping she'd trick herself into thinking she wasn't really trying to go to bed.

Five minutes later she started to cry. And knew that wasn't going to work. She had to sleep. More than anything.

She was a medical professional. Understood the importance of proper rest, most particularly during times of crisis. If she wanted to have the capacity to cope, she had to sleep.

If she'd had a sleeping pill, she might have taken part of one. What she had was a bottle of wine Brandon had brought her from San Francisco several months before. It was in the cupboard above her refrigerator.

A quarter glass of wine would calm her. The effect would be more instantaneous than anything else she could think of.

So she poured—and felt odd doing so in the early hours of the morning. But she drank it. And when it didn't work as quickly as she liked, she carried the glass—and the bottle—into the living room with her. She'd lie on the couch and sip slowly until the wine took effect. If it happened in the next ten minutes, she'd still have half an hour to sleep before Grant arrived.

NERVOUS AS HELL and hating the fact, Grant knocked on Lynn's door ten minutes before their scheduled meeting that morning. In jeans and his Bishop

Landscaping polo shirt he could have been facing any other day.

But the only thing familiar about his day so far were the clothes.

Lynn didn't answer his first knock so he knocked again. Maybe she wasn't back from the main building yet. He was early, after all....

He heard the door click. She'd unlocked it, pulled it from its jamb and left it hanging there.

Catching a glimpse of her through the crack she'd made, he pushed his way in. The back of her bright green scrubs preceded him into the living room. So he followed, a bit concerned when she sidestepped and almost hit the lamp on the side table.

It wasn't until he'd skirted the couch where she'd dropped, ready to sit beside her, that he noticed the half-empty bottle on the table.

"You're drinking?" She didn't drink much. She'd told him once that she couldn't tolerate the loss of control.

And unless he was missing his mark, he'd say she'd just consumed half a bottle of wine before eight in the morning.

"I couldn't sleep." She didn't sound drunk. Or even particularly upset.

Maybe if he'd had more sleep, Grant would have held his tongue. He doubted it. His life had come unglued and he went right along with it.

"What's with you?" he asked, sitting on the edge

of the couch, a good foot away from her, his elbows on his knees.

"What do you mean?" Her gaze was steady as she looked at him.

"You are the most controlled individual I have ever met. Nothing fazes you. Not even your daughter's disappearance." Once he started, he couldn't stop, as weeks of pent-up tension erupted inside of him. "Oh, you were concerned, I'll give you that, but you stood there completely engaged at all times."

"If I wasn't how would I help find her?"

"That's just it, Lynn. You were thinking about helping to find her at a time when most mothers would be catatonic with fear and grief. But not you. You just stay right there in your mind, keeping control of everything, moving forward and solving the world's problems."

The words were unfair. He knew it. He wasn't as good as her. He'd tried to maintain control and lost it completely.

"Don't you ever just feel? So much that it drowns out all rational thought and you do something crazy?" Like ranting at the woman you loved when all you really wanted to do was take her to bed and lose yourself in her arms.

"Crazy like drinking at eight in the morning?" she asked, calm as ever.

"I'm sure you had a rational reason for doing so."

"Rational?" Lynn jumped up so fast she spilled wine down the front of herself. And did nothing to clean it up.

It was going to stain.

"You think I'm rational?" She wasn't screaming, but her voice was raised louder than he'd ever heard it. "I was ironing clothes at three in the morning. Socks, Grant. I ironed socks! The elastic melted. I think I ruined my iron."

Pacing the room, her nearly empty wineglass still in her hand, she turned her back to him.

If he hadn't been so upset, he might have grinned.

"The first thing I did after I got Kara to bed and said good-night to Maddie was run to my bathroom, curl up in the corner and sob." She turned around.

And the tears in her eyes stabbed him to his core.

"If you want to know the truth, I'm scared to death most days of my life," she said, standing in the middle of the room, crying openly. "I'm scared to death that if I don't stay focused, stay calm, I'm going to fall apart so badly I'll never get myself back together."

He stood. And she held out her hand—sloshing the remaining wine over her wrist—holding him off.

"And then who would look after Kara? She's just a little girl, Grant."

"I know."

"Do you?" She gestured with the glass again,

and he watched to make sure that none of it got on the carpet.

"Do you also know that I'm jealous of Darin and Maddie?" she asked, her tone accusatory, wild and hitting him in the heart. "They made love and they're having a baby!" Her voice raised another octave. "Do you know that's all I've ever wanted? To be in love, make love and have babies with the man I love?"

He knew he wanted to be that man. And to run out the door and disappear at the thought.

"Do you know that you're that man, Grant? The one I dream about and make love with every single night when I close my eyes?"

His throat dried up on him.

"And do you have any idea…" Her voice broke. She sniffed. And then, very softly she finished. "How incredibly scared I am of the power my intense and illogical love for you gives you?"

He moved forward a step.

She took a step back.

"Because someday, you could be just like Brandon, changing your mind about who you are and what you need out of life, and there wouldn't be a single damn thing I could do about it."

She sipped from her empty glass. Didn't seem to notice that there was no wine left and continued to hold on to the glass.

"If you were even still in my life, that is," she

amended, frowning as she backed into the wall. And stood there, leaning against it.

Her hair was pulled back tightly and neatly as always. She had no makeup to cry off. And her clothes were pressed. But she didn't resemble, in any way, the calm, controlled woman he'd come to know and…love.

The admission that he didn't just care—that he was in love—was easier to accept knowing that she loved him, too. It wasn't as if the concept was new to him. Just the admission.

"We're a pair," he said aloud.

Her frown grew.

And he said, "So are you giving Kara up? Giving Brandon full custody of her?" He tried to sound as if they were talking about the weather when he knew the question was crazy. But he hoped it would prove a point that was only now occurring to him.

He was fighting for something bigger than life here.

"Of course I'm not giving her up!" His half accusation, half assumption hadn't sat well with her. "Why would you even suggest such a thing?"

"Well, just yesterday you were facing the possibility of losing her."

"You think I don't know that? You think I haven't been up all night, reliving that horror over and over and over again?" Fresh tears sprang to her eyes. And Grant needed to hold her.

And to be held.

"Can I tell you something?" He needed her to listen. He might not find a way to get the words out a second time.

She nodded, watching him. Not quite suspiciously, but almost.

"Last night, while I was sitting at home, thinking about Maddie and Darin's situation, I couldn't focus. I couldn't face the thought. It's like I had this barrier inside my chest that stretched up to my mind."

Her gaze softened. He couldn't describe how, but he felt the change in her. And something within him pushed farther forward. "But coming here this morning, knowing that I was going to discuss the situation with you, it wasn't overwhelming. I wasn't daunted at the prospect. I'm not happy about it, mind you, but I can...believe that, together, we'll find a solution."

The first step she took forward was a little shaky. "That's how I was yesterday," she told him softly, sounding more like the woman he knew. And loved. Really, really loved.

"The whole time Kara was missing I was leaning on you, touching you, drawing all of my strength from you," she said, coming slowly closer.

The words were uttered simply, but there was nothing simple about them. She stopped a couple of feet from him.

He took a step toward her. "Maybe, in loving, what we give up in control, we gain in strength to sustain us through the things we can't control."

She seemed to be giving the thought serious consideration.

"Sounds easier than it is, huh?" She was looking him straight in the eye. And his old Lynn was back. "I love you, Grant Bishop."

"And I love you." He'd never said the words to a woman before. Hadn't ever thought he'd do so.

And they hadn't killed him.

CHAPTER TWENTY-EIGHT

"HOW MUCH TIME do we have?" Grant hadn't come any closer, but the hungry look in his eyes brought him right inside her.

Setting down her empty wineglass, she looked at her watch. Darin's therapy was over in twenty minutes. Kara and Maddie would be in day care a bit longer than that.

"Fifteen minutes."

His hands went to his belt buckle. She took off her top. And felt wild and sexy when he stared at her breasts in her lace bra. Her nipples were already hard.

Maybe because he'd released his fly, giving her the first real look at his penis, leaving absolutely no doubt that she turned him on.

Really turned him on.

"I showed you mine, now you show me yours," he said, leering at her. Reaching behind her, she unfastened her bra, letting it fall off her arms. She should be shy. She'd been so uncomfortable the first time she'd let Brandon see her naked.

She couldn't get naked fast enough, for Grant.

He took off his shoes. Let his pants drop and stepped out of them, leaving them with his briefs on the floor.

She pulled her pants down, too. Leaving her underwear on. Because teasing him was fun.

It made her feel powerful.

And turned her on like she'd never been turned on before.

This beforetime, the foreplay, was exquisite. They'd had weeks of it. And she was so hungry she was shaking with it.

"You owe me one more. Take off your shirt," she told him and couldn't believe her luck when he revealed pecs that were so clearly defined she had to touch them to make sure they were real.

So she did. Reaching out, she buried her fingers in the hair on his chest, teasing his nipples, squeezing muscles that had been built through years of hard work.

She was hot and wet and ready to take him inside her. Except then…it would be over.

"Condoms." She barely got the word out, thinking of the ones she'd stashed in her bedside table weeks ago, in preparation for his visits.

"I have a couple in my wallet." He didn't move. As though he knew she didn't want to end the sweet torment. Like he agreed with her.

Still focused on his chest, she was shocked when

the tip of his penis pressed against her pelvis. And again. Knocking. Seeking entrance.

"I…" She licked her lips. They hadn't even kissed. And all she wanted was his penis inside her. For now. Forever.

She wanted the world to end. Right then and there.

While the moment was still perfect.

GRANT THOUGHT ABOUT waiting. The first time shouldn't be rushed. Not when they would remember it for the rest of their lives.

Not when they had the rest of their lives…

He pushed harder against her. Sliding himself between her legs. In and out, rubbing his penis against her inner thighs. Lynn's knees gave out and he caught her, lying her down on the floor and settling himself on top of her.

"The condom," she choked, opening her legs to let him between them.

"I was thinking, let's not use one," he told her. "I'm thirty-eight years old. I don't want to wait much longer to be a father."

Had he just said that? Really?

His penis urged him on. Eyes wide, Lynn stared at him, but she didn't push him off her. Or tell him to protect himself. He didn't take back his words, either.

He pushed the head of his penis just inside her opening. "Will you marry me?" he asked.

Arching up, Lynn took him inside her.

"Yes," she said, and within seconds she was pulsing around him.

Awash in sensation, he lost himself inside her. Moving on instinct and emotion and crying out in a voice he didn't recognize as he finally emptied himself inside of her.

He'd had a lot of sex.

But he'd never made love before.

LYNN WAS UP so fast she was still breathing hard after she'd gotten fully dressed. She picked up the wineglass and the bottle, disposed of one and washed the other. She wiped the counter and looked out the window into the backyard, thinking that she should pick the weed she could see growing out there. She rushed around so fast she made herself dizzy and still kept moving.

Grant reached out and placed his hand on her shoulder, turning her to face brown eyes that were filled with so many emotions she started to cry.

"Are you sorry?" he asked, his voice hoarse.

Would he understand if she told him she was? But told him why she was?

"You aren't obligated to marry me, Lynn." His deadpan voice was a giveaway. She'd hurt him.

It was the last thing she'd wanted to do.

"Well, you're obligated to marry me," she said, trying to maintain control, to mask her fear. Just like always.

But this wasn't always. And she wasn't the old Lynn anymore.

"I'm… It was incredible, Grant," she whispered, tears in her eyes again.

With a tender finger, he brushed back a few stray hairs that had come loose from her ponytail, and used his thumbs to wipe the corners of her eyes. "Then why these?"

"Because…"

She was going to tell him. And choked.

Her strength was in him. And in herself, too. Her strength was in trusting herself to handle whatever came her way.

"Brandon… I…"

He looked confused. "What? You think he won't want Kara to have a stepfather? You don't want to disappoint him? What?"

"No! Brandon will be thrilled. He feels so guilty and…it doesn't matter. No matter how Brandon felt, it wouldn't affect my choices where you're concerned. It's just…I'm so afraid…." The words tumbled over themselves.

"You aren't the only one, lady." With a hand on either side of her head, he held her steady as his mouth plundered hers. And in his kiss, she forgot about being afraid.

"I… The way I feel about you… It's so much more than I ever felt for Brandon. Even the love-making… Especially the lovemaking…" She was making a mess of this whole conversation. "I fell apart so completely when Brandon left. I'm scared to death of what would happen to me if you ever did. How would I cope?"

"I don't know the answer to that. I'm not going to walk out on you. Ever. But I can't guarantee that fate won't take me away. What I do know is that if it happens, you'll be given the strength to cope."

The conviction in his words reached her right where she loved him most.

"I suspect that the love we feel for each other will be there even when we aren't physically together," he said. "So no matter where I am, or you are, in this life or beyond, we'll have it to draw on."

"And it's a well that never runs dry," she said slowly, thinking about her love for Kara, too. How someday Kara would grow up and be off living her own life and Lynn would still have the strength of her daughter's love to carry her, too. How she'd probably be gone from this earth before Kara was and how her love would continue to nurture her daughter even then.

And then there was Grant. As she allowed the floodgates of emotion he'd brought into her life to open, she lost her balance and held on to him.

Just as she always would. No matter where he was.

He was right. "With you in my life, my well will never run dry," she said.

"I love you, Lynn Duncan, soon to be Lynn Bishop."

She was getting married.

He gazed deeply into her eyes, and her trust started to grow.

They were going to be okay. Really okay.

And suddenly, she couldn't wait until bedtime. Every bedtime. Or mornings, either. For the rest of her life.

GRANT SET THE table for lunch. He told Maddie where she was going to sit. Next to Darin. And Kara, because Kara had asked to sit next to Maddie. He was sitting next to Lynn.

She put the plate of sandwiches on the table. Ladled everyone a bowl of soup.

"Why are you grinning like that, Grant?" Darin eyed him like a man who knew. And Grant knew that he would never get used to seeing the glimpses of the Darin who'd once been in the eyes of the Darin who now was.

"You'll find out," Grant told him, still grinning. If Darin saw a new man in him, a less serious, less rigid man, then he was just going to have to get used to it.

"Did you get the test results, Lynn?" Maddie asked before Lynn even sat down to eat.

"Yes, I did," Lynn said just as calmly. But Grant wasn't fooled. He knew how nervous Lynn was about the changes descending on them.

And how excited she was, too.

They'd had sex so quickly they'd had time left over to talk.

"And I'm pregnant, right?" she asked.

Darin dropped his spoon into his tomato soup, splashing the liquid over the sides. He slid back from the table and stood up, his hands on his hips, looking down at Maddie.

"You're pregnant?" His voice squeaked like an adolescent going through a voice change.

"Yes," Lynn said.

"Woo-hoo!" Darin whooped so loudly that Kara jumped and missed her mouth with her peanut butter–smeared bread. He danced and jigged and wiggled his hips and threw his arms about, going around and around the table and into the kitchen. Maddie laughed so hard she had drool at the corners of her mouth.

Watching them, Kara started to laugh, too.

GRANT WASN'T SURE he'd get his older brother to calm down enough to have the conversation they'd planned on having before his next therapy session. But he knew he had one shot and he needed to use it.

"Sit down, Darin, we need to talk about your

responsibilities here." He made his voice purposely stern. "You're going to have to marry Maddie."

Hurrying back to his seat, Darin sat with so much force his chair rocked back. Grant's stomach sprang to his throat as he lunged for the back of the chair, righting it before Darin fell backward.

"I'd have caught it, Grant," he said, his tone perfectly serious. "And I agree, it is my responsibility to marry Maddie. That's why we've been trying to make a baby first. I'm glad you understand."

If Grant hadn't been so boneheaded, he'd have realized long ago that Darin's fate had been taken out of his hands the second Darin had met Maddie.

And known that because he loved his brother, he had to relinquish what he could of Darin's life back to him.

"Here is what we propose," Grant said, and the room grew completely still. Even Kara was watching him, her mouth filled with peanut butter.

"Lynn and I are going to get married. And you two will get married. We will add on to the bungalow here for now...."

"Lila might not like that," Maddie said. "She likes the bungalows to be the same because—"

"It's okay, Maddie," Lynn told her. "We've already talked to Lila."

"Oh. Okay." Maddie took a bite of her sandwich.

Grant looked from Maddie to Lynn and continued. "And we will all live together here." Because

Lynn and Grant would have to help raise the baby Maddie was carrying, while they watched over Darin and Maddie, too.

"With Kara, too," Darin said.

"Of course," Lynn said as her daughter shoved more bread into her mouth, seemingly unaware of the changes taking place around her.

Because Kara was the one person who really got it. She knew she was loved. That she'd be taken care of.

And she didn't worry about the details.

"So, is everyone okay with the plan?" Grant asked.

"I'm okay with it, Grant," Darin said, and took a bite of sandwich.

"I'm okay with it, Grant," Maddie said right after him, carefully spooning soup into her mouth. "But I want to sleep in the same room with Darin because when we're married we'll sleep in the same bed. I don't like having intercourse on the beach."

"That's right," Darin said. "We want to have sex in bed."

Grant looked to Lynn, not quite sure they were up for this. She was busy helping Kara to another sandwich quarter, but looked over at him and smiled.

The whole world was changing. They were all going to be different. And everyone just sat there and ate.

"Darin?"

"Yes?"

"You still want to get married, don't you?"

"Of course. I have to get married. Maddie and I did it on purpose."

"So you're happy?"

"I'm happy, Grant. And I have to eat because I have to go to therapy."

Life for Darin was what it was. And if it wasn't what he wanted it to be, he got his girlfriend pregnant and made his world rosy.

"I made a picture today," Kara announced.

Grant thought about asking to see it. And realized he still didn't know what happened to pictures.

"What was the picture?" Lynn asked.

"Sand castle!" she yelled out, clasping her hands together.

It was about the cutest thing Grant had ever seen.

"What happens to all these pictures?" he asked.

"They're put in a folder and the mom gets them at open house," Maddie said, in between bites. "But now I think you'll get them, too, because you're going to be Lynn's husband, which makes you the dad at the open house."

He was going to be a dad. Or at the very least a stepdad and an uncle, too. He'd never even changed a diaper. Or watched someone change one.

He had a lot to learn. But he'd get it all. Eventually.

Lynn's hand found his thigh under the table and

moved upward. He was feeling her. She was hungry again. And not for soup and sandwiches.

"Are you happy?" She whispered the words into his ear, sending a bolt of desire straight through him.

"It's not nice to tell secrets, Lynn," Maddie said.

Darin burped.

And Kara giggled. "Say 'scuse me!"

He didn't get a chance to give Lynn his answer. But he had it ready for the next time she asked.

Yes.

He, Grant Bishop, the boy who'd lost both of his parents before he graduated from high school, and the man who was one hundred percent responsible for his handicapped brother, was happy.

Because of her.

He could have told her something else, too.

He, Grant Bishop, was going to spend the rest of his life, every minute of every day, doing what he could to make her happy, too.

Because together, they could handle anything life handed them.

Together, they were one.

Lynn was wiping Kara's hands and mouth. "Ready for your nap, little one?" she asked.

"It's not time for her nap." Maddie was frowning.

Lynn glanced at Grant. And her look told him exactly what was on her mind.

"You and Darin have to get to the day care and

therapy, don't you?" he asked, innocently enough to pass by the two of them.

Darin glanced at his watch. "Yes," he said. "And now that we're having a baby and getting married, you're going to let us walk there alone, aren't you?"

Darin's look was pointed, serious.

"Yes." Grant's answer was just as serious.

He wished they'd hurry up and get out of there. He knew what Lynn had in mind for the two of them during Kara's naptime—and while it might involve a bed, it wasn't napping.

"Tell everyone goodbye," Lynn said, Kara on her hip.

"Bye," Kara said to the room, rubbing a hand across her eyes. And then she looked at Grant.

"See you soon, Mister, I love you."

"I love you, too, Kara." The words came out of his mouth.

And it was then that he fully recognized the truths that endured even when a guy tried to control what *couldn't* be controlled. Couldn't be contained.

He'd worked hard his whole life. Feeling in control. Providing everything he'd believed he needed.

But love had been waiting there for him, and he finally had it all.

* * * * *

LARGER-PRINT BOOKS!
GET 2 FREE LARGER-PRINT NOVELS PLUS
2 FREE GIFTS!

HARLEQUIN

super romance

More Story...More Romance

HSRLP13R